Acclaim for Ruth Reid

"Reid's second series installment (after *A Miracle of Hope*) works well as a tender romance with a bit of suspense. A solid pick for fans of Beverly Lewis and Melody Carlson."

—*Library Journal* on *A Woodland Miracle*

"Ruth Reid is skillful in portraying the Amish way of life as well as weaving together miracles with the everyday. In this book, she writes a beautiful tale of romance, redemption, and faith."

—Beth Wiseman, bestselling author of the Daughters of the Promise series, on *A Miracle of Hope*

"Ruth Reid pens a touching story of grace, love, and God's mercy in the midst of uncertainty. A must-read for Amish fiction fans!"

—Kathleen Fuller, bestselling author of the Hearts of Middlefield series, on *A Miracle of Hope*

"Reid gives readers the hope to believe that there are angels with every one of us, both good and evil, and that the good angels will always win."

—*RT Book Reviews* on *An Angel by Her Side*

"*An Angel by Her Side* brings together not only a protagonist's inner struggle, but the effect on the character from outside forces. In short, the reader rises, falls, grows, and learns alongside the story's champion."

—*Amish Country News Review*

"Reid has written a fine novel that provides, as its series title claims, a bit of 'heaven on earth.'"

—*Publishers Weekly* on *The Promise of an Angel*

"If *The Promise of an Angel* is anything to judge by, it looks like she's going to become a favorite amongst Amish fans."

—*The Christian Manifesto*

"Ruth Reid captivates with a powerful new voice and vision."

—Kelly Long, bestselling author of *Sarah's Garden* and *Lilly's Wedding Quilt*

"Ruth Reid's *The Promise of an Angel* is a beautiful story of faith, hope, and second chances. It will captivate fans of Amish fiction and readers who love an endearing romance."

—Amy Clipston, bestselling author of the Hearts of the Lancaster Grand Hotel and the Kauffman Amish Bakery series

THE *Promise* OF AN *Angel*

Other Books by Ruth Reid

THE *Promise*
OF AN *Angel*

RUTH REID

THOMAS NELSON
Since 1798

Published in Nashville, Tennessee, by Thomas Nelson. Thomas Nelson is a registered trademark of HarperCollins Christian Publishing, Inc.

Thomas Nelson books may be purchased in bulk for educational, business, fundraising, or sales promotional use. For information, please e-mail SpecialMarkets@ ThomasNelson.com.

Scripture quotations taken from THE NEW KING JAMES VERSION. © 1982 by Thomas Nelson. Used by permission. All rights reserved.

Publisher's Note: This novel is a work of fiction. Names, characters, places, and incidents are either products of the author's imagination or used fictitiously. All characters are fictional, and any similarity to people living or dead is purely coincidental.

ISBN: 978-0-7180-8477-6 (repack)

Library of Congress Cataloging-in-Publication Data

Reid, Ruth, 1963–
    The promise of an angel / Ruth Reid.
        p. cm. — (Heaven on earth ; 1)
    ISBN 978-1-59554-788-0 (trade pbk.)
    1. Amish—Fiction. 2. Michigan—Fiction. I. Title.
    PS3618.E5475P76 2011
    813'.6—dc22   2011006178

Printed in the United States of America

16 17 18 19 20 RRD 6 5 4 3 2 1

Dedicated to my grandmother, Florence Gunderson, who thirty-five years ago gave me my first briefcase to store my stories in, and to my mother, Ella Roberts, who stayed up late to type all those stories. You both are godly women who greatly influenced my life—I am blessed.

For He shall give His angels charge over you,
to keep you in all your ways.

Psalm 91:11

Pennsylvania Dutch Glossary

abvoahra: serve
ach: oh
aemen: amen
aenti: aunt
bloh: blue
boppli: baby
daed: dad
denki: thank you
drauwa: trust
Englischer: a non-Amish person
es: is
fasavvahra samling: sour the gathering
fashprecha: promise
fraa: wife
gayl: yellow
geh: go
greeya fatt: get away
guder mariye: good morning
guder nacht: good night
gut: good
haus: house
himlish-engel: heavenly angel
Ich: I
Ich veiklich: I truly
jah: yes
kaffi: coffee
kapp: a prayer covering
kumm: come
kumm mitt mich: come with me

leddich: unmarried

mamm: mom

mammi: grandmother

maydel: girl

meidung: shunning

meiya: tomorrow

mich: me

muscht: must

nacht: night

nau: now

nay: no

nett: not

onkle: uncle

Ordnung: the written and unwritten rules of the Amish

Pennsylvania Deitsch: the language most commonly used by the Amish

redd-up: clean up

rumschpringe: running-around period that begins when the person turns sixteen years old and ends when the young person is baptized into the Amish faith.

saund: sound in doctrine

shiklich: appropriate, suitable, proper

shul: school

vass: what

veiklich: truly

vinsha: wish

wedder: weather

wundebaar: wonderful

yummasetti: A traditional Amish dish made with hamburger, egg noodles, and cheese

zudie shul: to school

zvay: two

Chapter One

Mecosta County, Michigan

The maple tree's crimson canopy offered shade for the children in Judith Fischer's charge, and a perfect place to stitch her quilt while viewing Levi Plank as he worked with the men building the barn. With the structure nearly complete, soon the supper bell would ring. Judith glanced toward the house. Her friend Deborah was busy preparing the outdoor tables for the meal. Judith enjoyed helping with the food preparations, but she loved sitting with the children and entertaining them with stories more.

Six-year-old Rebecca pulled on her sister's sleeve. "Tell us another story."

Judith turned back and eyed the tight circle of smiling children. "What color dress will the *maydel* wear?"

"Yellow," said Rebecca.

Little Emily looked down at her own dark dress. "Not black or blue?"

A leaf fluttered from the branch above them and landed on Judith's lap. She picked it up and twirled it by the stem. "In stories, people wear bright colors." She tucked the red leaf into her tightly wound hair, leaving it to dangle from under the head covering. "Storybook characters can also wear wildflowers and colorful ribbons in their hair."

Rebecca raised her hand to shield the late afternoon sun from her eyes as she looked up into the branches. "What's her name?"

Judith repositioned the younger girl's bonnet, then removed the leaf from her own hair and tucked the stem under Rebecca's head covering. Feeling a tug on her other arm, she looked down at her five-year-old brother's gap-toothed smile. "*Jah*, Samuel?"

"Name her Judith."

The girls chimed in their agreement.

Emily's eyes widened. "I'll name the boy in the story."

Judith glanced toward the barn and spotted Levi on the roof. She watched as he removed a nail he'd been holding between his teeth and hammered it into the wood. Judith couldn't help but smile. Levi would make a perfect storybook hero.

"Let's call him Andrew," Emily blurted.

"Andrew?" Judith echoed louder than she intended. She followed the child's gaze to Levi's cousin, Andrew Lapp, and watched as he measured a piece of lumber. He paused, holding the pencil in place against the wood, and smiling, turned toward the children. As his eyes met Judith's, he lifted his hand from the board and touched the brim of his straw hat.

2

Rebecca scrunched her freckled nose as she looked at Judith. "Why is your face red?"

Judith touched her warm cheeks. Before she could think of how to answer, she heard her sister Martha giggling behind her.

"Supper's ready," she said. "That is, if the daydreamer is ready to eat?"

Judith set the quilt section beside her and stood. Since Martha turned seventeen last month, her entire demeanor had changed. Judith hoped her father would notice the way Martha sashayed to the barn. He'd have something to say about that.

Judith lined up the children to brush the grass off their dresses, meanwhile watching Levi climb down the ladder out of the corner of her eye.

"Am I done?" Emily asked.

She looked at the girl's dress. "*Jah*, run to your *mamm*."

Martha had managed to be at the foot of the ladder as Levi reached the ground.

Sarah, Emily's older sister, fanned her dress by pulling on both sides, then twirled in place. "What about me?"

After a few swipes, Judith sent her on her way. Her jaw tightened as she heard Martha and Levi laugh. She should be the one exchanging pleasantries with him, not Martha. She was the one turning nineteen tomorrow. She shooed the other children toward the house without inspecting their clothing, but held back Rebecca and Samuel.

"Samuel, you stay with Rebecca and me. *Mamm* doesn't need to chase after you today."

He pointed to the supper tables. "I'm hungry."

Judith could see Martha, Levi, and some other girls their

age moving in her direction. She pretended to brush grass off Samuel's clothing. "*Mamm* wouldn't want you to *kumm* to the table covered with grass. *Nau* hold still."

"Hello, Judith." Levi paused near the tree, Martha and the others clustered around him. "You sounded happy being surrounded by children all day."

Judith blushed. He had noticed her under the tree. She thought she'd seen him gaze in their direction a few times.

Martha sighed. "She was filling their heads with nonsense again."

Judith gritted her teeth and didn't comment.

"She's going to lead the children astray. They'll all want to wear lacy gowns and ribbons in their hair." Martha pointed to Rebecca. "See, she has our sister wearing colorful adornments."

Rebecca's lips puckered, and Judith quickly patted the girl's slumped shoulders. "It's okay. Martha used to listen to stories too."

"Before I turned seventeen."

Judith crossed her arms. "And you think seventeen makes you grown?"

Martha planted her hand on her hiked hip and shot her nose into the air. "At least I don't dream of fairy tales. I—"

Judith hadn't noticed Andrew joining their group until he cleared his throat and stepped forward. He reached into his pants pocket and knelt in front of Samuel. "I have something for you."

"For me?" The little boy beamed.

Andrew handed him a galvanized nail. "After supper, I'll help you pound that into a piece of wood."

"Really?" Samuel rolled the nail over his palm, eyeing it as if he held a fistful of candy.

Andrew stood and dusted the dirt from his patched knees. "Sure. You want to build barns someday, don't you?"

Samuel nodded. "And furniture too."

Rebecca peeked around Judith's dress. "Andrew was the name of the boy in Judith's story."

Judith's breath caught as she glimpsed Andrew's raised eyebrows. She sent a furtive glance in Levi's direction, but he and the others were heading toward the house.

Andrew squatted and picked up the quilt Judith had been sewing. "Ouch!" He shook his hand. "I guess I stabbed myself with your needle." He handed her the fabric, taking care to point out where the needle was stuck. "I hope I didn't dirty your work."

Judith looked down at the squares. "It'll come out in the wash." She hoped. When she married, she wouldn't want her wedding quilt marred.

She reached for Samuel's hand and caught Rebecca before she darted away. "You two need to wash for supper." Avoiding eye contact with Andrew, she hustled the children toward the house.

As was the custom, the men stood on one side of the table, the women and children on the opposite side. While Bishop Lapp thanked God for the meal, the completed barn, and the day's fair weather, Judith glanced across the table at Levi.

His thick broad shoulders gave him a towering build. Hat in hand and head bowed, his sandy-brown hair, damp with sweat, curled into ringlets and fell forward, covering his eyes.

She stifled the sigh that threatened to escape. If her father caught her staring at a boy instead of giving thanks to God for their new barn, she would hear about it. She tried to keep her eyes closed, but as the bishop's prayer droned on and on, she couldn't keep from peering at Levi again.

His eyes opened. He tipped his head enough to look between his coiled locks.

Her heart quickened. Tomorrow she'd be nineteen. In her dreams, she had already accepted his courtship invitation.

His glance passed over her toward the opposite end of the table.

She leaned forward on her tiptoes and craned her neck to see what he was looking at. His gaze had stopped on Martha. Her long, batting lashes and perfect, rose-glowing cheeks stole his undivided attention.

Judith looked again at Levi. He shook his head as a broad grin spread across his face. She wondered what her sister had asked him, and snapped her head in Martha's direction to see her sister's lips form an exaggerated pout. Disgusted at her inappropriate behavior, Judith turned her attention back to Levi to see him shrug at Martha.

Judith squeezed her eyes shut and bit her bottom lip.

This wasn't how she dreamed things would be when she turned nineteen. While a few of her friends dared to speak of what it would be like to live outside the Amish community, Judith valued household duties, knowing they prepared her for marriage. She performed each task with vigor, even unpleasant chores like scrubbing barn-soiled clothes against the washboard, while pretending to be Levi Plank's *fraa*.

Now his playful gestures toward her sister were unbearable. He'd talked about courting *her* once she turned nineteen. She had expected he would ask to take her home after the next singing.

Judith felt a tug on her dress and looked down at Rebecca. "Where's Samuel?" the little girl whispered.

Judith brought her finger to her lips. Even at age six, children knew not to interrupt the blessing.

She glanced to her other side, where her brother was supposed to be. Samuel was gone. She scanned the immediate area. He wasn't with her parents or with the other children. He wasn't— anywhere. She drew a deep breath. Once the prayer ended, she would search for him. He wouldn't go far. She looked again at Levi, but a blur of blue in the distance caught her attention.

Samuel was squatting on the barn roof with hammer in hand, tapping a board.

Judith moved away from the table and ran toward the barn, prayer or no prayer.

"Samuel!" Her voice boomed in the near silence.

Samuel jerked upright, arms flailing. In the time it took to blink, he disappeared from view.

Judith sprinted to the other side of the barn. *Please, God, let him be okay. He's just a child.* She pushed herself to run faster.

She rounded the corner of the barn and skidded to a halt. A man, an *Englisch* man, was kneeling next to her brother.

The man lifted his head away from Samuel's face. "The boy's alive."

Judith collapsed to her knees as she stretched her hand to Samuel's pale face. "Samuel."

Her brother didn't respond or open his eyes.

The *Englisch* man rose to his feet. "Have faith. Samuel's steps are ordered by God."

When she looked up at the man, his eyes flickered with a bright, wavering light. Her throat tightened, and she was unable to speak.

Then the sound of the others approaching pulled her attention away. Her older brother, David, reached them first.

"Samuel, wake up. Please." Judith wrapped her arms around Samuel and clung to his limp, unresponsive body. "God, please," she murmured.

David's strong hands lifted Judith and set her aside as others swarmed around Samuel.

"No, please don't—" Judith felt herself being pushed aside.

"Don't cause problems," David warned.

She drew in a hitched breath and wiped the tears from her eyes to clear her vision. From somewhere nearby, a voice resonated in a language she'd never heard. While everyone's focus remained fixed on Samuel, she turned a complete circle in search of the source. The voice sounded like that of the stranger she'd found next to Samuel. How had he known her brother's name? And where had he gone?

Filled with an urgent need to find him, she followed the sound of the harmonious chant and spotted the man crossing the pasture, heading into the apple orchard without looking back.

She moved cautiously at first, then with a surge of determination she lifted her skirt and broke into a full run. She lost sight of him, cloaked as he was in the undergrowth of the dense branches and an emerging thick haze that seemed to seep up from the ground. The fog turned solid at her feet, preventing her from following his tracks. He had disappeared.

She shivered at the memory of his penetrating stare. As though she'd looked at the sky through an icicle, his frosty-blue eyes etched her senses. Oddly, her core warmed with an inner peace.

A whoosh of wind, followed by a sound like sheets flapping on a clothesline, startled her. The murky vapor had cleared, and now shadows from the low-hanging branches filled the empty void. Somehow she knew it was pointless to follow, and she turned back.

Once clear of the grove, she sprinted across the pasture, hoping that no one had noticed her absence. Her heart still pounding hard, she steadied her breathing before she edged back into the crowd.

Her father was raising the rear wooden panel off the market wagon as the men lifted a board that held Samuel. They carried his limp body like pallbearers carrying a pine box.

Judith raced to catch her mother before she climbed into the buggy. "Where are they taking him?"

Mamm lowered a handkerchief from her face. "He needs a doctor. You'll stay with your sisters."

Judith saw Rebecca clinging to Martha. Both stared blankly as they looked on in silence.

Then she glanced at Samuel's white complexion. Eyes closed, unresponsive. The vivid impression embedded itself into her mind.

"Judith."

She looked up at her father.

"Keep your eye on the girls."

His stony expression drove a nail through her heart. It was her failure to supervise Samuel that had caused the accident. Her eyes welled up at the thought of her brother dying on her watch. As the buggy pulled away, her vision blurred again with tears.

Chapter Two

Judith cupped her hands over her mouth, muting any outward emotional display. She understood the scriptures; God's will for Samuel would prevail regardless of what bartering she offered on his behalf. Yet with her mind swirling with what-ifs, she had to offer. *Take my life in exchange. I'm to blame.*

Aenti Lilly tugged Judith's sleeve. "*Kumm*, we'll *redd-up*."

She drew in a snagged breath and nodded. Perhaps if her hands had work, she'd ward off the temptation to question God's ways.

Judith followed the women back to the food-laden tables. Surely after the men had labored all day they would wish to eat. At the moment they were still hovering near the barn, no doubt discussing chore duties. In their tight community, all hands pulled together in times of crisis. She'd spent several days herself helping with household chores for the Trombleys when all five of the children came down with chicken pox. Judith smiled, recalling how little Emily had begged for stories to take her mind off the itching.

Martha elbowed Judith's ribs. "Samuel almost died and you're smiling?"

"My mind wandered briefly, is all." Judith picked up a pan of beef casserole. The cheesy top layer was stiff. Much of the food would require reheating.

Martha came along beside her, carrying a crock of baked beans. "We know what happens when your mind wanders, don't we?"

David's wife, Ellen, stopped midway up the porch steps and spun around. "Leave the finger pointing be, Martha. What has happened cannot be undone." Her gaze switched to Judith, and her eyes were warm with sympathy. "Once I make up some plates of food to take along, I'll take Rebecca and Martha home with me for the night."

"*Denki,*" Judith replied. She certainly had no energy to hold her tongue while Martha barraged her with insults all evening.

Martha let loose a wayward sigh and stormed into the house.

"I'll ask your brother to speak to her," Ellen said.

Despite her sister's poor behavior, Judith didn't wish David's discipline to fall on her. He used to be mild-natured, and Judith had loved his sense of humor. But after he became a church deacon, he held his siblings to a sometimes unreachably high standard of obedience. Working with the bishop to keep the sheep from straying and the fold intact meant he kept a watchful eye over his immediate family.

Judith stepped inside the crowded kitchen, where the women were quickly bringing order out of kitchen chaos. Dishes were passed hand to hand in an assembly-line style, making plates available to take home and reheat.

Judith found a place to work next to Deborah.

"So what did he say?" Deborah's head bobbed at the window facing the barn's direction. "Levi," she mouthed. "Under the tree?"

Judith wrapped up two plates of food and handed them to Deborah, then picked up two more. "Ellen, we're taking these out to your buggy." She motioned for her friend to follow.

The screen door hadn't snapped closed before Deborah asked, "Did he say anything about you turning nineteen *meiya?*"

Judith shook her head. "I thought he might later, but—"

Deborah's eyes widened. "*Ach*, poor Samuel."

"*Jah*, I feel awful."

Deborah gently elbowed Judith's arm. "You're not to blame."

"He was under my watch." The strain in her voice made it barely audible, but she forced herself to continue. "I was more interested in watching Levi." Silence fell between them until they reached the buggy. "And guess who Levi was watching." Judith opened the back hatch and set the plates on the floorboard.

"Who?"

Judith closed the buggy door. "Martha."

"*Nay*, are you sure?"

"*Jah*." Judith gazed off in the distance at the setting sun as tears welled. She'd waited patiently to court Levi, planned their wedding in her dreams, and now her sister had gained his attention.

Deborah patted her arm. "Your faith is strong for Levi being the one. Besides, according to your parents' rules, Martha isn't old enough to court, is she?"

"I hope she cannot change their minds." She wiped her eyes. "I have no business to speak of Levi when my brother's fate is unknown. Please don't think poorly of me. My mind's flushed with scattering thoughts. Did you see the *Englischer*?"

"*Vass?* What *Englischer*?" Deborah's brows arched.

"He was kneeling beside Samuel."

"I couldn't even see Samuel. Not with so many people crowding around." She looped her arm with Judith's as they strolled to the house. "There was an *Englischer* with him?"

"*Jah*, strange, isn't it?" Odder still that she didn't hear anyone else talking about the man. As though he'd slipped through the entire crowd unnoticed.

"Did you talk to him?"

Judith was about to tell her friend what the man had said, when the door opened. The chatter of children filled the air as they chased after one another over to the row of buggies.

Deborah's mother came up beside Judith. "Be sure to send us word about Samuel."

"*Jah*, I will."

Judith glanced at the house as more womenfolk stepped outside. She caught sight of Martha craning her neck in their direction. This wasn't the time to share what the stranger had said. Her sister would accuse her once again of spreading stories.

She leaned toward her friend. "I have more to tell you later."

A wide smile spread across Deborah's face. "*Jah*, you better." She turned and caught up with her mother.

14

Ellen came up beside Judith, and they waited as several buggies passed them on the driveway. "*Aenti* Lilly is arranging a women's get-together."

Rebecca reached for Judith's hand. "Will Samuel die?" Her pale blue eyes probed Judith's, awaiting an answer.

Judith gulped. "*Nay*, Rebecca. He will be all right."

But Ellen picked up Rebecca and guided her into the back of the buggy. "That will be up to God." She motioned for Martha to climb in, then turned to Judith. "It's hard sometimes to accept His will."

Judith bowed her head. She hadn't intended to discount God's sovereignty. She just wanted to comfort her little sister and offer her hope.

Ellen touched Judith's arm. "Samuel is in God's hands."

"That is true, I know." Judith glanced into the buggy. Rebecca had nestled into Martha's arms. "You girls be *gut* for Ellen."

Ellen scanned the yard. "Where did my boys run to?"

Judith glanced toward the barn. Doubtless the new building had offered the nine-year-old twins a wonderful set of discoveries to explore.

"Want me to look for them?" Martha already had one leg out of the buggy.

"I'll go." Judith hurried away, hoping Ellen would keep Martha from following.

The scent of fresh-cut lumber met Judith the moment she stepped into the barn. She drew in a deep breath, allowing the aroma to penetrate her senses. Most of the men had packed up their tools and were heading home to complete their own evening chores, but she could see Levi scattering straw over the calf pen and Andrew and *Onkle* Amos milking cows.

Judith lifted her gaze to the empty loft. "Have you seen James and Jacob?" she asked Levi.

The boys poked up their heads from behind one of the horse stalls. "We're helping, *Aenti* Judith." James came out from the stall and wiped the hay dust from his pants. The boys, although not identical twins, both had their father's thick mop of sandy-colored hair.

Judith motioned toward the door. "Your *mamm* is ready to go."

Jacob leaned the pitchfork against the wall, and James passed Levi the feed bucket. With David having gone with Judith's parents to the hospital, the twins would have plenty of farm chores to do at home.

Judith followed them to the door, then paused and looked over her shoulder. "There's plenty of food in the *haus*." She made it a general invitation, but she hoped Levi would stay.

Levi crawled out from the calf pen. "I could use a *gut* meal when I finish here."

Judith smiled. "I'll ready a heated plate."

Back outside, the evening air had turned chilly. Judith shot a short wave at Ellen pulling out from the driveway, then wrapped her arms around herself. She wished she'd remembered her cape.

Her thoughts drifted to Samuel and how pale, even cold he looked with the bluish hue around his lips as he lay stretched out on the board. She hoped one of her mother's quilts was in the buggy for him to snuggle under during the ride home.

Judith walked back to the porch. She'd need a light to gather firewood. Even if her parents returned tonight, her father would be too exhausted to stock the woodbox.

After locating the wooden matchsticks on the windowsill, she readied the wick on the lamp. Shielding her hand around the lit match so the breeze didn't blow out the flame, she held it over the wick.

The sound of someone clearing his throat caused her to jump.

"I didn't mean to startle you." Andrew motioned to her hand. "Watch out, it's—"

Before he could finish his statement, the flame reached the end of the match and burned her fingers. She threw it from her hand, and they both stomped. Andrew's shoe smothered the flame and Judith's shoe slammed onto his.

"*Ach*, I'm sorry!"

He motioned to her hand. "Did you get burned?"

"*Jah*," she replied and jammed her fingers into her mouth to soothe the pain.

"*Kumm*, put water on it." Andrew motioned to the well pump.

"I'll be okay," she insisted, but Andrew had already turned and walked to the well. He pumped the handle to prime the well while she held her hand under the spigot. He worked the pump with such force the water gushed out, splattering Judith's dress and soaking her shoes.

"I'm so sorry." He released the handle, but the primed water continued to pour out.

Judith chuckled. He didn't seem to know his own strength. Anytime she primed the pump, she needed to put all her weight into each thrust, and it still took five or six times before water started spitting out. "I guess this is what I get for stomping on your foot."

"How is the burn?"

Numb, if she dared to complain. Dousing with icy well water during the fall season had a tendency to deaden the nerves.

Poor Andrew worked his hands together like he was wringing water from a rag. His nerves seemed as flimsy as the threadbare patches that covered the knees of his pants. Although older than the other unmarried youth, he didn't seem to have many social skills around women. He was shy, Judith supposed, or maybe just contentedly single. In any case, he was known to be more studious of the Bible and considered wiser than the other young men in their community, probably because his father was the bishop.

He surprised her by reaching for her hand. "Let me look."

"I, um . . ." Now she was trembling. "I'm all right." Besides, hadn't it dawned on him that he couldn't see if a blister had formed now that the sun had set?

"Your hand is cold." He dropped her hand as if the reality of his action had startled him. "I'll be by in the morning to do your *daed's* chores." His words ran together as if he were the one now shivering.

"*Denki. Daed* will be grateful to have help."

"I'll be praying for Samuel," he said.

A lump formed in her throat, and Andrew took a step closer as if he sensed how difficult it was to reply. He jammed his hands inside his pockets. "I'll be praying for you too."

Judith sucked on her bottom lip and nodded. She wouldn't

deny needing prayer, but Andrew's mention only amplified her feelings of guilt.

The barn door closed hard and caught their attention. Levi jogged over to them, then lifted his lantern to illuminate their faces. "Can you give Judith and me a few minutes?" Levi asked his cousin.

Andrew nodded and turned.

"Don't leave without eating." Judith motioned to the house. "There's plenty of food inside."

Levi handed Andrew the lantern. "We won't need the light."

Andrew trained his eyes on Judith, then left without saying a word.

Levi motioned with his thumb in Andrew's direction. "What did he want?"

Judith flipped her hand palm side up. "I burned my fingers on a match."

Levi reached for her hand. His touch caused a coal-oven of heat to disperse over her, and any thought of needing a cape passed.

He released her hand. "Let's walk."

She ran her hand along her arm to smooth the goose bumps that had formed from his touch.

"Are you all right?"

She'd be all right if she could calm herself before he noticed her nervous fidgeting. "I'm worried, is all."

"About Samuel?" He stopped her hand from brushing her sleeve and held it.

While Andrew's hands had a calming effect, Levi's hold was unsettling. She shivered more, and not from the cool air. He squeezed her hand when she didn't reply, and his smile spread wide. "*Kumm mitt mich.*"

Judith freed her hand from his. "I need to stay close to the house." What would people say if they were seen wandering off into the dark? "Besides," she said, "there is food inside to put away and . . . and you haven't eaten." Her stomach had rolled so many times, she feared anything she attempted to eat wouldn't stay down long.

"I'll eat later. *Kumm*, I won't keep you long."

Levi's convincing arm-tug overrode her apprehension, and Judith followed him beyond the spread of the porch's lantern light. They stopped under the low-lying branches of a maple tree.

"From here we can still see the porch."

Judith glanced in that direction. With the lamp lit, she could easily see the last of the women milling outside on the porch with *Aenti* Lilly.

"You spent a great deal of time under this tree today," he said.

She tapped the tree trunk as if patting the hand of a good friend. "The shade kept the children cool." She hid the real reason. From under the tree, she'd had an unobstructed view of him as he worked on the barn. Judith leaned against the tree. She'd spent endless hours in this same spot dreaming of the day she'd be alone with Levi.

He rested his shoulder against the trunk and faced her. "Children love you, don't they?"

"The way my sister batted her lashes at you during prayer, I'd say children love you too."

He chuckled. "Rebecca is sweet."

"I was referring to Martha."

"Martha's seventeen. She's hardly a child anymore."

While to most members of their settlement, turning seventeen meant one had reached courting age, Judith's parents developed their own guidelines. They had requested that she wait until age nineteen, and she assumed the same restrictions would apply to Martha.

Levi leaned forward, his breath warming her face. "It's *nett* the Lord's will to be jealous of your sister."

The ridges of bark pressed against her spine as she held her reply.

He sighed. "I wish I could see your expression."

Judith swallowed. If the darkness hadn't masked her face, he would see the truth. The ugly, sinful truth. She was jealous of her sister. Any unmarried man in the settlement would line his buggy up to drive her home from singing. Martha's smooth skin and long dark lashes made Judith feel plain. And clearly Martha already knew how to gain male attention.

Judith tipped her face higher and changed the subject. "Did you see the *Englisch* man today? I followed him into the apple orchard."

"*Nett* so."

"He disappeared into the fog."

Levi chuckled. "There was no fog in the air today." He moved closer, touched the dangling tie-string of her prayer *kapp*, and slid his fingers between the strings to the ends. "God doesn't want you to tell stories," he said while tying the ends into a bow under her chin.

Judith untied the head covering. "I saw a man."

He reached for the bottom of the string.

She tilted her face downward and waited, sure he would again silently remind her that lies were sin by retying her *kapp*. Instead, he coiled the string around his finger.

"How many children do you want?" he asked. "A dozen?"

"More."

Her quick reply stopped his coiling midway up the string. Neither spoke. If they were courting, such a personal question wouldn't sound odd. Still, his asking about her future was a pleasant surprise.

He continued to gather the string around his finger. "More than a dozen?" he asked, unguarded confidence in his playful tone. He released the string and tipped her chin upward. "Do I have to wait until you're nineteen *meiya* to kiss you?"

Patches of moonlight spread through the maple tree's leaves, spotlighting his wide smile. She couldn't answer without first catching her breath.

But Levi didn't wait. Before she blinked, he'd kissed her. Although it ended much quicker than she'd dreamt her first kiss would, her heart clapped all the same. Even the leaves overhead, unsettled by a swift breeze, seemed to applaud.

"I want more than a dozen too."

"Why do you tell me that?"

He ground his boot into the dirt like an unsteady horse. "If you'd learn how to kiss, you'd be closer to making your dream come true."

Resentfully she moved away from the tree. "You're comparing me to those *Englisch* girls I hear you've kissed during your *rumschpringe*."

He not only didn't deny her accusations, he didn't even hang his head in shame. Instead, he smirked.

"I intend that my husband teach me the ways of kissing." She turned. "I have to go."

He clutched her wrist. "Those girls didn't mean anything."

Judith inhaled a sharp breath. He kissed girls without it meaning anything? Why did he kiss them, then? And of greater importance, why had he kissed her?

He drew her close. "My *rumschpringe* is over. I want to—"

"Levi?" Andrew stood at the edge of the path with a lantern held high in the air.

"I have to go. Andrew's giving me a ride home." He leaned forward, but instead of kissing her again, he tugged the string of her prayer *kapp* and tromped off.

Andrew climbed into the buggy and waited for Levi to come out from the woods. He would give his younger cousin a few more minutes, but he didn't intend to wait half the night. Levi would have to walk if he lingered much longer. Andrew had his own chores to do, and he'd promised to return in the morning to do the Fischers' milking. He would do more if it released the burled knot that had formed in his stomach after Samuel's accident. He should have never given the boy the nail.

"*Ich* didn't have time to eat." Levi climbed inside the buggy. "And you have poor timing." He plopped down on the bench and folded his arms.

Andrew didn't dare imagine what that meant. Something

told him the comment had nothing to do with missing his meal. At twenty years of age, his cousin had much to work out with the Lord prior to gaining church approval. Not that Levi had requested baptism. But certainly he had to make the commitment someday soon.

Andrew caught sight of a form moving from the wooded area over the moonlit lawn. "You left Judith alone in the woods?"

"At the edge."

Andrew shook his head. "I'll wait if you want to walk her to the door."

Levi didn't budge from the seat. He motioned toward Judith. "She's in the yard *nau*."

"You don't know how to treat a woman, do you?" Andrew waited until Judith reached the porch, then tapped Patsy with the reins.

"No lectures, Bishop Junior." Levi laughed. "Besides, how much practice have you had?"

His cousin had a point. Compared to Levi, Andrew had no experience with women. The friendship he'd shared with Esther would have matured into marriage had she not died. Had his heart not died with hers.

Levi elbowed him. "You should've used your time before baptism more wisely."

"Wise is not sampling women like a new flavor of ice cream." Andrew clicked his tongue, encouraging Patsy into a faster trot. There wasn't anything wise about the wayward decisions his cousin made, but Andrew dared not discuss them for fear of passing judgment.

He pulled back on the reins once they neared Levi's house,

and Patsy slowed her pace until they were in the drive. "I would think with Judith turning nineteen, you're ready for a serious commitment."

"She's *shiklich, saund*, and"—Levi stepped out of the buggy, chuckling—"not fun. *Jah*, I suppose I will marry her."

"You don't sound all that sure it's a *gut* idea."

"*Jah.*" Levi grinned. "Let's just say, there's a distracting reason not to be baptized yet."

Fire.

Judith pushed away from the kitchen window and rushed to the door. "The barn's on fire! Get the others!" She sprinted toward the glowing structure, her mind whirling. The calves, horses . . . Rusty . . . she had to save Samuel's horse.

Inside, Judith skidded across the straw on the floor to a stop. Behind her the wooden door slammed closed.

The barn was illuminated, but not from a fire.

It was him.

The *Englischer* she had seen at Samuel's side. An unearthly glow hung suspended around the stranger. The blinding light was more than she could look upon, and Judith lifted her arm, hiding her face in the crook of her elbow.

The barn filled with rich voices chanting, "Holy, Holy, Holy is the Lord God Almighty."

Still Judith didn't dare open her eyes, and she sank to her knees.

The chanting stopped.

"Everything is possible for those who believe," said a deep baritone voice.

Fully aware of the trance suspending her, Judith remained silent. Deep within, every fiber of her being trembled. She sensed the man near, as though his breath surrounded her as he spoke.

"To everyone a measure of faith has been given."

A rush of wind pelted her body with the straw and dust stirred up from the floor, followed by a serene stillness and peace. Opening her eyes, she watched the image grow faint as the light faded. Then he was gone.

A commotion and voices at the barn door alerted her senses fully.

"It's all right," she called out as *Onkle* Amos and *Aenti* Lilly dashed inside carrying buckets.

Onkle Amos turned to her, his head cocked sideways. "Where's the fire?"

Judith looked at her *aenti*. "Did you see the bright light radiating from the barn? I was worried about Samuel's horse. And the calves."

Aenti Lilly stretched out her arms to Judith. "*Kumm*, let's go back to the *haus*."

Judith leaned against her aunt's shoulder. "You didn't see the light?"

"Shh . . . I know." Her aunt led her to the door. "I'll take you inside where you can rest."

Judith stopped. "They're okay, the animals, *jah*?"

"They're fine, Judith. Nothing happened."

"*Ach*." A wave of dizziness washed over Judith, and she

lifted her hand to her forehead. "I don't understand. I saw the light from the kitchen window. Didn't you see him?"

"Who?"

"The angel."

Aenti Lilly opened the door to the house. "You need to lie down." She turned to *Onkle* Amos, who had followed them into the house. "She's overcome with grief. It'll pass. She needs to lie down and rest." *Aenti* Lilly guided Judith by the elbow down the hallway to her bedroom. "Should I stay with you tonight?"

"*Nay*, I'm going to sleep *nau*."

Aenti Lilly paused at the door. "I'll check on you in the morning."

Judith crawled under the covers. This day was too much. Her head collapsed against the pillow and she closed her eyes.

To everyone a measure of faith . . .

But how large was her measure?

Chapter Three

Judith never dreamed she'd spend her nineteenth birthday alone. The empty house seemed dull and drafty as she padded to the kitchen in her stockings. She emptied the cold ashes from the side of the cast-iron cookstove into a bucket and carried them outside to sprinkle over the harvested area of the garden.

Mamm insisted that wood ash mixed with barn muck supported an early spring sprout. Though the *Englischers* who bought from her garden stand told her she had the best produce in the county, she had warned Judith not to become prideful of people's compliments. "God provides the sunshine and rain," *Mamm* always said, "and those elements necessary for life are never in our command."

Judith admired the pink blush of morning sky and prayed. "God, please spare Samuel and let him come home. He needs his family. *Aemen.*" Her eyes were raw from lack of sleep and crying, after she'd spent a sleepless night petitioning God.

She watched as the fine powder of ash dust settled over the brown, frost-damaged vegetation. The small patch of celery had succumbed to the cold temperature, and that saddened her the most. Next planting season she planned to double the crop size. She wanted plenty of creamed celery for her anticipated wedding feast.

She turned back to the house. While dreaming about marriage helped take her mind off her brother, it sure wouldn't get the chores done.

Judith filled the woodstove with kindling and brewed a pot of coffee. Except for the pan of sourdough biscuits baking in the oven, breakfast was prepared when a knock on the front door sounded.

"*Guder mariye.*" Andrew lifted up the full milk buckets.

She opened the screen door, and as Andrew stepped inside, she looked toward the barn for Levi.

Andrew wiped his boots on the rug. "It sure smells *gut* in here."

She glanced over her shoulder at him, then closed the door. Trying not to show her disappointment, she smiled. "I hope you're hungry." She led him to the kitchen, where she gestured for him to unload the milk buckets.

"You didn't have to fuss on my account."

Judith rose to her tiptoes in front of the sink window. "No fuss." She craned her neck to look around the lilac bush toward the barn. "Wasn't Levi going to *kumm* today?"

Andrew mumbled something incomprehensible.

Judith turned away from the window. "Did you say—"

His eyes widened like Samuel's did when he was caught sneaking a treat off her cookie sheet. Only instead of giggling like Samuel, Andrew broke into a coughing fit.

"Can I get you some water?" She removed a glass from the cabinet and pumped the handle of the well several times.

Andrew's face looked somewhat flushed, and he avoided eye contact with her when she handed him the glass. "*Denki.*"

He must have been thirsty. He drained the water in one gulp.

She reached for the glass. "Let me pour you more, or would you rather have *kaffi* with breakfast?"

"That isn't necessary. I have other chores—"

She pulled out a chair from the table. "You have to eat. Have a seat, and I'll make you a plate."

Andrew held her eyes in a long gaze, then cleared his throat, nodded, and took a place at the table. "How's the burn?" He motioned toward her hand as she placed a cup of black coffee on the table in front of him.

Judith chuckled. "I suppose all that water you doused on me kept it from blistering." Opening the oven, she took in a long whiff of baked biscuits as a blast of heat washed over her face. She heaped a serving of fried eggs, potatoes, and hot buttered biscuits onto a plate and handed it to Andrew, who stared at her, then at the plate, but said nothing. Until today, she'd never noticed that he had a sheepish sideways grin. His demeanor was typically more starched than playful. She wasn't sure what had gotten into him today.

He cleared his throat and bowed his head in a silent prayer.

Out of respect she should have closed her eyes. Instead, she studied the waves of chestnut hair that rippled around the crown of his head.

Andrew lifted his head and grinned, and her cheeks warmed when she realized he had caught her staring.

"Any word on Samuel?"

Judith brushed her hands against her apron. "*Nett* yet."

He paused between forkfuls of potatoes and stared.

At first, she couldn't decipher his expression, then she understood. His empty look wasn't bewilderment, but pity.

"I'm sorry."

"He'll be all right. I saw—" How could she go on? She didn't doubt what she saw, but how could she expect Andrew to believe her when Levi hadn't?

Andrew's brows lifted. "What did you see?"

Judith looked down at her hands, clasped in front of her. She wished he hadn't asked. How could she describe her experience so that Andrew would believe her? A stranger with magnetic blue eyes . . . a blinding light . . . a presence . . . fog . . . chanting.

"Judith, what's wrong? You're so pale. Are you ill?"

Good. At least the embarrassing blush had faded.

A knock on the door saved her from having to explain. She rose from the chair and went to answer. The sight of Levi standing on the other side of the screen door brought a wide smile to her face.

"I milked your brother David's cows first so I could spend more time here." Levi followed her into the kitchen. "Any word on Samuel?" He pulled out a chair and sat.

Judith turned to the stove. *"Nay."* She filled a cup with coffee and brought it to him.

Levi looked at Andrew. "How long have you been here?"

Andrew shrugged. "Chores are done."

"Did Judith ask you if you saw an *Englischer* yesterday?"

Andrew lifted his gaze to Judith. *"Nay."*

"What about fog?" Levi continued as though he had a checklist of questions. He turned to Judith. "You did say the man disappeared into the fog, right?"

Judith turned toward the cabinet, feeling as though a clammy blanket of dread had been wrapped around her shoulders. Maybe if she ignored the question, he'd drop it. She removed a plate from the cabinet.

"Did you notice any fog, Andrew?"

"Nay."

Judith cringed. Why must Levi tell the bishop's son, of all people? She removed the lid from the cast-iron skillet, piled the plate with fried eggs and potatoes, and brought it to the table, pretending not to notice both of their stares.

"Andrew didn't see any man or fog."

"So I heard." She slapped the plate on the table in front of Levi. What was his purpose in asking Andrew . . . to make her look delusional? She eased into the chair at the end of the table.

Levi leaned over the plate and took a deep breath. "This smells *gut*." He looked at Andrew. "What do you think, Bishop Junior—will she make a fine *fraa*?"

Andrew glanced at Judith and then at Levi. *"Jah."*

Levi turned to Judith and winked. "I spent a *gut* share of last night wondering why you made up the story of the *Englischer.*" He speared potatoes with his fork. "Because of Martha, *jah?*"

Judith cuffed her hand behind her neck, trying to thwart the anger she felt boiling up inside her. Her muscles tightened while she applied steady pressure and willed herself to keep silent.

She shot up from the table and grabbed the pot holder on the counter. With her shoulders squared, she proceeded to the table with the kettle. "More *kaffi*, Andrew?"

He wiped his mouth with a napkin and pushed back from the table. "*Nay*, I have to be going." He walked to the kitchen entry and paused. "Happy birthday."

Judith smiled, pleased he had remembered. "*Denki.*" She returned the kettle to the stove, then followed him to the door. "It was very kind of you to take care of the animals."

Andrew nodded and lifted his hat off the wall hook. "It was no trouble." His gaze drifted toward the kitchen, and she wondered what caused his now sullen expression.

He looked back at her. "Judith, don't take that from him. You deserve better."

She didn't know what to say.

His eyes widened. "Perhaps I shouldn't have spoken so forwardly. *Denki* for breakfast."

"*Jah*, have a *gut* day."

Judith returned to the kitchen. She picked up Andrew's plate and utensils and carried them to the sink. "I wish you hadn't said that about my cooking." She decided not to respond to his comment about Martha.

Levi put down his fork and crossed the room to meet her next to the sink. "That you'd make a *gut fraa*? Why?"

33

She shrugged. "Did you see Andrew's face? I feel sorry for him."

Levi cupped both his hands over her shoulders. "Don't feel sorry for him. There are many maids his age in the next district who would love to marry Bishop Junior."

Judith winced at the way he mocked Andrew, as though he were predestined to follow his father's ministry role.

Levi rolled his eyes. "But according to Andrew, there was only one person he'd ever marry."

"I know he spent a lot of time with Esther while she was ill." She wanted to add that she hadn't heard rumors of Andrew participating in *rumschpringe* or that he made a practice of meaninglessly kissing other women.

Levi stroked his hand over her cheek, and all reason to defend Andrew left her thoughts. Her eyes closed. Last night he had surprised her with a kiss. Today she'd be better prepared to respond.

"Are we alone?" he whispered.

"Uh-huh." She opened her eyes and leaned in toward him as his gaze drifted to her lips.

He leaned forward, but the squeak of the front door opening stilled them both.

"Judith?" *Aenti* Lilly called from the entry.

Levi stepped back, his eyes locked on her. "Would you spend time with me tonight?"

Every nerve in Judith's body flared to life. She steadied her fluttering heart with a deep breath. "Today isn't Sunday. There's no singing tonight."

He grinned. "I don't want to sing."

Aenti Lilly entered the kitchen. "There you are. Amos is driving me to the hospital to take food to your parents. I thought maybe you'd like to go along and see Samuel."

Judith wiped her hands against her apron. "*Jah*, I would."

Levi cleared his throat. "Tell your *daed* not to worry about the cows. I'll *kumm* back later this evening to milk them."

Judith smiled, looking forward to seeing him later. "I'll tell him, *denki*." She walked him to the door. *Sorry*, she mouthed.

Aenti Lilly removed Judith's cape from the wall peg and handed it to her. "We'll be gone the better part of the day. I have a few egg deliveries to make on our ride into town."

The twelve-mile buggy ride into town passed uninterrupted as Judith relived those few moments with Levi. Even the blaring car horns of the drivers behind their buggy didn't disrupt her daydreaming. She sighed, recalling how Levi said she'd make a good wife. Her life's purpose to serve God and her husband in faithful obedience would happen in the near future. How wonderful it would be when the others no longer viewed her as a girl, but as a married woman.

After making several stops to deliver eggs, they arrived in the city limits of Hope Falls.

Onkle Amos turned onto Oak Street and stopped the buggy at the front entrance of the medical center. "I'll see if there's a place to tie the horse," he said as she and *Aenti* Lilly stepped down from the buggy.

While *Aenti* Lilly asked the woman at the volunteers' desk

for Samuel's room number, Judith took in the new surroundings. She'd never been inside the hospital and marveled at how clean and modern the place looked.

Judith followed her aunt into the elevator and gripped the handrail until the ride came to a shuddering stop. Once the door opened, it was easy to see they had stepped into the children's ward—zoo animals decorated the walls. *Aenti* Lilly read the room numbers on each door aloud as they walked down the hall to Samuel's room.

Judith rushed to Samuel's bedside, eager to hear how he felt and what he thought of the hospital.

"He's asleep," David said from the corner where he sat. His tousled hair looked as if he'd combed his fingers through it most of the night, and his eyes were bloodshot.

"This late?" Judith's mouth dropped open. Samuel was an early riser. He never slept past seven. "Where're *Mamm* and *Daed*?"

"The neighbor drove them to the *haus*. They didn't sleep."

Aenti Lilly came around the other side of the bed. "What did the doctor say?"

David rubbed his beard. "The tests haven't come back for them to determine the full extent of his injuries. But they don't think his brain is swelling."

Judith swallowed. "Does that mean he's going to be okay?"

David shrugged. "Only God knows." He glanced at *Aenti* Lilly. "Do I smell roast chicken?"

Aenti Lilly held up the lunch tin. "Enough for your *mamm* and *daed* as well." She handed him the container and said, "There's no reason to sit here and juggle the food on your lap. Judith and I will sit with Samuel."

Judith gazed at how peaceful Samuel appeared while asleep, then looked over at David. "*Aenti* Lilly is right, you need to eat something. You've sat with him all night."

David seemed reluctant to leave the child's side. "You'll stay close to him?"

Judith nodded. "*Jah*, I won't leave him."

He turned to *Aenti* Lilly. "I am hungry."

Aenti Lilly walked him out, then poked her head back into the room. "I'm going to tell Amos what room Samuel's in. I won't be long."

Judith slid the chair that David had sat in closer to the bed so she could hold Samuel's hand.

"You *muscht* wake up, Samuel." She closed her eyes, feeling them fill with tears. "Your steps are ordered by God."

When she opened her eyes, a woman had entered the room. Dressed in what looked like a navy-dyed bedsheet made into a matching set of shirt and pants, the woman walked up to the bed rail.

"Hi, I'm Val, Samuel's nurse."

"I'm Samuel's sister Judith."

The nurse studied her watch while holding Samuel's wrist. Next she listened to his heart. Judith stood when the nurse removed what looked like a pen from her shirt pocket and aimed it into Samuel's eyes as she pried them opened.

"Why are you doing that?"

The nurse clicked the end of the pen, and the light went out. "I'm checking to see if his pupils react to the light and if they're equal size."

"What for?"

"It monitors for swelling after a head injury." The nurse removed a clipboard from the foot of the bed and jotted something on the paper. Then she injected a syringe into the plastic tubing, and yellow-tinged medicine went into the IV line.

"What are you giving him?"

The nurse tossed the empty syringe into a red box. "It's a steroid to help reduce the swelling around his spinal cord."

Judith gazed at Samuel. He looked frail and small beneath the bedclothes.

"I'll be at the nurses' desk if you should need anything."

Before Judith could ask what spinal swelling meant, the nurse had already left the room. Judith eased into the chair. "God, please take away his swelling."

Samuel whimpered then, and Judith rose from the chair.

"*Mamm?*"

Judith leaned over the bed rail. "It's Judith, Samuel. I'm here with you." She stroked his arm.

"Where am I, Judith?" He sounded frightened, disoriented.

"I'm going to get the nurse," Judith said.

But Samuel clutched her hand. "I'm afraid. Don't leave me."

Before Judith could reassure him that she would be right back, the door opened and David entered the room. "He just *nau* woke up."

David pivoted around. "Stay with him. I'll fetch the nurse."

Within seconds, the nurse entered with David on her heels. She walked over to Samuel's bed and addressed the boy. "My name is Val. Can you tell me your name?"

"His name is Samuel," David answered for him.

The nurse frowned. "I need him to answer." She turned her attention back to Samuel and smiled. "Can you tell me how you feel?"

"Where's *Mamm?*"

David bent closer to the bed, impatience etched across his face. "Samuel, answer the nurse. It's important."

"I hurt. I want *Mamm.*"

Samuel started to cry, and Judith reached over the rail and stroked his matted hair away from his face. "Samuel, tell the nurse what hurts."

"I need to ask you a few questions." The nurse reached for Samuel's hand. "Will you try to answer me?"

"Yes, he will," David responded.

The nurse sighed. "I know you're concerned about your brother, but I'll have to ask you to leave if you answer for him again. It's important after an accident of this nature that he answer for himself."

David exhaled. "I see."

"Samuel, can you squeeze my finger?"

Judith held her breath as she tried to gauge the nurse's expression.

David leaned over the bed rail. "Are you trying, Samuel?"

Judith thought it was the sound of frustration in David's voice that caused Samuel to pull his hand away from the nurse and lodge it under his opposite armpit. She wanted to nudge Samuel herself to reply, but in a nonintimidating way. David's impatience, likely due to his lack of sleep, showed.

The nurse looked up to the ceiling. "Can you point to the elephant?"

Judith looked up and for the first time saw the jungle scene painted on the tiles above them.

Samuel's eyes lit up at seeing the colorful artwork. With

reluctance, he withdrew his hand from its guarded position and pointed. His gaze roamed the ceiling with boyish curiosity.

Judith smiled, wondering if the paintings reminded him, as they did her, of the Bible stories of the Garden of Eden.

"What about the colors on the butterfly? I see red. What other colors do you see?" Val moved down to the foot of the bed as Samuel studied the painted butterfly.

"*Gayl* and *bloh*."

Judith looked to the ceiling. "*Es gut*, Samuel." Her words slipped out, and she bit her lip. She didn't want Val to reprimand her.

The nurse pulled back the covers to expose Samuel's feet. "Will you try wiggling your toes for me?"

Samuel's toes didn't move. Judith's focus shifted to Val, but the nurse kept her expression neutral.

Val removed a pen from her pocket and, with the capped end, slid it from his heel upward.

David moved from the foot of the bed back up to the head in one quick step. "Samuel, can you feel what she's doing to your foot?"

"*Nay*." His voice squeaked.

"He's frightened. He's never been in a hospital," Judith volunteered.

Val nodded, then returned the covers over his feet. "I'll page the doctor and see if he's on the floor."

Once the nurse left, David pulled the covers back again to view Samuel's feet. He touched them. "Samuel, do your feet feel cold?"

"Do I have socks on?"

Judith's throat tightened. Samuel's feet were bare.

She turned to David, unable to verbalize the question in her mind. David blinked several times as though he might cry. She'd never seen him break down.

David took Samuel's foot in both hands. "Do you know if my hand is on your foot or not?"

Lying flat on his back, Samuel raised his head to see his feet. His nose scrunched, and he turned his gaze upward. "I see a lion."

Judith began to sob. How could he not know if David was holding his foot?

"Judith, hush." David released Samuel's foot.

"You know the colors of the butterfly." A quiver rose in her throat. She looked at David. "He knows where the lion is in the bushes. His thoughts are together. *Why doesn't he know if he's wearing socks?*"

David leaned close to her. "Don't frighten him," he whispered.

The door opened, and a doctor entered with the nurse following. "Hello, I'm Dr. Finch." He reached out and shook David's hand first, then Judith's. "I hear young Samuel is awake."

"*Jah.*" David glanced at Samuel.

The doctor approached the bedside. "Can I ask you a few questions?"

Samuel nodded.

The doctor chatted with Samuel for a minute, then he said, "Now, Samuel, tell me if you can feel this." He ran the cap of his pen from Samuel's heel to his toes.

Samuel's tear-soaked eyes darted from Judith to David. "I can't move my legs. I don't feel anything."

The doctor tapped a rubber hammer on several areas of

Samuel's legs, pausing each time to monitor Samuel's expression. By the time he tapped the little boy's knees, Samuel was crying hard, yet hadn't complained once of feeling any pain.

"None of this means anything. Samuel will be all right. I know it." Judith's declaration caused the doctor to stop his examination and look at her. She avoided looking at David, who had growled something under his breath. Still, she had to share her hope with Samuel. "An angel told me so," she blurted.

Samuel's eyes widened. "He did?"

David's stare hardened. He reached for Judith's elbow and bobbed his head toward the door. "We're going to step into the hallway." He smiled at the doctor as he steered Judith away from the bed.

Samuel held his hand up and whimpered for her not to go.

David tugged on her arm. "I have to talk to Judith. You listen to what the doctor says. We will be right over there." He nodded toward the door.

Judith looked back at Samuel as she followed David. She shouldn't have to leave Samuel's side. He was frightened. If only Ellen were here, she'd be able to calm David's moodiness.

He kept the door ajar to be within earshot of the doctor and nurse and leaned into Judith to whisper. "It's in God's hands whether the boy walks again, so don't go filling his head with ideas that may be outside of God's plan." David glanced into the room, then turned back to her with a tightened jaw. "What is this talk of an angel?"

"The day Samuel fell off the barn. The angel was with Samuel when I came around the barn. He knew Samuel's name." She closed her eyes. *David hasn't slept. He's irritable because he's tired*. Calming herself, she decided not to mention the angel's second appearance in the barn.

David pinched the bridge of his nose and closed his eyes. "Don't tell him make-believe stories." He pulled his hand away and opened his eyes.

Judith blinked back tears.

"Judith, I'm sorry for sounding harsh. But Samuel wouldn't be in that bed if an angel had come."

With his tone softened, a hint of the old David returned. The wise brother she loved and admired for his wit. The David before he became the church deacon.

Aenti Lilly walked up with two cups of coffee. "Amos is staying outside with the buggy." She handed David a cup. "You look to need this more than me." She motioned to the other cup in her hand. "I thought I'd take Amos something warm to drink." Her brows knitted. "Is something wrong?"

"Samuel woke up." He leaned closer and lowered his voice. "Judith told him she'd seen an angel kneeling at his side."

Aenti Lilly sighed. "*Nay*, Judith. This is not the time to tell the child stories."

Judith searched their faces, hurt and frustration building. "It wasn't a story."

Her family had a strong belief in God. They knew God dispatched angels to help people in a time of need. Surely this was such a time. Why didn't they believe her?

"Your family has been through too much already." *Aenti* Lilly looked at David. "I fear Judith's story would only further upset your *mamm*. After almost losing Samuel, she would worry about Judith's state of mind."

"I agree." David turned to Judith. "You will not speak of this again. Do you understand?"

Judith looked at the floor tiles. No one wanted to listen to her. But how could she simply stop talking about the angel? *Wouldn't it be like not talking about You, God? I'd never deny You.*

David stepped in closer to Judith. "Answer me."

"*Jah,* I understand." *Please forgive me, God.*

He turned to *Aenti* Lilly. "Will you take Judith home *nau?*"

Judith walked to the elevator, thankful for her aunt's silence. She pushed the down button, and a moment later the doors opened. Several people filed out of the small space before Judith and *Aenti* Lilly could enter. It wasn't until she was inside and had turned to face the closing doors that she noticed the mesmerizing blue eyes of the *Englischer* staring at her from outside the elevator. His gaze bored into her, while a blinding light shone around him. Her arms prickled with tingly bumps. She opened her mouth to acknowledge him, but her voice caught.

Her vision hazed with floating spots.

Her knees buckled.

She heard *Aenti* Lilly's voice coming from a great distance, and the elevator compartment went dark.

Chapter Four

"Samuel's legs are paralyzed."

Andrew edged closer to the barn wall after overhearing Jonas Fischer tell of his son's condition to the bishop. What felt like a crushing weight of bricks pressed against Andrew's chest as he strained to listen. A dull string of heartbeats passed in silence.

"Hannah is . . . not so well." Mr. Fischer's voice trailed off.

"I'm sorry to hear this news. The community will see that your pumpkin crop goes to market. Andrew will milk the cows."

His father's list of how the community would pull together droned on. Not that it wasn't a blessing for the Fischers to have church members to rely on for support, but Andrew had to wonder if any of it offered comfort or even mattered in relation to his son losing the use of his legs.

"Judith concerns me as well." Jonas let out a long sigh.

Andrew held his breath. Was Judith ill? She acted normal during breakfast yesterday. Although when he returned later in the evening to milk cows, he hadn't seen her, nor was there any smoke curling out from the stovepipe.

"She passed out in the elevator at the hospital. Then when she awoke, she was rambling about having seen an angel. She told Samuel he would walk." Brother Fischer sighed. "I know she blames herself for his accident, but—"

Andrew leaned against the barn wall, his stomach aching as though he'd been kicked by a horse. Judith told stories, but never ones she believed. He found it difficult to think she would make up a story about seeing an angel just in an attempt to cheer Samuel's spirit.

His father and Jonas were walking off now, and Andrew couldn't hear any more of their conversation. He drew in a steady breath and stepped out from the barn.

"Andrew." His father waved him over.

He looked down at the brown grass as he met them at the buggy.

"When you were at the Fischers' house, did you hear Judith talk of seeing an angel?"

"*Nay.*"

"I told Jonas you would keep up the chores."

"*Jah*, I will." Andrew looked up long enough to catch a glimpse of Mr. Fischer's down-turned mouth.

"And if you hear any talk of angels . . ." His father cleared his throat.

If they were asking for a report on Judith's suspicious behavior, they might better probe Levi. Then again, after the way Levi hounded Judith the day before, Andrew wouldn't wish to give him the task of interrogating her. "Judith doesn't say much to me."

"I'm taking Hannah back to sit with Samuel at the hospital. *Denki*, Andrew." Jonas turned to his buggy.

His father waited until the Fischer buggy was out of view before he said, "I want to know what Judith is saying about an angel." He shook his head. "Brother Jonas doesn't need to handle problems with his daughter at a time like this."

Andrew silently agreed. But if Judith really was telling stories, surely her brother David would speak to her.

"I didn't make up the man. I saw him next to Samuel." Judith poured hot water from the kettle into a line of cups. She leaned back to glance from the kitchen into the sitting room, where the womenfolk were chatting as they quilted. She turned back to Deborah and lowered her voice. "He's an angel."

Deborah bobbed the tea bag into the hot water. "Judith, you know I believe you, right?"

Judith nodded.

"But as your friend, I think you had better keep this to yourself. There's so much talk *nau*. If you keep insisting that you saw an angel, it will only hurt your family more."

Judith gulped. If the community were talking, it meant she'd brought condemnation on herself. Shame on her family.

"You know it's hard for me to keep quiet," she said. Judith shook her head slowly. Samuel's frightened expression came to her mind. She'd only meant to comfort and encourage him.

"I know this is upsetting. But the talk will pass." Deborah patted her arm. "You mustn't blame yourself for Samuel's condition."

"*Ach*, how can *Ich nett*?" She pointed to the sitting room. "With every stitch I sew into the quilt we're making for him, I pray for forgiveness."

"And *mei* prayer is for you to understand and accept God's will for Samuel."

"Don't pray for me. Pray for Samuel, please." Judith picked up two cups to take to the women and motioned for her friend to do the same.

After serving everyone, Judith sat down and sipped the tea. Her mother had gone in to the hospital to stay with Samuel, so *Aenti* Lilly took charge. She kept a tight rein on the conversation, steering it away from Samuel's accident and quizzing the women about their canning of winter squash and how many acres of pumpkins they'd be sending to market.

Eventually, though, someone said, "Samuel will find comfort with this blanket."

"*Jah*, what a fine idea for us to sew it together," Deborah's mother said.

The bishop's wife agreed. "It shall keep his legs warm in the winter, *jah*?"

"Would he know if they were cold?" Martha asked softly.

Judith winced, and Rebecca poked her head up from the corner where the children were playing with rag dolls. "Is it true that Samuel won't ever walk again?" her little sister asked.

The women exchanged glances with one another.

Rebecca sidled over to Judith. "Please, tell me if it's true."

Judith placed her arm around her sister and leaned closer. "I believe he will walk," she whispered.

Rebecca's eyes brightened. "He will?"

The women immediately began to murmur, and Judith felt her lungs tighten.

"Judith's not well," *Aenti* Lilly said quickly. "She hit her head when she fainted in the elevator." She looked at Judith. "Isn't that right?"

Rebecca started to whimper. "Will you have to go to the hospital too?"

"*Nay*, I'm fine."

Ellen set her cup on the lamp table and lifted Rebecca into her arms. "God is looking after Samuel."

Judith scanned the women's worried faces. "I saw a bright light outside the elevator," she began, but caught her words before saying what she knew would only bring her grief.

The bishop's wife looked at *Aenti* Lilly. "Didn't you say she saw a strange light in the barn as well?"

Aenti Lilly closed her eyes and nodded.

Judith couldn't help herself from blurting, "I saw an angel." She looked at Rebecca cuddled in Ellen's arms. "And Samuel will walk."

"Judith," Mrs. Lapp said calmly, "it is not our place to dictate to God what *muscht* happen. We *muscht* accept His will as it comes." She looked around the room at the others, then brought her gaze back to Judith. "None of us wants you to blame yourself. We know how much you love Samuel."

Martha began sniffling, and *Aenti* Lilly handed her a hankie. "I don't understand. Samuel's just a child," Martha said, blowing her nose. She wiped her puffy eyes and glared at Judith, then she stood and bolted out the door.

An uneasy silence fell over the women. A few shifted in their chairs. Some fumbled with their bonnet ties. Finally *Aenti* Lilly set her cup on the empty wooden chair beside her and reached for her sewing hoop. "It will be *gut* to have this blanket done for Samuel to *kumm* home to."

Deborah's mother passed her empty cup to her daughter. "Why don't you and Judith collect the dishes."

As Judith stood, a numbing sensation traveled the length of her body. It all seemed like a dream. First Samuel's accident, then fainting in the elevator, and now the women busying themselves with their needles to avoid eye contact with her.

Deborah handed her some empty cups. *"Kumm,"* she said, motioning her to the kitchen.

Still dazed, Judith followed.

Deborah set the dishes in the sink. "I thought you were going to let it go. *Nau* the bishop will get involved."

Judith sighed. "I don't know what compelled me." She glanced into the sitting room, then turned back to her friend. *"Jah, Ich* do. He told me Samuel's steps were ordered by God. Only an angel would know what God said."

"Judith, please. It isn't *gut* to talk as though you know how God thinks. It's dangerous. What would the bishop say?"

"I fainted from the radiating glow of an angel. And he was on the children's ward to see Samuel. I just know it's true." Judith paused. "I need to talk with Martha."

Even as a child, Martha was often overly dramatic, espe-cially when her parents weren't around. But Judith knew that her sister's angry departure was only a cover for the hurt and anxiety she felt for Samuel.

"She's taking this hard." Deborah made a shooing gesture with her hand. "Go talk to her. I'll wash the dishes."

"*Denki*." She peeked into the sitting room. "It looks like they're finishing up."

Lord, I need a large portion of kindness, Judith prayed. She sucked in a deep breath and stepped outside.

She found Martha sitting under the maple tree. Her hands covered her face and her shoulders shook. The closer Judith came to her sister, the tighter her throat felt.

"Martha," she said softly.

Her sister looked up, swiping the wetness from her face.

"Samuel will be—"

"It's all your fault." Martha stood and crossed her arms. "If you weren't so nosy during prayer, you would've seen him wan-der off."

"Let's not talk about this *nau*," Judith said, using the smooth-est tone she could muster. She glanced over to the field at Levi, who was loading pumpkins into the wagon.

"Why? Because you know you were wrong?"

"Martha, you and I both know the truth." She reached for her sister's arm and swept her hand gently over it. "You were flirting with Levi."

Martha jerked her arm away. "Maybe he doesn't like you."

Judith resumed looking at Levi, who just at that moment looked in her direction and smiled. Her chest filled with warmth.

She remembered his asking her to attend a singing shortly after she'd turned seventeen, so he could take her home. At first he had seemed angry about her parents' refusal to abide by the community's usual standards. But two years had passed . . . and two days ago he had surprised her with a kiss under this very tree.

Judith turned to Martha. "*Jah*," she said. "He does."

Chapter Five

Andrew cleared his throat when Levi didn't immediately take the pumpkin from his hand. Following the direction of his cousin's gaze, Andrew assumed it was Judith's friendly smile that had captured his cousin's attention.

The sewing get-together had apparently ended. The womenfolk milled on the porch and near the buggies. That meant he and Levi would lose the younger boys' help.

Andrew called to the crew carrying pumpkins out of the field. "James, Jacob, Peter, Noah—your *mamms* are ready to go."

The boys hurried to the wagon, deposited their pumpkins, and headed toward the women.

Andrew nudged Levi. "I guess it's just us *nau*."

"I'll recruit more hands." Levi called to Judith and Martha, "Any chance you two want to load pumpkins?"

Although the girls didn't hesitate, Andrew wasn't sure whether they'd be more of a distraction to Levi than a help with harvesting the field.

"Where do you want us?" Judith directed her question to Levi.

He jumped off the side of the wagon. "Andrew will cut them off the vine and hand them to you. You can pass them to me, and I'll bring them to Martha, who will arrange them by size in the wagon."

Judith nodded and looked at Andrew. "What row are we working in?"

Andrew motioned for her to follow him while Levi showed Martha how to arrange the pumpkins in the wagon.

Andrew squatted down and cut the ripe pumpkin. "Sewing group ended early?"

"*Jah.*"

Andrew could see that Judith had been crying. He guessed that whatever had triggered her tears was also responsible for the early end to the gathering. Normally the womenfolk worked together for several hours. Today they hadn't made it much past noon.

He handed off two small pumpkins and continued down the row. He had more cut when she returned from relaying the others to Levi.

Her expression strained as she went to pick up a large pumpkin.

Andrew helped her lift it and gently released his hold. "Too heavy?"

She jostled it in her hands. "*Nay*, I can manage." She glanced over her shoulder at Martha and Levi talking.

Andrew paused to watch Judith teeter down the dirt row and pass the pumpkin to Levi. Martha went to receive the pumpkin and, with a wink at Levi, planted her hands on top of his.

Judith snapped around, her smile gone. She grasped the back of her neck, kneading the muscles. He'd seen that gesture before—she probably didn't even realize she was doing it.

This current handoff arrangement wasn't going to work.

Andrew knelt and cut a few more pumpkins. "You all right?" he asked when she returned.

"*Jah*, why do you ask?" She fiddled with the ties of her head covering.

He supported the pumpkin on his knee. "You keep turning the strings like that, you might choke."

"If only I could."

Her words were spoken under her breath, but he smiled.

She released the ties. "Sorry, I didn't mean for you to hear that."

"You don't have to silence your words around me." He understood how Martha and Levi's exchange would have annoyed her.

"My mouth has already gotten me into trouble today." She pointed to his knee. "Are you going to hand me that?"

He nodded, held up the pumpkin, then, taking her hint, returned to cutting vines. "We should have the wagon loaded shortly."

"*Jah*," Judith said, but her attention was back on Martha and Levi.

Andrew cut another pumpkin. "You want me to suggest changing places? We could break them up."

"*Nay.*" Judith turned back to Andrew. "Martha's young and just acting out."

That might be Martha's issue, but Levi was twenty and old enough to avoid such forwardness from a girl. But Andrew kept those thoughts to himself. It wasn't his concern anyway. He was there to help harvest the crop before a heavy frost destroyed the produce. He didn't intend to interfere in his cousin's affairs.

Another handoff, and Levi landed his hands atop Martha's. The games continued for several more passes. Judith didn't respond to it, pretending either not to see it or not to care about their lack of discretion.

Andrew carried the last pumpkin to the wagon himself.

Levi latched the wooden tailgate. "Martha wants to see Samuel." He faced Judith. "I thought maybe the four of us could drive into the hospital. I haven't seen him yet." He looked over his shoulder at Andrew. "Have you?"

"*Nay.*" Andrew turned to Judith. "I'm willing, if you think Samuel would like that."

Judith smiled. "*Jah*, he'd be happy for the visit."

"Let's go, then," Levi said.

Martha looked at her dirt-covered hands. "We'd better wash up first."

They all agreed and headed for the pump. Judith and Martha went first as Andrew pumped the handle. When Levi took a turn, he cupped his hands to collect water and tossed some playfully at Judith, bringing a wide smile to her face. Her eyes darted nervously as Levi came up beside her and dabbed his wet hand over a smudge mark on her cheek.

Then Martha's heavy sigh summoned his attention. He grabbed her wrists and played like he planned to drag her under the spigot.

Andrew stopped pumping.

"Whose side are you on, Bishop Junior?"

Andrew gazed at Judith, the trusting soul. If he had to choose sides, he'd take hers. His cousin's actions were shameful. Before Esther died, Andrew wouldn't have dared be playful with anyone but her.

"I'll harness Patsy," he said and walked toward the corral where the horses grazed.

"And leave me two against one?"

Andrew shrugged. His thoughts shifted to Samuel, wondering if the boy would feel up to having company and whether he knew his condition was permanent. Andrew coaxed Patsy to the fence with a handful of grain he'd taken from the barn. He took his time harnessing the horse.

Judith came to the buggy first with a baggie of cookies in her hand. "Samuel's favorite," she said.

"You're a thoughtful sister."

"Would you like one?"

"*Nay.*" He leaned over to loop the leather strap under the horse's girth. "Are they *kumming?*"

"*Jah.*"

Andrew glanced over Judith's shoulder at Levi and Martha strolling toward them. "You're nicer than most," he said.

Judith looked behind her. "At least she's smiling *nau.*" She turned back to Andrew but wouldn't hold his gaze. Her eyes darted up to the sky, around the yard, and to the buggy. She reached for the buggy door and said, "I'll wait inside."

Judith took the backseat. Andrew climbed into the front. They waited silently as Levi and Martha got in.

On the ride to the hospital, Levi and Martha's playful banter continued. Andrew focused his attention on seeing Samuel. He suspected Judith was dealing with the same dread. Then again, perhaps Judith's silence had more to do with the way Martha giggled at every word Levi spoke.

"This is the long way into town," Levi commented.

"*Jah*, I always go this route." Ever since Esther passed away, Andrew had avoided the road leading to her house. The road he had traveled every day for a year. The one that led to her resting place, yet offered his soul no peace.

"This way will take another forty minutes." Levi twisted on the seat. "Was something wrong with the other road?"

"I don't go that direction." Andrew hoped his cousin would remain silent for the rest of the trip, but after a long moment passed, Levi leaned closer.

"Esther?" he whispered.

"*Jah*." He tapped the reins, and Patsy picked up the pace.

After a few more minutes passed, Levi turned his attention back to Judith and Martha and, to Andrew's relief, didn't mention anything more about Esther.

Once they reached the hospital, Andrew found an area away from the traffic to tie the horse. He would use Patsy as an excuse not to stay in the room long, he decided, walking into the main lobby.

Levi pushed the elevator button. "Is this where you fainted?" he asked.

"*Jah.*" Judith closed her eyes, either avoiding more of Levi's questions, praying, or possibly feeling nauseated by the upward motion.

The elevator stopped, and they stepped out. The paintings on the walls drew their attention.

Judith pointed ahead. "His room is down this hall."

Martha's pace slowed. Her face contorted, and she sniffled as they reached the room.

Judith opened the door, and Samuel saw them enter and brightened at once.

She held up the baggie. "I brought you some cookies." She looked at her mother sitting next to the bed. "If it's okay with *Mamm.*"

Mrs. Fischer gave her daughter a slight smile and nodded.

As Samuel reached into the baggie to choose a cookie, Martha edged closer to the bed. He paused and raised his brows at his sister. "What's wrong with you?"

"I was worried about you." Martha rubbed her eyes.

Samuel's smile widened as he withdrew a peanut butter cookie. "I get to eat in bed here."

All of them chuckled nervously, and the tension in the room eased a bit.

"Don't get used to that," Mrs. Fischer warned. She looked over to Judith. "How are things at the *haus?*"

"*Gut.*" Judith looked around the room. "Where's *Daed?*"

"He read in the paper the *wedder* is expected to change, so he headed to David's *haus* to ask his help to bring in the crops."

Andrew stepped forward. "I'll help them."

"*Jah*, me too," Levi added.

"*Denki*." Mrs. Fischer gave them a weary smile. She asked about the pumpkins and thanked him and Levi for the work they'd done. She asked if Rebecca was still with Ellen and David and if Lilly was dropping by to check on them. But she didn't mention anything regarding Samuel's condition.

Several silent intervals passed where no one found a topic to discuss. Samuel ate his cookies, seemingly unaware of how uncomfortable everyone felt. After an hour lapsed, Andrew wasn't sure he could bear another passage of awkward silence.

"I should check Patsy." He tapped Samuel's foot. Even through the covers, his foot was stiff. Cold. Andrew withdrew his hand. "You get well."

"It's getting late. You should all go," Mrs. Fischer said.

Samuel swept his hand over the blankets, and crumbs spilled onto the floor. "Will you *kumm* back to visit me again?"

The boy's gaze pierced Andrew's heart. "*Jah*, soon." He turned away the moment Mrs. Fischer stood to straighten Samuel's bedcovers. As he headed for the door, Judith and Martha were saying their good-byes, and Mrs. Fischer was softly scolding Samuel for messing up the hospital floor with his crumbs.

Levi followed, and once they were in the hallway, he blew out a breath. "That was hard."

"*Jah*," Andrew replied.

Judith and Martha came out, shutting the door behind them. They took a few steps away from the room before Martha broke down, sobbing.

"I can't see him like that. He's just a boy." Sobbing harder, she turned into Levi's arms and buried her face against his chest.

Levi patted her back. "It's hard, but you need to stay strong. Do it for Samuel."

Martha lifted her head off Levi's chest. Still, they stayed practically nose-to-nose as they talked. "Why would God do this to a child?"

Levi guided her head back to his embrace and rested his chin on her head. "I don't know."

Andrew looked at Judith, standing off to his side. She too was weeping. What was he supposed to do, hold her? He should've checked on the horse sooner. He couldn't comfort her, not the same way Levi had with Martha. He leaned toward Judith. "There's a water fountain down the hall. Maybe a drink would help."

She nodded and walked away with him.

"I'm sorry," Andrew said.

Judith wiped her eyes. "For what?"

"Samuel." He pointed at Levi and Martha. "Those two."

"She's taking it hard."

Andrew stared at her. Was she really so blind? Levi should be comforting her, not her sister. He glanced back at the two standing close, talking. For Judith's sake, he hoped his initial impression was wrong . . . but seeing them, he couldn't be certain Martha hadn't fallen into Levi's arms for attention.

Judith pressed the fountain lever and sipped the water. When she finished, Levi and Martha were walking toward them.

Martha bent to drink from the fountain, and Levi stood with Judith.

"She's mad at God for doing this to Samuel," he said.

Judith sighed. "Did you talk sense into her?"

Levi shrugged. "I tried."

Andrew tossed his head. "We need to go."

They rode down to the bottom floor in silence and spoke little on the ride home.

Andrew stopped the buggy near the Fischers' porch. "Tell your *daed* I'll *kumm meiya.*"

"*Denki*," Judith said, stepping out of the buggy. She glanced at Levi. "See you *meiya?*"

"*Jah.*"

Martha delayed getting out. When she did, she paused near Levi's door opening and leaned in to whisper something Andrew couldn't make out. He wasn't sure he wanted to hear if he could.

Levi grinned at Martha. "Maybe so."

Whatever words they shared caused Martha to giggle. Suddenly, she was no longer the grieving teenager seeking comfort.

Then again, maybe she was.

Chapter Six

At the first hint of dawn, dozens of buggies filed into the drive. Judith's heart sank, remembering the excitement she'd felt on the morning the community arrived to build the barn. Similar chattiness carried over the air. It wasn't the same today. But how could it be, with Samuel in the hospital?

Martha met Levi's buggy in the drive. He glanced over her shoulder, flashed a smile to Judith along with a quick wave.

Judith's smile widened as she waved back. Surely the day would be brighter now that Levi had arrived.

Andrew walked up behind Levi and tapped his shoulder, and the two headed toward the field.

Judith greeted Deborah as she climbed out of her parents' buggy.

"How did your talk with Martha go?" her friend asked once they were alone.

Judith shrugged. "Martha is Martha. She blames me. She blames God. I think she's in love with Levi. I know she's had a crush on him probably since she turned twelve." Judith slowly shook her head. "Lately, *Ich* don't know what has *kumm* over her. She used to be a sweet girl."

Deborah slid her arm under Judith's. "It's the world. Didn't you say she's been singing *Englisch* songs?"

"*Jah*. But you know Martha. She's talked about what it would be like living outside the community for the past two years *nau*."

"She'll get over herself."

"So *Ich* hope. But mad at God . . ." Judith shook her head. "It's *nett* healthy."

Deborah leaned closer. "I have something to tell you." She looked around. "Ben asked me to the next singing *nacht*. That's *wundebaar, jah*?"

Judith squeezed her friend's arm. "I'm so happy for you."

Deborah's gaze moved across the field until it stopped on Ben. He worked the team of four draft horses in the corner opposite Levi. "Well," she said, pulling her eyes away from the field, "we should find ourselves something useful to do."

"*Jah*, I suppose work will help pass the time." Judith leaned closer. "Maybe we can volunteer to run water out to the field in a while."

"*Gut* idea."

Judith and Deborah joined the other women. Deborah seemed oblivious to the women's aloofness, but Judith wasn't. Their faces crinkled with concern, fear, indifference—she wasn't sure what they were thinking. But as the day continued, it became plain to see there was tension every time she entered a room.

Judith pulled Deborah aside. "Why are they avoiding me?"

Her friend's face turned serious as she leaned closer. "Whatever you do, don't bring up the angel. Nothing about seeing an *Englischer* either. They think—" She bit her bottom lip.

"What? Deborah, you *muscht* tell me."

"They think the stress has addled your mind."

Judith swallowed hard. "Do you?"

"*Nay!*"

At least someone believed her. Judith bobbed her head toward the kitchen. "Let's take water out to the field."

As Judith opened the kitchen cabinet and removed two gallon-sized glass pickle jars, several of the younger children entered the room and circled around her.

"Will you take us outside for a walk?" Emily asked.

"Perhaps, after I take water to the men in the field."

"Can we *kumm* with you?" Rachel asked.

Emily bounced on the balls of her feet. "Please."

Martha entered the kitchen. "What are the jars for?"

"Water." Judith took the containers to the sink.

Emily tugged Martha's dress. "We're going to take water out to the field with Judith."

"And she'll probably tell you stories of seeing an angel too." Martha's voice grew louder. "Would you like that? Would you like to hear stories of how she followed an *Englischer* and he disappeared in the fog?"

Silence fell over the kitchen.

Then Ellen intervened. "Stop telling the children that," she said.

Emily leaned her head against Judith's arm. "She's a *gut* storyteller." She turned to her *mamm*. "Can we take water out to the field with Judith?"

"*Nay, nett* a *gut* idea." She redirected Emily toward the sitting room.

"She can go with me. I'll take water out," Martha suggested.

Emily spun back around. "*Jah*, please, *Mamm*?"

"I suppose their water jugs are empty by *nau*." Emily's *mamm* looked down at her daughter and smiled. "You can go with Martha, but stay away from the horses."

"*Jah*."

Martha cast a gloating smirk at Judith. "I'll take the jars."

Judith's eyes darted from one woman's down-turned head to another. Without saying anything, she turned and went outside.

Deborah followed. "I don't understand your sister. Didn't she know not to bring up that subject of storytelling?"

"She knows exactly what she's doing. And she knows how much I love spending time with the children."

Deborah rested her hand on Judith's shoulder. "I know you do. And they love your stories. But . . . if you want a marriage proposal, you need to change your storytelling image."

"You know I want to be married more than anything. It's all I've ever wanted." She glanced at the house. She didn't want to be on the porch when Martha came outside. "I'm going to take a walk."

"I'll *kumm*." Deborah stepped off the porch.

"*Nay*. I don't want to get you into trouble too." She motioned to the house. "I just need a few minutes away from everyone. I won't be long."

"Find a place and pray. This all *muscht* blow over or I fear you'll end up *leddich* like Katie."

For years the girls had heard Ellen despair of her sister Katie's unmarried status. And they both pledged not to follow Katie's unfortunate footsteps and be disappointments to their parents. Judith turned and walked toward the barn, but with the men stocking the loft with hay, she couldn't hide inside with the horses.

She rounded the corner of the barn and paused at the place where she'd found Samuel unresponsive. *Please forgive me, Lord. I've managed to embarrass my family. How will I ever earn their respect? They all think I'm telling stories. But I did see an angel, didn't I?*

She continued to walk across the pasture toward the apple orchard. At the end of the grove, she followed the footpath that weaved between the yellow-leafed poplar trees down to the river. This summer she had been busy with garden work and hadn't spent time at the river as she loved to do. Today wasn't warm enough to remove her shoes and soak her feet in the water, so she stayed up on the grassy bank.

God, even the parents want their children to stay away from me. What do I have to offer my church? What do I have to offer You? I might as well be openly shunned by my community. No one believes me. Judith turned her face into the direction of the breeze. Tears trickled down her face.

The leaves rustled overhead as though a storm brewed in the distance. But when she looked up, the sun was shining and the sky was blue. Judith closed her eyes and welcomed the breeze that dried her tears.

"What's troubling your soul, Judith?"

The baritone voice caused Judith to jump. Bounding to her feet, she turned in a quick circle. No one. The question had come as if from someone next to her, yet she was alone. She released her breath. The rustling leaves must have tricked her mind.

"Tell me what troubles you."

This time when she spun toward the voice, the angel was beside her. Petrified by his towering stature, she broke out into a cold sweat and her teeth began to chatter. Today he appeared even more gigantic. One look at the keenness in his deep-set eyes caused Judith to raise her arm and bury her face in the crook of her elbow while dropping to her knees, cowering.

"Do not be afraid." The richness in his tone hailed as a choir of a thousand.

Lying prone and breathing in the scent of the earth, she trembled. He said not to fear, but hearing the earth groan beneath her, she wished she could wither away, sure that at any moment she'd be swallowed into the earth's core. *"Himlish-engel."* Heavenly angel.

"Judith, do not worship me. Stand up, for I come on God's command."

She gulped. Apparently she had caused more problems than she thought. God had sent His angel concerning her. After hesitating a moment, she pushed off the ground and stood. With her eyes aimed at the caked dirt on her shoes, she waited for what would happen next.

"I will not destroy you if you wish to look upon me."

Her heart fluttered against her ribs like a caged bird trying to take flight. In slow motion, she lifted her head. Her eyes widened and her pulse surged as she carried her gaze up to his broad chest and head. His neck looked as thick as the trunk of a river birch.

"Why do you cry?"

"I told them what you said about Samuel, but no one believes me."

"Ah, because they do not see with their own eyes, they do not believe." He walked to the riverbank and sat on a large rock. "Do you believe, Judith?"

"I . . . want to." Unable to gain control of the quiver in her voice, she swallowed. She wanted to believe this wasn't a dream. That she was indeed talking with an angel. An angel sent on God's command. Yes, she wanted to believe, but doubts interfered with her judgment.

When Judith glanced up, prepared to confess her apprehension, he was gone. She scanned the area toward the river's edge and saw him entering the heavy growth of ferns. "Why are you leaving?" She stood still for a moment. "I have questions for you," she called, walking in his direction.

If he had taken the path, she might have found him. But when she hiked into the dense undergrowth of brush, she had to concentrate so she wouldn't lose her footing on the rocky embankment and slip into the river.

A sudden movement out of the corner of her eye startled her. As her heartbeat returned to normal, she wasn't sure who was frightened more, she or the whitetail deer that sprang out of the ferns.

Finally her feet needed to rest. Judith sat in the midst of the ferns. Surrounded by the leafy canopy, she wrapped her arms around her legs and lowered her head against her knees. She listened to the sound of the rushing water, and her thoughts drifted to how God supplies the deer a place to bed by the stream of water. The psalm about thirsting for the living God came to her mind as heaviness closed her eyes. *When can I go and meet with God?*

A profound silence dulled her senses, deadened her thoughts. Like a creature spooling into a dormant state, she lay, fetal position, on the ground. With her eyes closed, she heard chanting. Those same lulling sounds she'd heard after Samuel's accident were causing her eyes to close . . .

The sky cracked open, releasing pea-sized ice pellets. When they landed on her, they changed into a warm liquid and spread. Soon long, pointed icicles hung from her arms, dripping liquid that froze as it touched the ground, weighing her down like iron shackles. When her eyelashes froze to her upper lids so that she could not close her eyes, an angel appeared. His wool-spun hair was white and his skin bronze. He hovered so that his feet did not touch the ground.

He placed a road under her feet. Although her feet remained stationary, the road moved her through time—two cycles of seasons passed before her eyes. Without warning, the road split three separate ways, and a voice told her to choose. Both the rocky road to the left and the paved one to the right were wider than the center, which was a mere footpath. Unable to see beyond the turns, she felt her heart thump against her icy armor.

The angel spread his hand before her eyes, and everything in sight turned to shades of gray. The center path, however, glowed. Trees, top-heavy with golden-colored leaves, glittered against the blue sky as they convulsed. Persuaded to follow the voice calling her name, she tried moving closer to the center path. Her feet, however, frozen to the three-pronged junction, forced her to stay planted, and her heart cried out to God . . .

Chapter Seven

J udith woke with her cheek against the damp ground. She blinked several times as she tried to bring her surroundings into focus. Seeing the daylight fading, she realized she'd been out for a while. Her mind fogged over as she tried to recall the details of the dream. Three roads to choose . . . what did it mean?

A prickling sensation slithered down her spine.

Dozens of ravens perched in a nearby tree suddenly took flight. Their wings flapped and their raucous caws echoed in the stillness. Judith scrambled to her feet. Why ravens? Why didn't she wake to the cooing of doves or the sound of sparrows? Ravens with their loud, alarming calls were unnerving. As she moved through the brush, unable to keep close watch on her footing, her heart hammered and her breaths turned jagged.

It wasn't long before she reached the wood-lined path that led to home. She pushed herself to run faster, refusing to let the shifting shadows of the woods hinder her progress. Focused on the trail, she didn't notice the figure ahead until his strong arms caught her midstride. He brought her to an abrupt halt as he pulled her off the trail. Gulping for air and unable to scream, she thrust her fists against his back. Her legs crumpled, and the figure caught her before she hit the ground.

"I'm sorry. I didn't mean to frighten you," Andrew said, releasing his hold.

Judith struggled to regain her breath. He should have spoken sooner so she knew it was him.

"Are you okay?"

"You practically tackled me. Why did you have to knock the wind out of me?"

"You almost plowed me over. I didn't think you were going to stop." He leaned around a tree to look in the direction she'd come from. "What were you running from?"

Andrew's father was the bishop. How could she tell him that she'd spoken with an angel? She'd be shunned—if the community hadn't already decided to dismiss her. If she shared what she'd witnessed, *meidung* was more than a possibility.

The crack of branches above them caused her to flinch. Startled by the noise, she bolted into what felt like a wall—Andrew's thick chest.

His sturdy arms surrounded her. "You're trembling," he whispered, tucking her head against him.

She listened to his heartbeat, steady and firm. His affection caught her off guard. He was usually so reserved.

Levi had mocked Andrew, saying the girls found him boring. Obviously, Andrew hadn't recovered from Esther's death. Perhaps he never would, seeing how Levi said even the bishop couldn't persuade his son to find a mate.

Andrew eased her back to arm's length. "Are you okay *nau*?"

Judith nodded. "What was that? Please tell me it was a squirrel."

He glanced up at the limb overhead and chuckled. "Would it be less frightening to think it was a furry rodent lurking in the darkness?"

She crossed her arms. "You think that's funny?"

He shrugged, and his lips twitched as he tried to hold back his laughter.

She groaned. Not him too. Andrew Lapp never poked fun at people.

"I'm sorry," he said sincerely. "It was a raccoon." His lips twitched again.

Judith wanted to hold on to her annoyance, but the silliness of the situation hit her, and soon she was laughing with him.

He stood with his hands jammed in his pockets, rocking back on his heels, a sheepish grin splayed across his face. "You have a nice laugh."

She covered her mouth with her hand long enough to compose herself. "What are you doing out here?" She hoped her tone didn't sound as ruffled to him as it did to her.

Andrew looked toward the trail. "I was looking for you. Everyone is."

Everyone. Had a search group been called? David, in

particular, would be upset with her for worrying their parents and for disregarding supper preparations.

"*Kumm*, I'll walk you to the *haus*." Andrew pulled his hand from his pocket and placed his arm around her long enough to turn her toward the path. "Where have you been anyway?"

"I . . . got lost." *Following an angel through the ferns.*

He stopped and stared at her, longer than she liked.

She began walking to break the awkwardness of his gaze.

After several moments, he broke the silence. "We've all been down to the river a thousand times. How did you get lost?"

His tone didn't sound accusing, yet she felt the weight of his probing question. She slowed her pace, scuffling her feet and kicking up leaves as she walked. She was grateful they were deep into the woods and the sun had set, so he wouldn't see the turmoil on her face.

"I wasn't lost. I was hiding."

He blew out a breath. "From who?"

She continued to walk. "Some of the parents . . ." Her words trailed off, and she wished her thoughts would fade with them.

A light flickered in the distance. Her leg muscles locked.

Andrew halted at the same time. "What's wrong?"

"Did you see that?" She wouldn't have to explain her vision if the angel appeared now. Andrew would have his own story to tell.

He nudged her shoulder. "You're getting awful jumpy."

Jumpy, he says. If he'd seen what I did, maybe his nerves would be on edge too. After concentrating her focus on that section of woods and not seeing another flash, she let out her breath. With Andrew at her side, her muscles recovered and she could walk without her legs feeling like noodles.

At another flicker of light, she gasped. "Did you see that?"

Andrew's chest expanded protectively, and he shielded her with his arms before he took a step forward. "Levi, is that you?"

"*Jah.*"

Judith sighed so hard, she was sure Andrew felt her breath on the back of his neck.

Twigs snapped in the wooded area, and Levi's light became visible. "Did you find Judith?"

Andrew turned, his breath warming her face. "She's with me."

A pine branch sprung forward, then swept back as Levi emerged. He directed the flashlight in her direction. "What have you been doing?"

"What are you doing with a flashlight? You frightened her," Andrew said.

"I keep one in my buggy for when I'm out late." He turned to Judith. "I was worried about you."

Her heart lightened at the thought. She longed to see the sincerity in his eyes, but the beam of light aimed at her face blacked everything out.

"Martha said you created quite a stir in the *haus.*"

Martha said . . . Her stomach knotted.

Levi directed the light over to Andrew. "She was making more claims that Samuel will walk."

Judith had a full view of Andrew's raised brows.

Levi flipped the light back on her. "I told you, Judith. There wasn't any fog that day, and no one saw a man standing at Samuel's side."

"He was kneeling," Judith corrected.

"Kneeling," Levi echoed in a mocking tone. "Did you tell Andrew what this man said?"

Judith raised her hand to block the beam. Why was Levi doing this to her? She thought he cared about her. Her thoughts swirled. How could she love a man who didn't believe in her?

"You don't have to tell me, Judith." Andrew stepped onto the trail. "We all should get back."

"Her imaginary man told her Samuel would walk." Levi chuckled.

Andrew's abrupt stop caused Judith to plow into him. His hand reached out to steady her balance. "Don't laugh at Samuel's condition," he replied before turning and trudging toward the house.

"Hey, Andrew." Levi waited for him to turn. "Catch." He tossed the flashlight to Andrew. Judith started to follow, but Levi reached for her arm and held her back. "I'm sorry. I wasn't laughing about Samuel's paralysis."

She looked at the trail and watched the beam of light grow faint as Andrew moved farther away from them. "I know you didn't intend to be mean-spirited." She glanced again to check Andrew's distance. "But why did you try to make me look foolish? I just saw the *Englischer* again. Only—"

"Only what?"

"He's an angel."

"*Ach, nett* so."

Judith pushed past him.

"You spent time with a man at the river?" Levi grabbed her arm and stopped her. "Answer me."

"Why?" She jerked her arm away. "You wouldn't believe me anyway."

"So this is your choice? You want to spend time with another man?"

Judith walked away. Levi had no idea what she wanted. She wanted to marry him. She wanted a houseful of children. She wanted to grow old in her community surrounded by her church family. She wanted him to believe her.

She couldn't answer his questions with the knot that formed in her throat. She increased her pace. Up ahead, Andrew stopped and pointed the light at the ground, illuminating the path's ruts from the tree roots.

Levi was right behind her and blew out a breath. "I'm still waiting to hear your choice."

"It's late. I don't want everyone to worry." She also didn't want to defend herself to him anymore.

Levi looked at Andrew. *"Nau* she thinks about that."

Andrew redirected the beam on the path. "She's right. It's late, and we have chores in the morning."

Judith whispered, *"Denki,"* under her breath. If Andrew heard, he didn't reply. He continued on the path home.

Once they rounded the back side of the barn, others circled her with lanterns lifted to get a good view of her face.

David moved forward. "Where were you, Judith?"

Andrew stepped between them. "She was lost. I found her in the woods."

"Humph." Levi stared at Andrew. "That isn't what she told me."

They all turned their eyes to Judith. Andrew's face held the only welcoming expression, but she didn't dare use him for support. She couldn't burden him with her problems.

Levi nudged her arm. "Tell them, Judith."

She looked over her shoulder, her stomach churning. Even the bishop had come to search for her.

God, if the angel was from You, please help me. I believe You sent him, but they won't.

Her father came forward. "Your *mamm* would worry sick if she knew about this."

"I'm sorry." Judith sidestepped toward Levi.

"What were you doing?"

Reflections from the lantern's tongued flame flickered across the ground. Whatever she said they would refuse to believe.

"Is this about Samuel walking again?" her father asked.

Lord, I need Your strength. Guide my tongue.

"I believe he will," she whispered.

"She said she heard that from God," David added. "God spoke to her."

Judith closed her eyes as the crowd gasped.

Bishop Lapp stepped forward. "Child, do you know what that statement implies?"

Judith kept her focus on her shoes. She'd heard that people in cults sometimes claimed they heard from God. Surely they wouldn't think she would join a cult or that she'd want to stray from the church. She loved God with her whole heart.

"Answer the bishop," her father demanded.

Judith bit her lip. "I spoke with an angel."

Her father leaned forward. "No one heard your mumbling. Say it louder."

She lifted her head. Her eyes darted from the bishop to her father to David, then settled on Levi. "I have faith that Samuel will walk. I was told that . . . he would."

"We *muscht* accept Samuel's outcome." The bishop paused. "It is what God has decided."

"God's decision is for him to walk." Judith regretted her words the moment she spoke. She should have guarded her mouth.

"You do not think like God thinks. To talk as though you have the power is blasphemy," declared the bishop.

Her father drew in a sharp breath and clutched his chest. He made a high-pitched wheeze, and Judith moved to his side. As he gasped for air, anger rose up in her chest. Her father hadn't had a breathing attack in months.

Why now, God?

"I'll be . . ." His breathing ragged, he leaned on David for support.

"Amos, would you help him back to the house?" David turned to Judith. "*Daed* doesn't need any more stress, ain't it so?"

She swallowed hard.

Her brother pointed toward the barn. "Wait for me in there. You and I will talk after the bishop and I finish speaking."

Judith walked with her head lowered. She didn't want to look anyone in the eye, especially Levi. Speaking out of turn to the bishop, she had shamed herself and her family. Entering the dark barn, she didn't bother to light a lantern. Somehow, the darkness felt comforting. Levi had told her to choose. After his public accusations, she understood. He had chosen for her. He would never marry her now.

Andrew pondered what gave Judith the nerve to speak up against everyone, including his father. She'd never planted discord and had always been compliant with the *Ordnung*, even content. She hadn't allowed him to cover for her whereabouts, and now she was at the hand of her brother. Where had her courage come from, if not from the Lord?

"Something about her has changed." Levi broke the silence.

Andrew turned from watching Judith walk to the barn to see Levi shaking his head. If anyone understood Judith, it should be Levi. Yet he seemed annoyed and impatient with her stressful family situation, rather than sympathetic.

Levi turned toward his buggy. Andrew walked alongside him.

"Why did you do that to her?" Andrew tried to mask his irritation, but Levi's smug attitude made him angry. He offered up a quick silent prayer for wisdom, then continued. "She deserves more from you."

"People need to know how sick her mind has become. I was planning to marry her." Levi motioned toward the barn. "But even if David was to whip her, it wouldn't change her mind."

"David said he planned to talk with her, not lash her."

"*Jah*, so he said. How much *gut* talk will do, I don't know." Levi's shoulders dropped. "Why was Judith the only one to see an *Englischer* the day Samuel fell off the roof?"

Andrew shook his head. He hadn't seen a stranger, but he had seen Judith run off into the pasture and head toward the apple orchard. He looked at Levi, but in the darkness he couldn't read his expression. Maybe his cousin was actually worried about Judith. There was no telling. But Andrew decided not to reveal how he'd seen Judith running off that day. Levi had caused enough heartache. Andrew wouldn't give him ammunition to hurt Judith more.

Levi's eyes narrowed. "If she's running around with an *Englischer*, I don't want to be made a fool."

Andrew looked over his shoulder. His father and the others had walked to their buggies. "My *daed* is waiting. I need to leave."

Andrew headed toward his father's buggy, remembering how frightened Judith had been in his arms. *Lord, please give David wisdom when he talks with Judith. If what she claims is true, let him see with his own eyes.*

Andrew hurried to his father's buggy and placed his hand on his father's coat. "I believe her," he said, loudly enough to cause David to glance in his direction.

The bishop steadied his hand on Andrew's shoulder. "What are you saying?"

What *was* he saying? Did he truly believe her?

"Tell David to *geh* easy with Judith. Please, Father. David will listen to you."

"What's this about my sister, Andrew? What do you know?" David had come closer, arms still crossed.

"I believe her." He turned from David to his father. "Why is everyone so willing to believe a doctor's report? Is he not a man who bases his judgment on man-made machines?" Not seeing any response from his father, Andrew turned to David. "You want to discipline her for having faith. What if what she says is true? Our duty is to pray for her."

"Andrew, watch your tone," his father warned.

He drew a deep breath. "I didn't mean to sound disrespectful."

David patted Andrew's shoulder. "Because *Ich* sent her to the barn, you think I'll punish *mei* sister?" He shook his head. "*Ich* plan to talk to her, is all." He looked at the house and then back to Andrew. "My *daed* has a weak heart and his breathing is poor. *Ich* don't want him hearing what *Ich* say to Judith. She needs direction is all, *jah?*"

"*Jah*, and prayer too." Andrew looked toward the barn. He wished he had a few minutes alone with Judith to gain her trust.

The bishop heaved a long breath. "It is late, Andrew. Let's be on our way."

Andrew placed his foot on the buggy step and paused. "I'll help Levi with your father's farm *meiya*."

David nodded, then headed toward the barn.

Andrew noticed his father's stern expression as the bishop flicked the reins. Despite his father's disapproval of his speaking out, Andrew couldn't leave without suggesting they pray for Judith. What if what she claimed was true?

Chapter Eight

Andrew anticipated his father's lecture would start once they were out of the Fischers' driveway, but they hadn't even passed the mailbox before he began.

"Don't ever do that again." His father kept his voice low and his eyes focused straight ahead.

"Judith is—" *Innocent . . . frightened.* He could describe her in so many ways, but none of them would satisfy his father now.

"She's trouble. I've never heard a child, and a female at that, speak to her elders with such blatant disregard. Others might become like her."

Andrew bit his tongue. Even at twenty-two years of age, he

knew not to argue with his father when he was speaking as the bishop. Tonight he had overstepped his bounds.

But he'd had to. Someone needed to defend Judith. "She loves God."

The idea of an angel did seem extreme, but Judith's conviction to stand against her family and community overpowered Andrew's initial disbelief.

"She's given the enemy rein to control her mind. Word came back to me that she's corrupting the children with lies about colorful dresses and flowers." His father slapped the reins.

"Those were make-believe stories. Told to entertain, not to harm."

"That's teaching vanity. It's a sin."

Andrew couldn't disagree with that statement. Vanity was part of the world they had chosen to be separated from. Still, Judith's humility was in solemn accordance with the *Ordnung*. Until her brother's accident, her stories had been considered harmless, not rebellious.

He shifted on the buggy seat as an image of Martha flashed across his mind. Now there was a girl who had become vain. Look at the way she had draped herself by Levi after the barn was built and again in the hospital. That girl must have found a mirror somewhere, because she was self-absorbed in her own beauty.

Judith, on the other hand, hadn't a clue of her own loveliness.

"She's not a girl for you to think about," his father said, interrupting his thoughts.

"I feel sorry for Judith."

"You've been baptized into the church. You *muscht* live according to the commitment and rules of the faith."

Andrew wanted to remind his father that Judith was currently attending the Dordrecht Confession classes and soon would be eligible for baptism herself. He kept his comment to himself, however, in fear that his father would remove her from the classes.

His father directed the horse into their drive. "She's brought condemnation upon herself."

Andrew swallowed hard, remembering that he had given Samuel that nail. His conscience pricked at him for the part he had played in what happened to Judith and Samuel.

"Whoa."

Patsy stopped in front of the house, and his father handed Andrew the reins.

"Tend to the horse, son. It's been a long day for me."

Grateful his father didn't want to continue the discussion, Andrew waited for him to step out of the buggy before directing Patsy to the barn.

Andrew unbuckled the harness, his mind still lingering over thoughts of Judith. He remembered how she had trembled in his arms. He wished more than anything that he could calm her fears. She might have gone to the river to hide, but something had caused her to become frightened.

Andrew slid the harness off the horse and walked it to the stud peg. The day Samuel fell, Judith had acted strangely, scanning the crowd as though looking for someone. He should have followed her into the apple orchard.

Andrew grabbed the horse's halter and led the mare into the paddock. If given the opportunity, he planned to find out more.

Humiliation clawed at Judith. She trusted Levi, and he had publicly abased her, causing the entire community to turn on her without giving heed to her claims. Maybe if she told them about the dream. But she couldn't explain the significance of seeing three roads. How could she expect anyone to believe she woke up knowing she would have to choose a path? Levi wanted her to choose between him and the angel . . . too many choices.

The barn door opened. Judith looked up from her seat on the milking stool long enough to see David enter, then she looked back down at the straw-covered floor. The lantern he carried didn't offer much light, but she didn't want to see his face. Outside, his eyes had narrowed when he looked at her. She didn't expect him to be kind now that they were alone in the barn. Judith had never given him reason to punish her. Until now.

He stopped in front of Judith, arms crossed and leaning heavily on one hip. "What do you have to say for yourself?"

Indignation welled within her. And hopelessness too, as she realized that no explanation would appease his angry mind-set. He wouldn't believe anything she said. She shook her head and watched from the corner of her eye as his arms uncrossed and his hands twitched at his side.

"Well?" His voice deepened.

What do I tell him, God? Judith kept her head bowed.

"How do you think *Mamm* and *Daed* will feel if you're forbidden to join the church? Leniency toward your outburst will not continue. You are of age to choose to follow God or the world."

Judith hadn't considered such consequences of her actions.

Her parents would be devastated if their daughter were adjudged by the bishop as offending God, and she were forbidden to stay within the fold.

"I don't want you seeing that *Englisch* man again."

David's tongue-lashing struck her heart as painfully as if he'd taken a strap to her. Then he did something she never expected. He bent to his knees in front of her, his eyes hooded with concern.

"Judith, I don't want you to destroy your reputation. But even more important, I don't want you going to hell because you opened your mind to deception."

Her throat swelled. False prophets deceive people. Pride, greed, self-ambition, and lust were all tactics she knew the enemy used to mislead those in the world. A world of which she wanted no part. Loving the Lord and serving Him all the days of her life was her goal. She wanted to be pleasing in God's sight. Judith bowed her head. She wanted to be pleasing in her parents' sight too.

David interrupted her thoughts by squeezing her folded hands, the first time in a long while that she could recall an outwardly kind gesture from him. "You need to pray and ask for forgiveness."

Judith nodded. She had several issues to pray about.

He stood, started toward the door, and stopped. "Don't ever let me hear you've been with the *Englischer* again."

She sat silent, her mind whirling with David's words of counsel. Once he left the barn, she fell to her knees. "Forgive me, God. Let my heart be not deceived with empty words. My desire is to be Your obedient servant. *Aemen.*"

Walking to the house, Judith silently repeated her prayer for wisdom. She sighed with relief when she saw that David's buggy was gone from the yard. She climbed the porch steps wondering what he had told her father.

Martha met her at the door with a smirk. "Did he use the thin leather strap?"

Judith groaned. "I'm nineteen, Martha." She scanned the room. "Where's *Daed*?"

Her sister's smile faded. "He went to spend the night with Samuel at the hospital, and David and Ellen took Rebecca home with them again."

Judith went into the kitchen. Feeling her stomach rumble, she realized she hadn't eaten supper. Several dishes of food brought by the womenfolk lined the counter. She peeled back the lid from a dish of beans, then looked inside the next container.

Martha came into the kitchen and leaned against the wall. "Did you really see an angel?" She rolled her eyes. "I told Levi that you make up so many stories, no one knows the truth."

"I tell stories to children, not adults."

"That isn't what I heard. Levi said you angered the bishop."

Judith closed her eyes, willing herself not to cry. Levi had told Martha everything. The two of them must have had a long laugh together.

"Another story I heard was that you spent all day with an *Englisch* man." She made a *tsk-tsk* sound. "What evil are you weaving in all your lies?" Martha turned and walked down the hall to her bedroom.

Judith brought her hand up to the back of her neck, applied pressure, then decided she wasn't restraining these words. Anger fueled her steps down the hall.

She swung the bedroom door open hard, slamming it against the wall. "I didn't lie." Her eye caught the lamp on the windowsill. "What are you up to, Martha?" She pointed at the lamp. "You don't think I know what it means to have a lamp lit in the window?"

Martha flipped her nose into the air. "I don't care. I'm seventeen, and you can't stop me from going out."

Judith walked to the window and turned the wick down to extinguish the flame. "You're a tease. I saw you flirting with Levi . . . touching his hand every time you passed him a pumpkin."

Martha laughed. "Then you *muscht* have seen how much he liked it." She raised her chin, removed the top two straight pins that held her dress together, and tossed them onto the dresser. Then she turned and swept out of the bedroom.

Judith stormed after her. "Where are you going?"

"Anywhere the world takes me. I plan to have fun. Not live a boring life like you."

Judith pulled Martha's arm. "The devil seeks those he can devour . . . and I hope you reap what you've sown."

Martha jerked her arm from Judith's grip. "My life's in my own hands," she said and fled out the back door.

Judith turned her face to the ceiling. "I suppose I'll be blamed for not stopping her. With *Mamm* and *Daed* gone, this will be my fault."

If there was ever a time to pray, it was now.

Chapter Nine

Andrew arrived at the Fischer house before daybreak to do the barn chores. When he saw no sign of lamplight coming from the kitchen window and no smoke from the stovepipe extending over the house roof, he went straight to the barn. It seemed improbable that the entire household would go to the hospital this early. Perhaps they had overslept.

Inside the barn he added the correct amount of powdered milk and warmed water into the feed pail, then rolled his shirtsleeve and hand-stirred the mixture, making sure there wasn't any sediment of powder caked on the bottom of the bucket before he fed the calf.

From the hayloft above him, the floor creaked. Footsteps

caused a fine dust of hay to spill between the boards. Andrew set the bucket of calf feed down and walked around the stall area to peer up the wooden ladder attached to the wall.

"Levi, did you hear something?" a female voice asked.

"Don't worry. Ready yourself," his cousin replied.

Andrew's throat tightened as the air in his lungs drained. He leaned against the wall, unable to comprehend what he had overheard. Hearing boots thump directly above, he dashed around the corner.

Levi whistled as he climbed down the ladder. He rounded the corner, pulling his suspenders over his shoulders. "How long have you been here?"

Andrew picked up the calf feed. "I should ask you that."

Levi cleared his throat. "I thought I'd get an early start." His eyes widened as a haze of dust sifted through the floor cracks directly above him.

"What did you get an early start doing?" Andrew didn't want his suspicions confirmed. He sucked in his breath, hearing Levi's companion tromping down the ladder.

Martha rounded the corner. Her unbound hair hung over her shoulders, her prayer *kapp* bunched in her hand. She flipped her hair to one side, exposing her long neck.

Levi took a step toward her, and Andrew moved into his path to block him. He pressed his hand against Levi's chest as he looked over his shoulder at Martha. "Go to the *haus* and make yourself presentable."

"Levi?" Her voice dragged into a helpless-sounding plea.

Levi groaned. "Run along. Andrew and I need to talk."

∽

"Where were you all night?" Judith trailed the swing of Martha's butter-colored waist-length hair as her sister sashayed down the hall.

"I went out." She entered the room and tossed her *kapp* on the bed.

"Why is your prayer *kapp* off?"

"I didn't go out to pray." Martha fingered her tangled hair and removed several pieces of hay.

Judith pointed to the head covering. "Put it on. You'll follow the *Ordnung* while you're living in our parents' house."

Martha laughed. "Like you do?" She picked up the *kapp* and twirled it by the strings. "Did you keep your head covering on when you met with the *Englischer?*"

Judith left the room without another word. David would have to deal with Martha's disobedience. Her sister never listened to anything Judith had to say.

Why did Martha choose now to make a point of proving her difference? The family needed to stand strong together for Samuel. Judith entered the kitchen as the kettle began to hiss. She blew out a breath, wishing she could be like the kettle and blow off everything pent up inside of her.

The back door slammed, and Judith looked out the window to see Martha walking toward the chicken coop. Relieved to see that her sister had put her hair up and that her *kapp* was in place, she returned to preparing the morning meal.

The heated bacon lard snapped in the cast-iron fry pan. Martha hadn't returned from gathering the eggs. Judith peered out the window but didn't see her sister. Now that the weather had turned cooler, the chickens were not laying as many eggs. It never took this long to collect them.

Judith removed the skillet from the stove as Martha entered the kitchen and placed the basket of eggs on the counter.

Judith selected a few eggs and rinsed them in a bowl of vinegar water. "I see you've made yourself presentable."

"Not because you told me to."

Judith dried the eggs with a clean dish towel and took them over to the stove. "I would hope you make yourself presentable to the Lord."

Martha clasped both hands behind her back and sighed as she always did when she wanted attention.

Judith wrapped the pot holder over the pan's handle and placed the skillet back on the stove. "I suppose you want me to ask what you did while you were out all night." She cracked the eggs into the pan, then looked at Martha when she didn't reply.

Martha smirked. "I don't think you want to ask." She sauntered toward the door.

Judith followed.

Her sister stepped outside onto the porch, then looked back through the screen door at Judith. "I was with Levi."

Judith froze. A knot formed in her throat as she watched Martha skip down the porch steps and head toward the barn. Judith tightened her grip on the door handle to steady herself. Martha must be lying. It couldn't be true. Judith leaned her head against the wall and closed her eyes until the scent of burned eggs consumed the room. She opened her eyes to see a haze of smoke drifting out from the kitchen.

She ran into the kitchen. Grabbing a pot holder, she removed the fry pan from the stove while leaning far away from the bacon lard as it spat. She placed the hot pan next to the sink and opened the window to let out the smoke.

Judith wiped her hands on the front of her apron. She needed fresh air. Now was as good a time as any, she decided, to find Martha and learn the truth.

"Back off." Levi pushed Andrew aside.

"Only a woman's husband should see her hair down."

Levi's face contorted. "What does that matter to you, Bishop Junior?"

Andrew's jaw twitched. He pinned Levi against the barn wall. "What about Judith? You said you planned to marry her."

"Back off!" Levi shoved Andrew's hand away. He thumbed his chest. "I want a *fraa* who is submissive to me."

Andrew stepped away from him. "You should want a *fraa* who is obedient to God."

Levi chuckled. "Judith is rebellious." He peered at Andrew. "Isn't that what the bishop said, Junior?" He shook his head, making a patronizing *tsk-tsk*. "If you keep defending her, you'll fall out of favor with your father."

Andrew loved and respected his father, but something deep within him believed Judith. He'd spent most of the night praying for her—and praying it wasn't guilt that led her to believe Samuel would walk again.

Levi walked to the barn door and paused. "I'm sure we'll

still get married." He swung the door open, then looked over his shoulder at Andrew. "But she needs to straighten out first."

Levi's smug grin provoked Andrew, and the veins in his neck burned as he grabbed his cousin by his suspenders. "Stay away from Judith."

Levi sneered. "What are you going to do, fight me for her?"

His fist balled, Andrew had to restrain himself from striking his cousin. How dare Levi say Judith needed to straighten out, yet lure Martha into sin? Levi's breath reeked with alcohol, and no doubt Martha's did too. With a slight shove, Andrew released his hold. "Forgive me." He ground out the words between clenched teeth. "I lost my temper."

Levi shook his shoulders to adjust his suspenders back in the right place. "It's nice to see you're human."

Andrew clamped his jaw shut. Since childhood, Levi had loved to provoke him in ways unpleasing to the Lord. Andrew had disregarded the behavior in the past, understanding that Levi was two years younger and hadn't matured. But now there was a good chance that Levi's actions would involve hurting Judith, and Andrew wasn't about to stand back and watch.

His devious gloat worried Andrew. Would Levi continue to court Judith just to spite him? He watched Levi leave the barn, shoulders straight with an obvious agenda.

Andrew closed his eyes. "God, protect Judith from him. Allow her eyes to open to his ways." He swallowed hard. "I don't know why, but she loves him . . ." A tinge of guilt rose up in him. Once her eyes were opened, she'd be hurt beyond repair.

Curious to see if Levi went to his buggy or the house, Andrew stood at the door and searched the grounds. He spotted

Levi leaning against the chicken coop. Martha rounded the corner and stumbled, falling against him. Levi's arms wrapped around her waist, and she leaned into his embrace.

The door to the house slammed. Andrew caught a glimpse of Judith standing on the porch with her hand shielding her eyes as she scanned the yard. He scratched the back of his neck as Judith stepped off the porch. Had the Lord answered his prayer so quickly?

Chapter Ten

J udith halted at the sight of Martha and Levi's compromising embrace. Her sister's body fit snug against Levi's chest, and both appeared deeply involved in kissing.

"You know public kissing is not permitted." Judith narrowed her eyes at Martha. "You're not even of age."

Levi's hands fell from around Martha. "Judith—we just—"

Judith held up hands to silence him. "Spare me the shameful details." No amount of talking would explain what she had seen.

She fled toward the back of the barn. Once she reached the orchard, she veered off the main path, not caring that the low-lying branches scraped her face. Her only thought was to run as far away from Levi and Martha as she could.

At the river she collapsed to her knees, sobbing. "Why, God? How much more can I take?" Her sister knew that Judith had waited two years to court Levi. Several times she had shared with Martha her dreams of marrying him. Martha knew how many hours Judith had spent working on her wedding quilt, planning a large garden for a wedding feast. All for what—for Martha? She wasn't sure how, but somehow Judith must have failed her family, failed her church . . . failed God.

When a deep sound of someone clearing his throat caught her attention, she looked up through tear-stained eyes and squinted into the light. His face masked by the backlight of sun, Judith recognized him by his enormous size.

"What troubles your soul, Judith?"

She drew in a deep breath, released it, and inhaled again to gain control over her voice. "My life has been . . . torn apart." Choking on her words, she couldn't continue. She couldn't explain how Levi and her sister had wronged her.

"Things are not always what they seem." He walked to where she knelt on the ground. "God sees beyond today." He knelt beside her and placed his hand on her shoulder. "Child, only He knows the beginning from the end."

Judith nodded. She understood from reading her Bible that God was the Alpha and the Omega. "I know," she whispered.

"But do you believe?"

She shrugged, unable to talk with a constricted throat.

He cupped her face in his hand, and peace washed over her as he passed his thumb over her eyelids and cleared the cloudiness from her sight. "God loves you."

She sniffled. "Do you have a name?" The reflective shades

of blue in his eyes sparkled like a transparent sheet of glass spread over Lake Michigan.

He moved his hands from her face and lifted them to the sky. "Did God not place the stars and call them each by name?"

"God is the creator of all," she said, barely above a whisper.

"I am Tobias."

Cautiously she lifted her eyes toward him. "Will you tell me about the different paths from my dream?"

Tobias touched her cheek. "Your dream has not yet been revealed to me."

"But God sent you. Why?" She didn't understand how God could send an angel to someone as plain and insignificant as herself.

Tobias stood. "You are wise and will gain understanding in time. When your eyes are completely open, then you will comprehend."

Judith opened her eyes as wide as she could. "I want to see God's purpose for my life. But I don't see anything different."

The boom of his laughter caused the treetops to shake their branches. An array of red and yellow leaves rained from the sky. "This is not the time, child. But do not be discouraged. For the Lord gives wisdom. From His mouth come knowledge and understanding." Tobias surveyed the wooded area to her right.

She glanced in the same direction, but not seeing anything, she turned back. Tobias had vanished. She scrambled to her feet and turned a complete circle. There was no trace of him.

Branches snapped behind her, and Judith's heart thumped like a horse trotting on pavement. She spun around and came face-to-face with Andrew.

She gave a loud sigh to warn him he wasn't welcome. His arrival must have caused Tobias to disappear. Now she might not ever learn her purpose. But then, without Levi, her purpose seemed dismal anyway. Maybe that was why Tobias hadn't revealed the answer. The truth would have been unbearable.

Andrew steadied his gaze on her. If his expression was intended to display his pity or to mock her pain, she didn't know and didn't care to find out. At this point, she didn't dare trust anyone.

She huffed, hoping he would take the hint and leave. When he didn't budge, she moved under a nearby birch tree for shade.

Andrew stood in the same place, head bowed. He must be pondering something. Not that it mattered. She just wished he'd take his thoughts and move downriver.

When he lifted his head, he ignored her glare and kept his focus trained on her as he moved closer.

Judith found it disturbing that she couldn't resist his dimples. Today, she found everything about his intrusion in her life disturbing. She narrowed her eyes. "What are you doing here?"

He studied the birch tree that she leaned against and peeled off a thin layer of white bark. "I was worried about you."

She bit her bottom lip, wondering if he'd seen Tobias, then disregarded that thought. If Andrew had seen a mammoth-sized *Englisch* man here at the river, he would have said something. But what if he had overheard only her side of their conversation? If he told his father, she'd be doomed. The bishop had already accused her of blasphemy. She'd have to leave the community . . . her family . . . leave—

"Judith, are you all right?" The groove deepened between Andrew's eyes.

Her gaze darted from his to the river to the area where Tobias had stood before he vanished.

Andrew tossed the bark he had peeled to the ground and studied her face.

Not wishing to be under the spotlight of his gaze, she lowered her head and looked at the film of dust collecting in the cracks of her leather shoes. *Lord, will You help me?*

"I know why you ran off." His words tore through the silence.

Judith jerked her head up, surprised by his statement. "Then why did you follow me here?" Her throat tightened. "I suppose you want a *gut* laugh too?" She pushed past him and stormed over to the river. She wasn't about to be mocked anymore.

Andrew caught up to her at the edge of the riverbank. His hand locked around her arm, and he pulled her back as sand shifted under her feet and spilled over the embankment. Once he'd taken her several feet from the water, he released her arm.

"Look at me," he said.

Judith brought her head up and stared into his russet eyes.

"I'm not laughing."

His jaw was set and his eyes focused, leaving no room for humor in his expression. He hadn't been mocking her pain. Still, she couldn't continue to look into his eyes and not cry in front of him. She didn't want his pity.

Andrew scuffed his boot in the dirt. "Don't become bitter."

Judith gritted her teeth. If he thought he could lecture her now, he was wrong. Planting her fists on her hips, she leaned forward. "Don't tell me how to feel." After she'd been betrayed by her sister and by the man she thought she loved, Andrew was worried about her becoming bitter?

"Apparently you didn't see them. They were——" Warmth covered her face. She turned her back to Andrew and masked her face with her hands.

"I know bitterness and envy will choke the life from you." He moved in front of her and pulled her hands away from her face. "Don't let that seed grow."

His sober expression reminded her of the bishop. Not only did he look like his father, but now he *sounded* like him as well. "What are you going to do next, tell me how I'm sinning?"

Andrew clamped his mouth. Good. She'd silenced him. Maybe now he'd leave her alone. She hiked back to the river, stopping before she reached the edge. A crimson maple leaf floating with the water current reminded her of Tobias. She looked up to the barren treetops.

God, I need You.

Andrew came up beside her. "You know bitterness and envy are sin. I don't have to remind you of that."

But he had reminded her, heaping guilt on her conscience. All she wanted was a few hours to wallow in self-pity. After all, even dogs were allowed to lick their wounds.

Judith pivoted to face Andrew. "They spent the night together. So they know each other quite well."

His stiff facial expression didn't change.

"Didn't you see them? Their tight embrace was——"

Andrew lifted his hand to cover her mouth, stifling the last part of her statement. "I know." He stared hard at her for a moment, then as though he realized his hand was covering her mouth, his eyes opened wide and he jerked his hand away. It took him a few breaths before the grim lines around his mouth relaxed. She saw his Adam's apple bob as if he had to force something down with a hard swallow.

"You know *what?*"

"I, um . . . I know." Sweat dappled his forehead as he stalled to reply. "I saw them together in the barn earlier."

His statement rolled over in her mind until her insides heated up and the tip of her tongue tasted fire. "Then preach to *them* about sin."

He stepped closer until he stood inches from her, then leaned forward even more. "Sin is sin."

"Are you implying that I'm to blame? They can't keep their hands off each other, and it becomes my fault!" She turned her back to him, then whirled around to face him with her finger wagging. "*Nau*, because of you, I have to add anger to my list of sins."

He backed up, but she followed. With fisted hands resting on her hips, she leaned forward. "Are you pleased with yourself, *Bishop Junior?*"

Andrew's brows furrowed for the briefest second before he closed his eyes. Then without speaking a word he walked away.

Chapter Eleven

Was he pleased with himself?

Of course Andrew wasn't pleased that he had fueled Judith's wrath. He kicked a rock along the path through the woods. He'd been too hard on her. The sadness in her eyes revealed her pain. Although finding Levi and Martha together had shocked Judith, his own remarks at the river added kerosene to her fire. He couldn't blame her defensive response, even calling him Bishop Junior. Her mocking didn't carry the same punch as Levi's words did. Andrew reached the rock he'd kicked and sent it farther down the trail. If he dwelled on Levi's name-calling, hatred could take root in him.

"Forgive me, Father. Once again, I repent of my wrongful attitude. For coveting what Levi takes for granted, Judith's love.

Please forgive me, but my heart still aches for Esther. And now on a different scale I find myself wanting to protect Judith from Levi. Show her how to forgive Levi and Martha. I don't want this hurt to consume her life. And once again, I ask that bitterness and envy do not consume mine."

Andrew looked behind him on the path, hoping to see Judith. He wanted the chance to explain. His intention of following her to the river wasn't to make her more upset. He was worried. Andrew kicked the rock with enough force to send it skipping over the pine-needle path several feet ahead. After he'd provoked her to anger and caused her to sin, she would never believe he wanted to be her friend.

He hated how Levi had crushed her heart. Judith deserved better. Levi's playfulness was deceptive—a trap. His cousin and Martha deserved each other.

Once he reached the Fischers' yard and noticed that Levi's horse was still tied to the post, he looked over his shoulder again for Judith. He didn't want her walking back to find that Levi hadn't left. Andrew might have lost his chance to keep her company at the river, but if she returned before Levi left, she'd need him as a decoy.

Judith sat on the large boulder and listened to the rush of water. She wanted to be alone, but in the solitude, thoughts of Andrew's expression plagued her. She shouldn't have spoken to him in anger. He wasn't Levi. It wasn't Andrew's fault that Levi was a cad.

Judith sighed, disappointed with herself. She glanced at the ground, and a speckled stone embedded in the dirt caught her eye. After digging it out and wiping it off, she rotated it in the palm of her hand, admiring its sparkling hues. She tossed it and listened as it plunked into the water. The current flipped the rock over, and she wondered where it would be downstream in a day, a month, a year.

She wondered if her sins could wash away so easily—if being baptized and dedicated to following Christ was similar. She'd been taking classes for baptism and to join the church, but now she questioned her intentions. She despised her sister and couldn't imagine forgiving Levi.

Andrew was right. She was bitter and envious. She was as much a sinner as those she accused; the same people she despised. How could God see her as anything but a sinner?

"God, I know I'm expected to forgive so that I too can be forgiven. It's hard. Levi and Martha might as well have snatched my heart and wrung it like a rag. I don't have love inside me for them." She paused and lifted her face toward the sky. "I am sorry for my behavior toward Andrew. He only desired me to recognize my sins. I am a sinner, but I need You to show me how to forgive."

Judith opened her eyes and bent toward the water. Even though the river wasn't more than three feet deep and was clear to the bottom, she couldn't locate the rock. Unable to find where it had traveled, she turned for home.

Judith rounded the corner of the barn and was startled to find Levi harnessing his horse to the buggy. Her rage instantly rekindled.

He should have had the decency to leave before now. She scanned the yard for her sister. Martha wasn't anywhere in sight.

"Judith."

Her spine crawled at the sound of Levi's voice. Ignoring his call, she picked up her pace, heading straight for the house. How could she receive forgiveness when his very presence triggered hatred?

Andrew stepped out of the barn and came up beside her. He nodded in Levi's direction. "Just pretend you're not mad at me, and I'll keep him away from you."

What was Andrew's intention—to protect her from lashing out at Levi in anger? She heard Levi approach but refused to look his way. She glanced at Andrew, who was keeping pace at her side.

"Don't let him—"

"Cause me to sin?"

"Let it go," he whispered.

"And how do I do that?"

"Pretend he doesn't bother you. Laugh. Pretend I said something funny."

The "bishop junior" suggesting he could say something humorous was funny in and of itself.

"Ha ha."

"That's a start." Andrew chuckled. "But I'm not that boring. You can laugh louder."

Judith couldn't help but laugh, seeing him exaggerate a grimace.

Andrew's willingness to help was admirable, especially after she'd been cruel to him.

Levi caught up to them. "Judith, can we talk for a minute?"

"This isn't a *gut* time, Levi." She kept her focus on Andrew, and Levi dropped back. Feeling an odd sense of strength, she laughed harder. Andrew's plan worked. She *could* pretend Levi didn't bother her. She glanced at the house. Martha might be harder to avoid.

Andrew walked up the porch steps with her and paused at the front door. "That wasn't too bad, was it?"

"*Ach*, does it surprise you that storytellers are *gut* pretenders?"

"I am pleasantly surprised," he answered.

"*Denki*."

He bobbed his head toward the door. "Are you going to be all right with her?"

"And what will you do if I say *nay*? Move in with us?"

He chuckled. "If *Ich muscht*." He tapped the brim of his hat. "I take my pretend role seriously too."

Judith turned the doorknob. "*Denki*, again."

Andrew looked past her through the opened door, then back to her. "Will I see you *meiya*?"

"I, um . . ." She leaned forward to whisper. "Are we still pretending?"

He shrugged.

Judith assumed Martha was standing somewhere near the doorway. "I'd like that."

She made sure her answer sounded convincing for her sister's benefit. She'd still have to convince herself that spending time with Andrew would be wise. Though she had to admit that even Levi had never made her laugh with such ease.

Chapter Twelve

Andrew wheeled the ax, splitting the oak into two sizable chunks. He turned the firewood slab on the stump and quartered it into usable stove pieces. With his thoughts concentrated on Levi's improper behavior and the devastated look in Judith's eyes, he hadn't noticed his father's buggy approaching until he readied another log to split.

His father climbed out from the buggy, Bible in hand. This was late for him to be out on visitation. Perhaps he'd been at a meeting with one of the deacons whose duty regularly involved reporting church trouble. Levi's and Martha's names came to Andrew's mind.

"You split all this today?"

Andrew lifted his hat off his forehead and used his shirtsleeve to wipe his brow. *"Jah."* He'd worked up a sweat in the chilly autumn afternoon trying to chop enough wood to fill the woodbox for the cookstove before nightfall.

"Did you milk the Fischers' cows today?"

"Jah."

"Any more talk from Judith about an angel?"

"Nay." He thought of telling his father about Levi and Martha, then decided against it. Besides, the news should come from one of the deacons. He'd speak privately with David if the opportunity arose.

Mamm opened the back door. "Supper is ready."

Andrew leaned the ax against the stump. He'd worked up more than sweat—he'd developed a hearty appetite. He loaded his arms with firewood and followed his father to the house. The scent of beef casserole grew stronger the closer he came to the kitchen. Andrew unloaded the wood and dusted his hands of bark chips, then washed up before joining his parents at the table. He bowed his head in quiet grace.

His mother ladled a spoonful of food onto a plate. "Any news of Samuel?"

"Nay change," his father replied.

Mamm passed the serving spoon to Andrew. "During our time quilting today, the womenfolk were filled with talk." She buttered a biscuit as she continued. "Some believe Judith, and others think she might be trying to gain attention." *Mamm* set her biscuit aside and sampled the food. She gave a slight nod of approval and continued. "She's overrun with guilt, if you ask me. Poor Samuel wasn't watched. What was he doing on the roof?"

Andrew glanced at his father. The bishop continued eating without showing any interest in his wife's conversation.

"I've always liked Judith, but I'm afraid the community is divided in their opinions. She wasn't invited to the quilting frolic for fear she would *fasavvahra* the *samling*."

Sour the gathering. Andrew cleared his throat, a subtle attempt to cause his mother to pause. "Shouldn't the women embrace Judith? She hasn't been shunned. She isn't even baptized yet."

His mother and father exchanged glances, and she lowered her gaze.

The bishop turned his attention to Andrew. "While leniency is encouraged, I won't permit church strife." He paused and folded his hands before continuing. "Once Samuel is home, you won't need to spend so much time at the Fischer home."

Although Andrew nodded, something strong tore at his heart. The Fischers would continue to require extra help on the farm. Did his father intend to withdraw the community support, or was he merely interested in Andrew keeping his distance?

Judith ran the bristled brush over Rusty's neck. *Daed* had given the old horse to Samuel after it had grown too old to be a driver. Her brother loved spending time in the barn, and she'd often find him inside Rusty's stall, brushing him.

"Your winter coat is thickening." She patted Rusty's neck and moved the brush to the horse's flank. As helpless as Samuel's condition left her feeling, somehow grooming Rusty offered comfort. And after finding Levi and Martha together, she needed the solitude of the barn. Her dreams of marriage had certainly shattered. Her heart would not ever mend.

Light entered the barn as David stepped inside. He startled. Apparently she'd taken him by surprise.

"I didn't know anyone was in here," he said, approaching the stall.

"How's Samuel?"

David shook his head. "*Nay* better." He reached for the harness dangling from the wall peg. "The boys and I are planning to take the pumpkins to market *meiya*." He leaned his elbow on the stall gate. "How are you doing?"

"*Gut*." She kept her focus on the horse. If she looked at him, her brother would see that something troubled her deeply, and this wasn't the time to tattle on Martha.

"I wanted to talk with you about Samuel *kumming* home."

"*Jah*." She stopped brushing and came out from the stall.

"I don't want you talking about him walking." His voice soft, he continued. "Judith, the accident wasn't your fault."

Tears collected in her eyes. She wished she could believe her brother's words.

He placed his hand on her shoulder and tipped his head to see her face. "I know you feel bad. We all do. But—"

She closed her eyes, bracing herself while he paused to collect his words.

"Judith, it is not *gut* for the family to make wild prophetic claims. I fear if you continue, you'll be sent away."

Judith's vision blurred.

He gently squeezed her shoulder. "Dry your eyes. We *muscht* be strong for Samuel."

Judith nodded, although she wondered where her strength would come from. Her faith had once been, or so she believed, a source of raw power. But lately her faith was as wilted as a trampled stalk of winter wheat.

David's voice perked up. "Have you seen Ellen?"

"*Nay, nett* lately."

"She has news to share."

"*Jah?*"

A wide smile spread across David's face, but he shook his head. "I promised I'd let her say." He pointed to the door. "*Kumm*, she and Rebecca are in the *haus*."

Judith set the horse brush on the shelf and walked with David to the house. The last time he'd sported such an exuberant smile, Ellen was pregnant with the twins.

Rebecca ran to the door as Judith entered. Her sister's little arms embraced her legs, bunching her dress at the seam.

"I've missed you," Judith said, stooping down to give her a hug.

"Me too."

"Did you find the cookies I baked?"

Rebecca broke her hold and darted off to find the treat. Chuckling at her sister's enthusiasm, Judith followed her into the kitchen and opened the cookie tin. She held up two fingers. "*Zvay.*" She waited for Rebecca to make her selection, then turned with the container and offered them to Ellen.

The moment Ellen turned from where she stood at the sink, Judith didn't need to hear the announcement. The glow on Ellen's cheeks gave her secret away.

"David said you have news."

Ellen patted her belly. "We're going to have a *boppli*. In the spring."

Judith smiled. "I hope it's a girl."

"That is my prayer." She grabbed Judith's hand and gave it a squeeze. "Your brother wants more boys." She leaned closer. "He wants his own construction crew."

"Did you tell him someone needs to prepare all the lunch pails?"

Ellen laughed. "And sew the aprons that hold their nails."

Judith set the tin of cookies on the table before filling the kettle with water to heat for coffee. "Maybe you'll have twin girls and even out the number."

"That would be fine with me." She sat at the table. "It's been too long since I held a *boppli*. I'll take them two at a time."

Judith pulled out a chair and sat next to Ellen. "This is *wundebaar* news."

"Will you *kumm* stay with me when it's time?"

Judith nodded. "*Jah.*"

"Your brother might have a tough exterior." Ellen lowered her voice at the sound of the door opening and footsteps. "But seeing Jacob's head, David crumbled."

"So much for his experience delivering all those calves."

"I heard that." David walked into the room and leaned toward his wife. "Are you telling the story of how I fainted?"

"*Jah,*" Ellen replied.

The kettle whistled, and Judith stood. "Would you like a cup of *kaffi*, David?"

"*Nay,* I need to be on my way." He tapped Ellen's shoulder. "You and Rebecca can drive the buggy home." He reached into the tin and grabbed a handful of cookies. "I'm sharing with the boys," he said, responding to Ellen's light hand tap. "Where's Martha?"

Judith shrugged. She assumed Martha had holed up in her bedroom. She'd certainly made herself scarce, but Judith wasn't about to complain.

"Is she helping you with chores?" David walked to the entrance and craned his neck down the hallway. He turned back. "Is she?"

Judith feathered her fingers over her neck. She dropped her hands when his brows arched questioningly. *God, couldn't You reveal her sin another way besides through me?*

David leaned into the hallway. "Martha?" He waited a moment before going to her bedroom door and knocking. "Martha, open the door . . . What are you listening to?"

Judith and Ellen leaned into the hallway as David came out from the bedroom, something dangling from his hand. He came into the kitchen, opened the side of the woodstove, and shoved a portable CD player and headphones inside. "Let me know if she gives you trouble."

Martha came tromping down the hallway toward the kitchen.

He pointed at her. "That music is of the world and not anything pleasing to the Lord. You and I will talk later." He turned to Ellen. "Please don't be long. It'll be dark soon."

"*Jah*, I'll *kumm nau.*" She waved at Rebecca. "Get a clean dress. You'll have your bath tonight."

Her little sister ran down the hall and returned with a gray dress bunched in her hand.

Once Ellen and Rebecca left, Martha glared at Judith. "You told him, didn't you?"

Judith glanced at the doorway. "*Nay*. Should *Ich* stop him so you can?" She wished David had prodded more into Martha's deceptive ways. Her sister dabbled in more sin than just listening to a musical device.

"I don't know why it matters if I listen to music. God doesn't care about anything. He doesn't care about Samuel . . . or you." Martha spun in the direction of the bedroom. "I'm leaving the Amish faith."

"Martha." Judith grabbed her arm. "Don't say such words."

Martha jerked her arm from Judith's grip. "How can I serve a God who takes away a boy's ability to walk? I won't."

Judith stiffened. Surely Martha didn't know what she was saying. How could she speak so boldly against God's sovereignty? Judith closed her eyes in fear for her sister. *Lord, only You can change her stony heart. Bring her to repentance.*

Rebecca charged back into the house. "I forgot my doll," she said, running past Judith.

Her sister's tattered rag doll hadn't spent too many nights outside Rebecca's grasp.

Judith stepped outside and walked to Ellen's buggy. "Rebecca will be out shortly."

"*Jah*, she cried so hard at bedtime, I had to put stuffing in one of David's socks so she had something to hold while she slept."

"Just think, if you have a girl this time, you'll be making rag dolls." Judith sighed.

Ellen reached for Judith's hand. "You're nineteen. It won't be long before you have a husband and family of your own."

Judith forced a smile. If it were not so sad, she would remind her of Katie, Ellen's unmarried thirty-year-old sister who had no prospect of a husband or children. Judith never wanted to walk in Katie's shoes.

Chapter Thirteen

Preparing breakfast didn't have the same appeal this morning. The other day Judith had wanted to impress Levi with her cooking skills. Today cooking felt like a chore. Instead of standing over the stove in an effort to keep the food warm and prevent it from burning, she removed the pan from the wood burner and sat with her quilting sprawled over her lap. She needed something to do with her hands, although stitching the binding on her wedding quilt seemed pointless now.

Someone knocked on the door, causing Judith to startle and stick herself with the needle. She pushed the quilt aside and sucked her finger as she went to answer the door.

Andrew greeted her, then motioned to her hand. "You didn't burn yourself again, did you?"

She plucked her finger from her mouth. "Needle stab," she explained as she waved him inside.

"How did things go with . . . uh . . . ?" Andrew looked down as he wiped his boots on the rug.

Judith put him out of his stuttering misery. "With Martha?"

His head shot up. "*Jah.* Did she give you a hard time?"

"We haven't spoken of it." She half expected a lecture about turning the other cheek, but Andrew said nothing.

He followed her toward the kitchen, then stopped at the entry.

Judith scooped up a generous portion of eggs and fried potatoes and set the plate on the table. "Aren't you hungry?" She pulled out a chair.

He gave her a firm nod as though he had been waiting for her invitation and sat in front of the meal.

Judith filled a cup with black coffee, steam rising, and set it next to his plate. Then she went to the window and rose to her tiptoes to see the barn. When she turned back toward the table, Andrew's gaze met hers.

"He'll be in after he finishes milking."

Judith groaned. Looking for Levi out the window was a habit she needed to break. "I wasn't—"

But she *was* looking for Levi, and Andrew of all people would chastise her if she tried to lie—even to fool herself. His face crinkled, and again she braced herself for a lecture. Instead, he slowly chewed a mouthful of food.

"*Ach,* I'm sorry," she said, realizing she'd dished up cold food for him to eat. "Let me fix you something hot."

He mumbled something she assumed was to stop her from the trouble, but she disregarded it and snatched the plate off the table.

He gulped his coffee to wash down the mouthful of food. "I would have—" His voice hoarse from the scalding coffee, he cleared his throat.

Judith filled a glass with water and handed it to him.

Andrew drank the water and pointed to the plate of food she was discarding into the tin of scraps for the pigs. "I would have eaten that."

"And have word get out that I'm a bad cook?" She placed the fry pan on the stove, worked the spatula to scrape the sliced potatoes off the bottom, and added more oil to refry them. She had set a fresh plate in front of Andrew when Martha raced through the kitchen to answer the knock at the door.

"*Guder mariye*, Martha." Levi's greeting traveled into the kitchen.

Judith wiped her hands on her apron, glanced at Andrew, then crossed her arms. She didn't care if he knew she was bitter.

Levi entered the kitchen, and his nostrils flared as he took in the breakfast aroma. "Smells *gut* in here," he said.

Judith spun her back to his wide smile. What audacity he sported, breezing in with his jovial greeting as if unaffected by yesterday's conflict. Complimenting her cooking wouldn't get him back into her good graces.

Judith bit her bottom lip. There were plenty of chores to finish that would put distance between them. As it was, Martha had already started slathering him with attention. Besides, she wanted to spend time at the river. Samuel was expected home tomorrow, and once he arrived there wouldn't be much opportunity to sneak off to look for Tobias.

She eyed the basket of wet clothes washed earlier, picked

them up, and headed outside to hang them on the line. It wasn't long before the door opened and Andrew stepped outside.

He walked over to the clothesline. "Thanks again for breakfast."

Judith snapped a towel hard. "Did you hear him?"

Andrew's brows rose. "Levi?"

She held the towel's edge to the line, then realized she didn't have a clip ready.

He reached for the towel's corner, touching her hand. "I got it."

She bent down to grab a clip from the bag. "He said my cooking smelled *gut*."

"It did." Andrew jerked his hand away from her clip.

Judith grunted, bent to gather another wet towel from the basket, and gave it a quick snap, spraying a fine mist in the process.

Andrew wiped his face. When another snap sprayed him, he took the towel from her hands and lifted it to the line.

"The other day, after he said my cooking smelled *gut*, he said I'd make a *gut fraa*. Can you believe his nerve?"

Andrew sucked in a deep breath. "Are you going to hand me a clothespin, or would you rather I hold this towel until it dries?"

His curt tone jolted her from her thoughts. "I'm sorry." She secured the towel and bent for another one. Standing back up, she lifted the towel to the line and glanced at the house. "I suppose you think I'm still bitter."

Andrew chuckled. "Don't walk me into that fight."

She lowered the towel from the line and placed it and her hand on her hip. "You do, don't you? Go ahead and say it."

Andrew tossed his hands in the air as if she held him at gunpoint, then lowered them. "If you'd listen to your own tone, you'd have your answer."

"Humph. I should've hit him over the head with the fry pan."

Andrew's mouth opened, but closed when she pointed her finger at him.

"Don't lecture me."

Andrew clamped his mouth closed and raised his hands in surrender. With caution, he reached for the towel she held. "It's dripping on your dress."

She looked down and patted her hand over the water spots. Andrew cleared his throat and motioned with his head to the towel that he held in place.

"*Ach,* sorry." She hurried to fasten the clip.

They both tried to reach for the last towel and promptly bumped heads. Catching sight of each other in their mirrored actions of rubbing their heads, they laughed aloud at how silly they must look.

Just then Levi stepped outside. He cocked his head to one side as Andrew continued to laugh.

He stopped once Levi reached his buggy. "I should leave *nau.* I have furniture to deliver."

"*Denki* again for keeping up with the barn chores while my parents were with Samuel."

He fidgeted with a spare clothes clip. "Have you heard when Samuel can *kumm* home?"

Judith smiled. "The *docktah* said maybe *meiya.*" She motioned to the barn. "I guess you'll be relieved of the barn chores." A tinge of regret worked its way along her nerves.

Andrew handed her the clip. "I thought I'd *kumm* do the second milking this evening."

"That's very kind, but I'm sure you have orders to fill."

Andrew's furniture business was the busiest in the area. People from all over Michigan came to buy his furniture and hire him to build custom kitchen cabinets.

"As you said, there won't be many more days to . . . help." He tapped the brim of his hat. "Maybe we could go for a walk when I *kumm* later?"

Judith half nodded. "All right," she replied. Why did he think she might still need his support? She made a quick scan of the area. Levi's buggy was gone, and Martha hadn't come out of the house.

Andrew turned before she could tell him they didn't need to pretend any longer.

Branches of the poplar trees bent with the breeze and shed some of their triangular-shaped leaves, littering the trail with bright yellow hues. Judith hugged herself, wishing she had remembered her cape. Once she was clear of the woods, she could see that gray clouds had developed and were hiding the afternoon sun.

Meandering along the riverbank, she looked down at the rushing water, wondering if she could locate the speckled rock. She followed the river around the bend, hypnotized by the flowing water.

A patch of loose soil gave way beneath her foot, and her arms teetered for balance. As she fell, a strong hand caught her, lifted her off her feet, then planted her firmly on the ground.

"*Denki*—"

Tobias released his hold and smiled. Opening his outstretched hand, he asked, "Were you looking for this?"

Judith eyed the speckled rock. "*Jah*, but—" She caught herself. A quick reminder of who had sent him settled that question.

"I believe this is yours," he said, releasing it to her.

The rock's jagged edges were gone. She turned it over in her hand several times in awe of its pronounced colors and smooth texture. "It's beautiful."

Tobias motioned to the rock. "Below the surface elements, the true color is exposed."

She turned her gaze back to the rock as a beam of sunlight cast a prism of colors. While she watched, it turned into a radiant gemstone. Her hands trembled such that she feared she would drop it.

Tobias pointed to the stone. "This is how God's children sparkle in His eyes." He lifted his gaze to Judith, and a pigment of indigo flickered in his eyes. "Those who seek to have a pure heart are a rare gem."

"I try to do what is right." But once she voiced her claim, she remembered wanting to hit Levi with the frying pan earlier. She knew that God wouldn't view her heart as pure.

He pointed at the river. "The current is like the cares of this world. If you do not guard your heart, you will be tossed downstream." Tobias motioned to the ground. "Sometimes you think where you stand is safe, but in another step, the sand shifts and the foundation crumbles."

She glanced at the ground. When she looked up to ask him what he meant, he was gone, and she saw Andrew walking toward her. She groaned inwardly. He took his role as her protector too seriously. His timing was all wrong. The fact that Andrew Lapp had become hard to ignore was a curious predicament.

"What are you doing way down here?" He scanned the area. "I haven't been this far downstream in a long time."

She blew out an aggravated breath. "I thought you were leaving. Why did you *kumm?*"

Andrew rubbed the nape of his neck. "I thought we planned to take a walk." He made another pass around the area with his eyes. "Who were you talking to?"

"You heard him?" She couldn't stifle the hint of excitement in her voice.

His brows arched. "I heard you."

Judith heard the caution in his reply.

"Was I supposed to hear someone else?" He made another scan of the area.

Judith shrugged. "I guess *nett.*" She turned to leave.

"Hey, where are you going?" He jogged up beside her. "I thought we were going for a walk *together.*"

"Don't you find it odd that I'd be talking to myself?" She found the entire thing odd. Why was she the only one who saw and heard Tobias?

Andrew shrugged. "I talk to myself sometimes." He grinned. "Sometimes I have to ask myself where I put the measuring tape. I know it sounds silly. If I knew where I put it, I wouldn't have to ask myself."

Judith smiled in spite of herself.

He leaned closer. "If you ask me, I'd say there are a lot of us who talk to ourselves." He nodded. "An odd bunch we are, *jah?*"

A strong gust of wind lifted Andrew's hat off his head. She chuckled, watching him chase after it. With a sudden change in the wind's direction, the hat rolled on its brim into the undergrowth of ferns. Judith ran after it, with Andrew following.

"Here it is." She picked up his hat and handed it to him.

"What's that you're holding? A rock?" Another brisk breeze threatened to take his hat away again, but he smashed it against his head. "*Kumm mitt mich*," he said, reaching for her hand. "We can find shelter in the woods." Once they were under a large beechnut tree, he stopped. Looking at her hand, he asked, "You collect rocks?"

She opened her hand and smiled at the brilliant stone. "Do you like it?"

"*Ach*, a priceless gem."

"You see the gem too?" She wasn't crazy after all.

Andrew winced, obviously unable to give an honest reply.

"So you don't see it." She moved past him. Again she'd made a fool of herself.

He caught her arm, and the rock dropped from her hand. "What's wrong?"

She turned, jerked her arm from his hand, and leaned against the tree with her face hidden in the crook of her elbow. Maybe she was losing her mind. If he saw the rock the way she did, he would've commented on its glow.

God, why do I feel like I'm teetering on insanity?

He patted her shoulder and leaned closer. "Tell me what I said wrong."

Judith turned, and his hand dropped from her shoulder. "It isn't you."

He scratched the back of his neck and glanced at her sideways. "Will you *drauwa mich* to be your friend?"

Despite the concerned look in his eyes, she didn't dare trust anyone. Not after what Levi had done. Protecting her when Levi was around was one thing, but Levi wasn't in the woods with them. Andrew didn't have to smother her with his friendship.

When she didn't answer, he shifted his weight. "When you showed me the rock, what did you want me to see?"

She lowered her head, pinning her chin to her chest. "Don't ask."

He moved closer, brushing his shoulder against hers as he leaned forward. "I believe you've seen an angel," he whispered.

Judith raised her head and studied him hard. His eyes didn't blink, and his lips didn't turn into a smirk. He squared his thick shoulders, startling her with how handsome he looked. "You do? You believe me?"

He made a stiff nod. "*Jah, Ich* do."

She wanted to believe him. Andrew's patience melted her heart, but she couldn't construe it as anything but simple kindness. Why would he believe when he was unable to see Tobias?

He broke the silence. "I'd like to hear about him."

She shook her head. "It would only get you in trouble."

"Then I'd be in *gut* company."

He grinned as if he knew the sight of his dimples would soften her attitude. And it almost did. She warned herself to guard her heart. Why would the bishop's son want to be in the company of someone like her?

"Did he have wings?"

"I was beginning to like you, and *nau* you're making this

into a joke. Levi would ask if he's chubby and wears a halo. I suppose you—"

"I'm not anything like Levi." He jammed his hands into his pockets and shook his head slowly. "I don't remember hearing Levi say he believed you."

Judith closed her eyes. Andrew was right. Levi never even tried to believe her. He was harsh, judgmental . . . and all the things Andrew was not.

God, please forgive me.

Judith opened her eyes and saw that Andrew had silently slipped off. She jogged to catch him.

"He didn't have wings," she said.

He glanced at her and kept walking. "Asking if he had wings wasn't unreasonable. Have you read Ezekiel lately?"

"I'm sorry. I thought you were—"

Andrew stopped. "I won't ask why you put up with Levi mocking you. But I'm not like Levi." He continued walking.

Chapter Fourteen

Thoughts of marriage hadn't crossed Andrew's mind in three years, but last night he couldn't dismiss the idea of what it would be like. He woke in a cold sweat.

Esther was dead.

Why had his dreams of the cabin returned?

He glided the sandpaper block along the wood grain of the table leg. He'd come out to the workshop prior to daybreak, but he found no peace. His busy hands couldn't divert his mind's commotion.

Instead of closing up the cabin, he should have sold it.

But he couldn't clutter his mind with the past. Nor could he bear to ask God again why His prompting to purchase the cabin came when Andrew knew Esther was dying. He built false hope believing for a miracle. He had planned to drive Esther to see the cabin the day she died.

He should have sold it.

Andrew worked the raw edge off the spindled wood, blew off the powdered dust, and stepped back to admire the placement of oak knots. The natural beauty of the sanded piece reminded him of Judith. Once God's love smoothed out her hurt and defensive pride, her heart would radiate.

Levi was a fool not to recognize her beauty.

Last night Andrew had drifted to sleep thinking about her, then his dreams shifted to the cabin. It practically glowed. A warm fire in the fireplace and the laughter of children filled the room.

God, I don't understand. Those dreams died when Esther died. Why do they haunt me now?

Perhaps the time had come to sell the cabin. But as he glanced around the workshop, he compiled a mental tally of his expected income once the unfinished projects were completed and delivered. The money would be enough to do the necessary renovations.

His mind continued to teeter until finally he shook his head. His customer orders had backed up while he spent more time than anticipated helping the Fischers with barn chores. He had to focus.

Besides, he hadn't stepped foot inside the cabin in three years. How could he possibly predict the cost of the needed repairs? He wouldn't go against his teachings and become mired in debt. Not for a cabin he didn't want to live in.

Andrew returned to sanding the furniture and worked with

renewed energy to finish the job. Those thoughts were too dangerous to ponder any longer.

He stayed focused on the projects until his stiff back reminded him he'd been bent over most of the day. He swatted the sawdust off his pant legs and stood to arch his back. Tomorrow he'd apply the wood oil, and by the end of the week, after the last coat of lacquer had dried, he'd deliver the dining room set to the Watsons.

The sun hung low in the sky when he pushed open the workshop door and went outside. He pumped the well handle for water to wash his hands and face. His thoughts drifted to Judith and how startled she had looked when he insisted he wasn't anything like Levi. He should have restrained his tone; she was already upset with him.

It was that stupid rock that started the problem. The limited light in the woods hadn't provided the best view. Its spots and discoloration were caused from iron deposits, but she held on to it like it meant something special. He'd never seen her eyes sparkle as brightly as when he called it a gem.

Andrew bent over the stream of water with cupped hands. Splashing his face with the cold water awakened his memory. He jerked upright. She wasn't holding the rock on the path. When she tried to bolt from him in the woods and he caught her arm, she must have dropped it. He rubbed his wet face against his shirtsleeve. If it hadn't meant something to her, she wouldn't have shown it to him. Her eyes wouldn't have held that sparkle.

The back door opened and his mother stepped outside. "Your father and I are going to the Fischers' *haus* to visit. Bless God, Samuel is *kumming* home tonight."

Andrew's attention perked up. "I'll harness the buggy." He wiped his wet hands on the sides of his pants and dashed to the barn. He looked forward to seeing Samuel. The boy must be excited to get back home.

Andrew rolled the buggy out from under the lean-to connected to the barn. As he did, he caught sight of the courting buggy collecting dust. It was waiting on him, the last of the Lapp boys. Eight brothers had courted their wives in the two-seat open-air relic. He had anticipated doing the same. A lump formed in his throat. The buggy had sat idle since he parked it after the day he took Esther for a ride—their only ride.

Andrew climbed over the plow blade to reach the stored buggy. He swept his hand over the seat cushion, removing a layer of dirt as the dust rose up. After years of nonuse, the wheel axles would need oiling. The aged vinyl on the seat cushion was cracked and in need of conditioning, but Andrew was confident he could make the old buggy shine once more.

Perhaps if he convinced Judith to take a drive with him, she wouldn't hurt so badly over Levi's betrayal. His heart raced. He took a breath and reminded himself the drive was to help Judith overcome her hurt—nothing more.

He glanced at the house and noticed his mother holding a baking dish with a dishcloth draped over it. He hurried into the stall and led Patsy outside to harness the mare. Then he brought the buggy up to the house.

His mother stepped off the porch and handed him what smelled like shoofly pie. "We won't be gone long," she told him.

His father came out from the house and climbed into the driver's seat.

"Would it be all right if I rode along?" Andrew asked. "I'd like to see Samuel too."

His father nodded. "We aren't staying late."

Andrew climbed into the backseat. He hoped they stayed long enough to get a slice of his mother's pie. His mouth watered for a taste of molasses. Although knowing his mother, she would have set one aside for him at home. To his embarrassment, his mother tended to dote on him, the last of her sons to remain home. She made no qualms about not nudging him out of the nest.

His father made a clicking noise, and the buggy lurched forward. "I saw you inspecting the courting buggy."

His tone of approval didn't surprise Andrew. He'd made it clear when Andrew turned seventeen that he expected his son to actively pursue finding someone to marry and fill a house with obedient children who served the church and God.

"It needs work," was all Andrew dared to admit. It'd be foolish to mention his thoughts of taking Judith for a ride. His father had stated adamantly that he wouldn't allow her "angel babble" to divide his district.

"Is that shoofly pie, *Mamm*?" Andrew asked, hoping to redirect the conversation.

"It is, and there's one for you at home cooling on the counter."

"You coddle the boy, Mary." His father's tone indicated there was more to his speech. "He's twenty-two years old. The boy *should be* a man."

Andrew knew what his statement implied. In his father's eyes, a boy didn't become a man until he was married and could accept his ministry responsibility.

"*Nau*, Zechariah, you were not interested in courting either, when you were seventeen." His mother failed to add that they had three sons by the time his father reached twenty-three. Andrew had none and no prospect of marriage.

"The boy's not seventeen."

Andrew hoped his mother would let it go. He would always be the son who disappointed his father until the day he joined the church, married. Most nights he prayed that God would release his burden of striving against his father's wishes. After Esther passed away, his father had encouraged him to find a mate. When he declined his father's choice of a baptized woman to wed, Andrew was charged with disobedience. And even though the charges were not formally made before the church, Andrew felt his father's disapproval.

The district's stagnant growth was a curse, but Andrew's eight brothers had done their part in contributing to the community development. His eldest brother's wife was pregnant with their sixth child.

The horse's hooves clapped the pavement, and Andrew gazed out the opening of the buggy. He wondered if the bishops in other districts pressured their youth to marry without being in love. Marry to populate their community, to ensure that the traditions of the Old Order church would continue.

As they pulled into the Fischers' drive, Andrew was determined to ask Judith to attend Sunday's youth singing. That was, if he could convince her that she wasn't still angry with him. His hands moistened. Convincing her to trust him would take work. It would take boldness. He drew a deep breath and rubbed his hands against his pants.

"Be bold," he coached himself under his breath. *Judith needs a friend, someone she can trust.*

His father stopped the horse in front of the house. Andrew jumped out and assisted his mother, then went to his father's side and waited for him to give Andrew the reins. With a quick glance at the buggies lined up near the barn, it was easy to see that the entire community had come to welcome Samuel home.

Andrew found a place among the other buggies to tether the horse. The thudding of his heart caught him by surprise. This was the size of the crowd when the community met for church service every other week. He knew everyone—he shouldn't feel nervous. But with every step he took toward the house, his hands became increasingly clammy.

Several of the men had gathered on the wraparound porch. Andrew rubbed his hands along his thighs again. If he were to shake hands, he didn't want to extend a sweaty palm.

As he stepped inside the house, he passed more men filtering outside to the porch. In the sitting room, the elderly women sat together with a shared quilt spread across their laps. With the constant flow of people coming inside and going out, the drafty house must have caused their thinned blood to congeal—at least that's what his grandmother always said. He saw her now, and she waved him over.

She cupped her hand against Mrs. Stoltzfus's ear. "This is Zechariah and Mary's *boppli*," she said, louder than he wished.

At twenty-two, he was hardly a baby, but he nodded at the confused woman. His grandmother introduced him to Mrs. Stoltzfus at every gathering, and each time the woman crinkled her face as though she'd never seen him before and then asked who he had married and which children were his.

He knelt at his grandmother's side and patted her hand. "Feeling *gut*, *Mammi*?" Since his grandfather's death, he'd made a practice to stop by his uncle's house and visit her often. However, since he had taken on the extra chores for the Fischers, he hadn't spent much time with her.

"Already feeling the cold in my hips." She sighed.

Andrew patted her bony hand. "Winter won't be long *nau*." He'd seen the ground covered with snow several times in October.

"You will *kumm* visit soon, *jah*?"

Andrew stood. "*Jah*, soon." He scanned the room for Judith, and when he didn't see her, he touched his throat. "I think I'll get a drink of water."

As he walked away, he heard Mrs. Stoltzfus ask who he'd married.

Mammi's disappointed reply traveled to the kitchen. Now he wished he would've stepped outside. The group of women in the room looked at him with pity in their eyes. It was bad enough that his mother held a long face, but Judith stood up from removing a roaster pan from the oven with the same sympathetic look. He restrained himself from defending his bachelor status. Explaining his contentment to remain single never helped his cause. Instead, it ignited a flurry of women challenged to find him a suitable mate.

He cleared his throat. "Could I have a glass of water?" An easy means to turn their attention toward something they did well—taking care of someone in need. He could have gotten his own drink, but he'd have to listen to them fuss over him anyway.

Three women turned toward the cabinet, but Judith wasn't one of them. She continued to baste the turkey with broth. His mother handed him a filled glass as Lilly called out to everyone that Judith's parents had arrived. Samuel was home.

The women all moved toward the door, and Andrew moved toward Judith.

"Have you forgiven me?" he whispered.

Judith cocked her head to one side. "For what?"

"Our conversation wasn't left on *gut* standing the other day."

She smiled. "You made it plain. You're nothing like Levi." She moved toward the others.

Andrew followed at her side, and when she stopped, he leaned closer to her ear. "I'm not like Levi, in all the ways that matter."

The door opened, and the increased noise level in the house hindered further conversation. Judith turned her attention to Samuel's arrival. Her mouth dropped and her eyes widened. Even to Andrew, Samuel appeared gaunt in David's arms.

Judith quickly turned back into the kitchen, away from the excited visitors. Andrew came next to her side as she dabbed her eyes with the hem of her apron.

"Are you all right?"

She nodded.

"Are you sure?"

She continued to blot tears from her eyes. "I thought he'd walk through the door."

Andrew wasn't sure how to respond. Everyone knew Samuel

was paralyzed. His father had been at the hospital with Judith's parents when the doctor explained the spinal injury. The extent of damages wouldn't be seen until the swelling subsided. Any lack of movement a month after the injury, the doctor explained, would be permanent.

She drew in a deep breath and forced a smile. "I should welcome him home."

Judith weaved through the crowd of people. She hugged her brother, kept her phony smile tight, and said no more than a few words. Then she edged her way around the others, but instead of returning to the kitchen, she made a hasty retreat toward the front door.

Judith kept her head down as she bolted out the door. The evening breeze caught in her throat as she stepped onto the porch.

The door creaked on its hinges behind her, and she wiped her face before turning to see who had followed her outside.

"Are you all right?" Deborah's teeth chattered as she rubbed her arms.

"I will be."

"It's cold. Why don't we go back inside?"

"Deborah, when was Samuel's quilt finished?" Judith asked her friend.

Deborah touched Judith's arm. "Let's go back inside, Judith. It's cold."

"Please, just tell me. Was I intentionally left out of the gathering?"

Deborah nodded. "I'm sorry. I had nothing to do with it."

"I know." Judith looked over her shoulder into the sitting room window. Deborah's mother was staring at them. "You better go inside. I don't want your *mamm* saying anything and upsetting mine."

"Kumm mitt mich."

Judith shook her head. *"Nett nau."* She needed a few moments alone. She had placed more hope than she realized on Samuel walking. Now what did she have left? If faith was the substance of things hoped for, she certainly lacked faith.

Chapter Fifteen

Andrew edged into the crowd, neck stretched to spot Judith.

"Andrew," Samuel called.

He turned and, seeing the boy's outstretched arms, made his way back through the sitting room. He took hold of Samuel's hand and squatted next to the couch. "I'm glad you're home."

"Will you still teach me how to build furniture?"

Andrew's throat tightened. Samuel had remembered his promise. A day hadn't passed that Andrew didn't remember he'd given Samuel the nail. If he hadn't given the nail to the boy, Samuel wouldn't have climbed to the roof. Wouldn't have fallen. Until Andrew ignited Samuel's interest in building, the boy had been content with playing games and listening to Judith's stories.

"Even if my legs don't work, I can still build, right?"

Andrew marveled at Samuel's cheerful disposition in spite of his bedridden condition. He'd do anything to keep the smile on Samuel's face, even if it meant limiting the time he spent in his workshop on his tasks. "When you're feeling up to it, I will."

The boy's eyes widened. "*Meiya?*"

Andrew glanced at Mrs. Fischer standing at the end of the couch. He didn't want to make any promises without her approval. Once she nodded, Andrew patted Samuel's hand. "Sure, I'll bring the tools," he said and stood. He headed toward the door before the tears welling up in his eyes spilled over.

Judith's cape was missing from the hook. No doubt she had slipped out of the house in avoidance of the icy condemnation she feared would be cast in her direction.

Andrew stepped outside and wiped his eyes. He took a deep breath and blew it out with a steady exhale. When he didn't find Judith on the porch, he suspected she'd gone to the river. He leaped down the steps and headed in that direction. But rather than take a chance that she would force him to turn back, he took another route, a shortcut through the woods.

He found the rock she'd dropped next to the tree they had stood under. With better light, he could see it was freckled with multiple colors. No wonder she admired it so much. He sat with his back against the tree and tossed the rock into the air. Catching it, he looked it over again before tossing it back up.

Several more minutes passed without any sign of Judith. He stood to leave, but a faint sound of dried leaves crunching underfoot caused him to stay put. Judith walked into the clearing with her head down. She sat on the boulder facing the river, oblivious to his presence. Andrew took a step, then paused.

Lord, I ask that You give me the words to comfort her.

He took another step, then hesitated again. She was upset the last time he interrupted her at the river.

"Turn me around, God, if this isn't the time," Andrew whispered as he inched toward her. Then he spoke aloud. "Judith."

She turned to face him and clutched her chest.

"I didn't mean to frighten you."

"Why are you always following me?"

Her curt words were not going to push him away. "I knew you were coming to the river, and I didn't want you to be alone." He surprised himself with such a direct answer.

Her teeth clenched. "But that's why I came here, Andrew. I want to be alone." She crossed her arms and turned her attention to the river.

Lord, help me, please. Andrew moved in front of her to block her view. "Why did you think Samuel would walk through the door?"

She looked up at him. Her eyes narrowed. "Andrew, you're in my way." She stared at him hard, then the scowling expression disappeared and her lips trembled. She whirled in the opposite direction, facing the woods.

"Judith." He waited, but she didn't respond. She needed a friend's support, but holding her wouldn't be the answer, he told himself. He fought back the urge to comfort her in his arms. "I watched your face turn pale when Samuel was carried inside. You looked shocked. Why?"

"Andrew, go away." She tried to turn away, but he held her shoulders in a firm but gentle grasp.

"Please, tell me what gave you that hope."

If an angel had told her Samuel would walk, he wanted Judith to share what was said. She was there when he gave Samuel the nail. Surely she must understand how important it was to him that Samuel walk again.

"I shouldn't have spoken out loud," Judith whispered. She lifted her head and used her sleeve to dry her tear-streaked face. "Will you please go? I came here to be alone and pray."

"I'll pray with you," he offered.

It didn't surprise him that she shook her head. He waited a moment, then, knowing he was standing in her way of calling out for God's help, he stepped aside. She needed God's unsurpassable peace. He only wished she needed his friendship too.

Andrew went as far as the edge of the woods and stopped to look back at her. She hadn't moved. He reached into his pocket and pulled out the rock he'd found by the tree. Should he go back and give it to her now, or wait? He took a step toward her.

"Tobias said Samuel's steps are ordered by You. So why isn't Samuel walking? I don't understand." She lifted a tissue to her nose and blew. "*Nau* I won't be approved for baptism or joining the church."

Andrew strained to listen. Who was Tobias? There wasn't anyone with that name in the community.

Her face lifted toward the sky. "I believe You sent an angel. But if Samuel isn't going to walk, why did Tobias come?"

Tobias is God's angel.

Andrew dropped to his knees. He lowered his face to the ground, inhaling deep breaths of decayed leaf scent. Only God knew of his struggle to determine if the angel was real or something developed in Judith's mind. He believed her simply because she'd never been one to draw attention to herself or speak against authority, yet she did so with conviction about the angel.

"Forgive me," Andrew whispered. "Forgive the others, too, for their disbelief. And, God, thank You that Samuel will walk again. If You sent an angel to say he would, I believe he will."

Judith started to sing a hymn, and Andrew rose off his knees. He'd always found her voice sweet. Today her praise was purely heaven bound. She wasn't singing to fulfill part of a church service, she was singing to God. Restored with joyfulness, her voice grew stronger.

"Thank You, mighty God, for taking her burdens away." He felt the urge to sing as well, but instead he hummed the tune.

Judith stopped singing and spun in a tight circle. "Tobias, is that you?"

He must have hummed louder than he thought. Andrew stepped out from the woods. "It was me."

She rested her hands on her hips. "You! What are you still doing here?"

Andrew blew out a breath. He'd set her off again. "I, um . . . I wasn't spying on you."

She narrowed her eyes. "*Jah*, you were."

He came closer. "I heard you praying."

"Eavesdropping? What is that if it's not spying? Is there a difference?"

He shrugged. "I guess not." He looked toward the river and drew a deep breath, then faced her once more. "I heard you mention the name Tobias and . . . and I was curious."

She raised her chin. "About what?"

"There isn't anyone in our community with that name."

Her stare made him wish he'd kept quiet. Only minutes ago she was happy. He should have gone back to the house.

"And you thought he was an *Englischer* too?" She stepped closer. "You thought I'd gone running with an *Englisch* man." She shrugged. "I'm nineteen *nau*, maybe I should go on my own *rumschpringe*. I can do that, you know."

"Stop it."

She straightened her shoulders. "What did you say?"

Andrew came within inches of her face. "I told you, I heard you praying. Don't tell me any foolishness about an *Englisch* man. I know who Tobias is. He's an angel."

Judith bit her lip and stepped backward. "Andrew, I don't—"

"The day Samuel fell, I saw you run across the pasture. You went into the apple orchard, and when you came out, you were frightened. Why?"

Judith turned her back to Andrew.

"You followed him, didn't you? What did he tell you?"

"Why is what I say so important to you?"

He swallowed his shame. She might think him cowardly for not speaking up sooner, but he had to confess for his own peace of mind. "Because I gave Samuel the nail."

Judith turned, and her expression softened. "Andrew, Samuel fell because of lack of supervision. Not because you handed him a nail." She sighed. "He's held a nail before."

She was being stubborn, trying to shoulder all the responsibility. "I'm your friend. Tell me what the angel said."

Judith lowered her gaze. "You don't know what you're

asking. If you say you believe me, the community will come against you too."

He tilted her chin up so that he could see her eyes. "I'm willing to accept that."

"You don't know what that means."

He did know what it meant to go against his father and her brother, and he would do it again. "It means I believe God over man."

She sighed. "Andrew, why didn't you go with Levi during *rumschpringe*?"

Andrew shook his head. What did this have to do with the topic? "I didn't need a period of running around to know that I wanted to serve God. *Rumschpringe* is for those still searching." He studied her empty stare. "You're nineteen *nau*, is that what you want to do?"

"I asked because I knew what you'd say."

His questioning brows must have relayed that she wasn't making sense.

"You've been baptized. You can't stand up for me." Her voice cracked. "You'll be shunned."

He wanted to protect her, and here she was protecting him. "I would not go against God."

"The church. Your father."

"He is not God," Andrew rebuked. Although he liked the thought that she cared enough to want to protect him, she had to know that only God would determine his fate.

She stood mute, her focus fixed on him, then she released a pent-up breath. "Tobias knelt next to Samuel when he fell off the roof. And you're right, I did follow him into the apple orchard, but he disappeared into the fog." She stopped.

Andrew wasn't sure if she paused to gather courage or if she'd changed her mind about telling him the rest.

"Go on."

"Tobias knew Samuel's name and said his steps were ordered by God. He told me to have faith." She looked up and searched his eyes. "What do you think?"

He brushed his hands over her wet cheeks. "I believe Samuel will walk."

She sighed and then cracked a weary smile. "Are you just saying that?"

Andrew slowly shook his head. He believed every word. "Angels speak what God commands them to say."

She released her guarded breath, and he smiled. He'd gained her trust.

"*We* have to do what he said and have faith." He was standing with her. Even if it meant he'd be shunned.

Chapter Sixteen

Andrew penciled the measurement on a piece of white ash, then readied the handsaw over the marking. When he arrived to teach Samuel, he wanted to have all the cuts made. He would work with the little boy on hammering the pieces together and sanding the finished project.

Andrew finished the last cut and swept the sawdust off the floor. Then he hurried through his morning chores with his thoughts concentrated on Judith. Was it possible that his feelings for her were more than friendship? The idea of loving again frightened him—enough to make him spend most of the night on his knees.

Andrew entered the house to eat breakfast before heading over to the Fischers' place. His mother was at the stove, his father seated at the table reading the Bible. Andrew sat across from his father, but kept his morning greeting to himself so he didn't disturb his father's devotions.

Zechariah looked at him over the rim of his reading glasses. "You don't plan to go to the Fischers' today, do you?"

"*Jah.*"

His mother set a cup of black coffee in front of him.

"*Denki.*" He picked up the cup and blew into the hot liquid.

"Samuel is home. Jonas said he doesn't need your help."

"*Jah*, but I promised Samuel I would build with him today."

"That is thoughtful." His mother set a plate of eggs, fried potatoes, ham, and a buttered biscuit before him.

His father's eyes flickered with annoyance, and Andrew thought it best not to prompt him in any way to speak his mind. Something told him that what his father would say would jeopardize his new feelings for Judith. Instead, Andrew bowed his head and said a quiet grace over the food and asked for wisdom.

He hadn't loaded his first forkful of food before his father asked, "Where did you go last night?"

Andrew swallowed.

Mamm took a place at the table. "Zechariah, let the boy be."

His father's eyes hardened on his wife. "He is a baptized member of the church. I am speaking as the bishop." Once *Mamm's* head dropped in submission, his father turned back to Andrew. "Answer my question. You disappeared from the Fischers' *haus.* Where did you go?"

"I saw that Judith was upset . . . I went to talk with her."

"I don't wish for you to carry on with her."

His mother leaned closer to his father, and even though

she kept her voice low, her interjection was clear. "Ask him, Zechariah, to give more light on the subject."

Over the years, his mother had taken his side on a few occasions, but never at the table. And never in front of him. She shared her views with his father in a private conversation behind closed doors.

His father eyed Andrew carefully.

"We only talked." Andrew sounded defensive, and for good reason. He didn't want any more problems to fall on Judith.

His father slowly shook his head. "I'm not so sure visiting with Samuel is a *gut* idea."

"I gave him the nail," Andrew said softly.

"What is this about a nail?"

"The day Samuel fell. I promised I would build with him. I gave him the nail. He wouldn't have gone up that ladder if I had not mentioned building . . . and if I had remembered to take the ladder down."

His father sighed. "Very well, build with the boy. But keep your distance from Judith." He stood and took a few steps toward the sitting room before pausing. "If you disobey, other arrangements will be considered."

Andrew lowered his head and stared at the yellow yolk that had spread into the mound of potatoes. He pushed the plate aside.

Mamm stood, ruffled his hair, then joined his father in the sitting room. He strained to hear their conversation.

"Work in unity with our son, that's all I ask. Andrew's spent three years grieving Esther."

"My son will conduct himself according to the tenets of the *Ordnung*."

"He isn't seeking an outsider. Judith is—"

"I am speaking as your bishop."

The room silenced.

Mamm appeared in the doorway, gazed a moment at Andrew, then continued down the hallway.

Chapter Seventeen

J udith eased Samuel's bedroom door open and peeked inside. Martha sat next to Samuel's bed, partly weeping and partly singing. Judith didn't recognize the tune.

She placed Samuel's breakfast tray on the dresser and tiptoed closer. Her sister saw her and quieted.

"Keep singing." Judith motioned to Samuel smiling in his sleep. "Your voice comforts him."

Martha put her hand over her mouth, but her teary eyes exposed her heartache.

Judith placed her hand over her sister's shoulder. "He's going to be all right."

"*Nay*, he's *nett*," Martha blurted and rushed to the door.

Judith looked up at the ceiling. Samuel had to get better. He had to walk again.

Even Andrew feels guilty. Somehow he's taken responsibility for my error. I don't wish for anyone to carry the burden, especially not Andrew. God, please have mercy on him and ease his conscience.

Samuel's small chest rose and fell under the bedcovers as he slept.

"I know with all my heart that he wouldn't have survived that fall without You, God . . . I know You sent an angel for him." Her prayer shifted to Andrew. "Please don't let my speaking out harm Andrew in his father's eyes. Without the support of family and community, how could a person survive?"

Judith collected Samuel's uneaten breakfast and headed back to the kitchen, where her mother was rolling piecrust over the floured table.

"I didn't have the heart to wake him."

"He's so weak. I hope the visitors yesterday didn't wear him out." *Mamm* repositioned the rolling pin and with long, rhythmic strokes smoothed the dough.

Judith glanced at Rebecca, who was perched on a chair, chin resting on the table, waiting for a sample of *Mamm's* dough. Judith came up behind her mother, reached around her waist, and pinched off a portion of piecrust.

Her sister giggled while her mother wagged the rolling pin at them both. "I won't have enough to cover my pie for the harvest supper if you two keep snitching dough."

Judith sobered. Every year she looked forward to the harvest supper, a time when everyone came together for fellowship before the long winter months shackled them indoors next to the woodstove. Because of Samuel's accident, the supper had been moved to later in the month, and this year's gathering would be in their barn after the Sunday service.

Mamm stood upright and eyed her dough. "That should be enough for four pies, don't you think?"

Judith nodded, then pinched off the corner nearest her and passed it to Rebecca.

Mamm waved the wooden roller again. "I think you should stir the stew and forget about sampling my crust."

Judith winked at Rebecca as she went to the stove. She lifted the cover and breathed in the aroma of stewed tomatoes and beef, then stirred the ingredients with the wooden spoon and replaced the lid.

"I spoke with your *daed* about your hosting a Sunday evening singing at our house." *Mamm* dusted the table with more flour. "I thought after the harvest supper would be perfect. If we wait any longer, the *wedder* will turn bad."

Judith forced a smile. Her parents didn't know how her dream of marrying Levi had been shattered. Attending a singing without him would be dreadful—but watching him flirt the whole time with Martha would be worse.

Mamm's head tilted sideways. "I know you've waited longer to court than the other girls your age." She smiled. "Did you think we forgot that you turned nineteen?"

Judith wished they had. How could she explain to her parents that she had started to question everything? Marriage . . . baptism . . . church . . . Things had changed. She didn't dare think about the future now; it would only lead to more disappointment.

The knock on the front door offered an easy escape. "I'll answer it."

Judith rushed out of the kitchen. She didn't want to discuss hosting Sunday's singing even if it was a few days away. She couldn't stomach the thought that Levi would come to spend time with Martha. No doubt her own role would be reduced to serving snacks and hot cider while her sister secretly courted. Angry at the thought of it, she swung the door open wide.

Andrew stepped back and eyed her. "*Ach* . . ." He lifted his toolbox, which directed her attention to the boards teetering under his arm.

"I'm sorry." Judith chuckled at how unwelcoming her grimacing face must have appeared.

Andrew smiled. He looked down at himself, then up at her. "Do I look that bad?"

"*Nay*, you don't." Judith reached for the boards under his arm to ease his load.

Andrew placed the toolbox on the floor. "You had me worried." He leaned toward her and whispered, "I do like hearing you laugh, though, even if it's directed at me."

A vibration trickled down to her toes when he removed his hat and the tips of his earlobes poked out from under his chestnut hair. When he placed his hat on the wall hook, his suspenders became taut over his broad shoulders.

She'd known Andrew Lapp all her life and never thought of him as having a muscular frame. Her eyes were still taking in the tightness of his shirt when he turned. His lopsided grin appeared at the same time that a rash of warmth settled over her cheeks.

Andrew reached for the boards. "I'll take those." His hand brushed against hers, and their eyes locked.

Judith wondered if he felt the jolt between them, or if her mind was tricking her. The current had only been on her side, she decided, when his expression didn't change.

"Who's at the door?" *Mamm* came around the corner, dusting her floured hands on her apron. "*Guder mariye*, Andrew."

He picked up the toolbox from the floor. "I told Samuel I would build with him today."

Mamm motioned to the bedroom. "I'll go wake him." She turned toward the hallway but paused when she neared the kitchen entrance. "Rebecca, time for *shul*."

Judith eyed the pieces of lumber Andrew held. "What do you plan to build with those?"

He glanced at the boards but shifted them to the side when Rebecca darted into the room and ducked under his load. "I was thinking Samuel would need a lap table."

"That's very thoughtful of you." Judith looked at Rebecca, who was squatting next to the shoes that were lined against the wall. "Where are your manners, child?" Without taking her eyes off her sister, she continued speaking to Andrew. "A lap table would be handy."

"*Jah*, I thought—"

"Rebecca, about your manners," Judith reminded.

Rebecca glanced up. "I'm sorry, Andrew." She put a shoe on and squealed in pain.

Judith squatted beside her. "No wonder your toes are pinched. You put this one on the wrong foot." She removed the shoe and motioned for Rebecca to lift her other foot.

"Will you *kumm mitt mich* to *shul*?"

Judith enjoyed the mile-long walk to the schoolhouse she had attended until eighth grade. Except for the days it sleeted or rained—then the distance seemed more like ten miles. Walking Rebecca to *shul* would give her an opportunity to talk with Samuel's teacher about the studies he would miss staying at home. If he could hammer a nail, he could hold a pencil.

She helped guide Rebecca's foot inside the black stiff-toed shoe. "*Jah*, I'll walk you. Put on your other shoe and we will go."

Mamm returned from Samuel's bedroom. "He's excited you're here," she said to Andrew.

Rebecca's lip puckered. "I want to stay home too. *Nay shul*."

Judith couldn't hold back a chuckle at her little sister's exaggerated face. "You need to learn." Judith held out her hand. "*Kumm*, let's go walking."

Samuel sat in bed with his back propped by several pillows. Andrew took a seat at the foot of the bed. "Are you feeling up to working with me?"

Samuel's eyes brightened. "*Jah!* What will we build?"

Andrew tapped the boards in his hand. "I've already cut the lumber." He motioned to the bed. "I don't think your *mamm* would be pleased if we got sawdust in your bed."

Samuel laughed.

"It would be like sleeping in the barn, but instead of itching from hay you would be itching from wood shavings." Andrew gestured to his back. "You'd be rubbing against the bed frame like a cat."

He liked hearing Samuel laugh.

"Have you done that?" the boy asked.

"*Jah*. Sometimes in my shop I get sawdust everywhere and my back will start itching so that I have to remove my shirt and give it a *gut* shake." Andrew stretched his hand to Samuel's head and ruffled his mop of hair. "Are you ready to get started?"

Samuel nodded, and Andrew laid out the pieces over the bed. Although he had made all the cuts and rechecked the measurements, he showed Samuel how to read the measuring tape. He also spread out the sketch he'd made of the lap table and explained each piece and where the wood needed to be nailed.

When the door creaked open awhile later and Andrew looked up, Judith poked her head into the bedroom. "Are the two carpenters hungry?"

"See what I'm making, Judith." Samuel tapped the hammer but missed the nail and hit Andrew's finger. "I missed."

"*Jah*." Judith entered the room. She looked at Andrew sucking his finger. "Has he been 'missing' all morning?"

Andrew withdrew his fingers from his mouth and smiled at Samuel. "Nothing I haven't done to myself many a time."

She reached for his hand. "Let me look."

Her touch fueled his heart like a horse with its belly full of oats. But any minute he expected his hand to turn clammy, so he quickly jerked it away. "It doesn't hurt."

She twisted her lips at his sudden reflex. "If you would carry Samuel to the kitchen, everyone is at the table ready to eat." She hurried away.

He hadn't intended to be rude, but he didn't want her to know the effect her touch had on him. He looked at Samuel and shrugged.

"I don't blame you for not wanting to hold a girl's hand," Samuel said.

Andrew moved the project from the boy's bed and placed it out of the way in the corner of the room. "I'll tell you a secret. I wish I hadn't pulled my hand away."

Samuel's eyes grew large. "Do you want me to hit your finger with a hammer again?"

"I hope that won't be necessary." He winked at the boy. "But maybe *meiya*." He slid Samuel into his arms. "Hopefully the *wedder* will be *gut meiya*, and your *mamm* will allow you to sit on the porch to do the sanding."

"Will you ask her?"

"*Jah*." Andrew chuckled as he carried his new buddy down the hallway and into the kitchen.

Mr. Fischer came in from the barn and joined the family at the table. He gave Andrew a warm smile but kept to the business of eating. When he finished his meal a few minutes later, he returned to the barn.

Mrs. Fischer talked enough for everyone. She asked how the building project was going and how Andrew liked the stew. She talked about the weather turning colder and the possibility of an early snow. After she'd exhausted every topic, she aimlessly shuffled the eating utensils.

"Judith, why don't you pour Andrew another glass of milk?" Mrs. Fischer watched him as though she could see into his soul. "Since Judith is nineteen *nau*, I thought she should host the next Sunday evening singing."

Judith refilled his glass without making eye contact with Andrew and returned to her chair.

Andrew looked across the table at her. She stirred her bowl of stew with a spoon, as if she were not giving attention to her mother's comment.

"I get to participate, don't I?" Martha bit into her biscuit.

"And me too," Samuel added.

Mrs. Fischer chuckled. "Absolutely not, Samuel. This is time for the youth to become acquainted." She looked at Martha. "And you will watch Samuel in his bedroom for the evening."

Martha crinkled her mouth into a pout.

Judith looked up, and her blue eyes brightened.

Andrew scraped the last spoonful of stew from the bowl. If he was going to spend time with Samuel tomorrow, he needed to get home and finish his work. Besides, he had a special project of his own he wanted to surprise Judith with.

Once Judith knew Martha wouldn't be allowed to attend the Sunday evening singing, she fluttered around the house completing the list of chores. She even dusted the baseboards and refilled the oil in the lamps. *Mamm* sent Martha to *shul* to walk Rebecca home, while Judith worked with her mother on the food they would need for the singing.

Judith reached across the table and touched her mother's hand. "Are you sure you're feeling up to this?"

Mamm looked up from the writing tablet. "You shouldn't worry. I feel strong."

Judith shifted in the chair. Ever since the day of Samuel's accident, she had wanted to ask her mother if she believed in angels. David had insisted that she not bring it up. But now Samuel was home, and *Mamm* said she felt strong. She looked strong too, now that the dark circles under her eyes had faded.

"What is it? Do you not want to have the get-together? I thought you were looking forward—"

"I spoke with an angel." Her stomach flipped, and it felt like a hundred pins pricked her at the same time.

Mamm drew a deep breath.

"And I saw a vision . . . or maybe I was in a trance." Judith's eyes never left her mother's. "Have you ever"—she swallowed and lowered her voice—"heard of a visitation like that?"

"No . . . but sometimes when we want something real bad . . ." Her mother sniffled and reached for a rag on the counter.

"I know what I saw, *Mamm*." Judith kept her voice steady. "I even heard chanting. I followed him into the apple grove."

Mamm took another calming breath. "I heard what you've told everyone." She bowed her head. "What you said about Samuel walking too."

"I believe he will."

Tears spilled down *Mamm's* face. "I don't want to lose you, Judith. I just can't lose you."

Judith's throat tightened. "Please, *Mamm*, don't cry. You won't lose me."

Her mother blew her nose. "You *muscht nett* speak of this again."

"But—"

"It's for the best. Why do you think I want to have the singing at our *haus*? I want you to find a mate. I want you to marry and have *boppli* and . . ." She reached across the table for Judith's hand. "And have the life God purposed for you."

Judith mustered a smile. Her mother probably assumed that Levi Plank fit into her daughter's future. She couldn't tell her there wasn't anyone interested in marrying her now. Besides, maybe marriage wasn't God's purpose for her life after all.

The *church* deemed marriage a duty to fulfill, but did God? Judith had accepted and anticipated her womanly role . . . anticipated being married more than she anticipated falling in love. And she couldn't deny that Levi had broken her heart. But was it losing the dream of marriage that left her feeling brokenhearted? The thought startled her.

"Judith, I know you've been worried over Samuel, but his accident isn't your burden to bear."

"I shouldn't have yelled for him to come off the roof."

"What is done is done." *Mamm* squeezed her hand. "There will be no more talk of angels in this *haus*."

"There were angels in the Bible," Judith said softly.

"*Jah*, and they fought battles and delivered very important messages. Don't you see? We are only a small group of plain people. Why would God send an angel to our district? We already share His gospel within our community, and we already follow His word." She thumped her chest with her thumb. "We have His law deep in our hearts."

Her mother's drawn-out gaze pulled at Judith's heart. She believed everything *Mamm* said, but it didn't explain why she'd seen Tobias multiple times.

She needed to see him again. She needed to know more about the message God sent him to deliver. *Mamm's* question was one she had been asking herself for days. Of all the plain people in their community, why had God chosen her?

Chapter Eighteen

Andrew veered his buggy into the Fischers' drive and sighed when he saw Levi's buggy already parked next to the barn. He had convinced himself to be bold around Judith, and now it seemed his efforts would once again be compared to Levi's. He might as well have been chaff on the threshing floor.

Well, perhaps it was for the best if he never found courage to talk with Judith about courtship. After all, his father rarely changed his mind.

Mrs. Fischer answered the door. It would be another hour before Samuel finished his physical therapy exercises. Not wishing to see Levi, Andrew declined the invitation to wait in the sitting room. He decided to leave his tools on the porch and go for a walk.

He took the shortcut through the woods and sat at the river until he thought Samuel's therapy would be over. Then he walked the path leading to the house. At the sight of Judith picking apples, he stopped and leaned against a tree. She tossed an apron full of fruit into the basket, then bent and selected an apple. As he watched her bite into it, Andrew's mouth watered for a cup of warm apple cider.

He was about to step toward her when he heard someone whistling. Levi.

As Levi neared Judith, his tune turned into a long flirtatious whistle directed at her. Judith turned her back to him, but Levi latched onto her elbows. "I've been looking all over for you."

She tried to pivot away, but his nose followed her neckline to her ear like a hound on a fox trail.

Andrew's chest deflated as he turned to walk away. Levi had won again. It shouldn't have come as a shock that Levi realized he wanted Judith—or she him.

Judith's voice carried. "I told you before. I don't want to hear what you have to say."

Hearing her in distress was enough to ignite Andrew. He spun around, blazing with fury as he saw her trying to push herself off Levi's chest.

"I just want to talk with you, that's all. Give me five minutes."

Andrew stormed toward them. "Let her go, Levi."

"*Greeya fatt*, Andrew." Levi looked at Judith. "Tell him we were just talking."

"Our talk is over. I was hoping to meet Andrew here, not you."

The moment Levi's arms dropped from around her, Judith rushed to Andrew's side. She slipped her hand into his and looked up at him with wide eyes. "Will you take me for a walk *nau?*" Her voice quivered, but her gaze bored a hole into his heart.

Andrew felt his insides stammering to reply. Vaguely aware that Levi was walking away, he held his focus solely on Judith, yet couldn't utter a sound.

She bounced up to her toes. "Please," she whispered next to his ear.

The warmth of her words sent a prickle along his spine. He turned his face toward her, and her lips brushed against his cheek. An accident or a kiss, he wasn't sure, but the touch of her lips against his cheek quickened his pulse.

"Were you really hoping I'd be out here?" he asked, his lips only inches from her face.

She tried to look over her shoulder to where Levi had been, but Andrew cupped her face in his hands. As he glided his thumb over her cheekbone, she tried to explain.

He leaned closer, her lips his focus. She was saying something, but he didn't hear her words. Unable to think of anything but kissing her, he stopped her speaking with his mouth.

Judith tensed and brought her hands up to his chest. Had she pushed against him, he would have stopped. She didn't. She eased into his embrace, responding to his kiss, and he lingered as long as he dared.

Andrew broke from the kiss first. They stared at each other a long minute, then, seeing her glance in the direction where Levi had been, his mind spun to find some way to explain his rash action. "Next time you want to fool Levi, make it believable."

Her attention snapped back to him. *"Ach*, that was pretend?" She covered her mouth with her hand.

"You and I both know it wasn't all pretend." He walked to the apple basket, picked it up, then turned to look back at her. *"Kumm* on. Levi will know it was staged if we don't walk back together."

Judith hesitated.

Andrew's stomach was in knots. He had prayed for boldness, but now he despised himself for behaving brashly like Levi.

"If it helps to know," he said, "I think Levi was jealous when he left."

"Gut." She looked at him sideways. "I guess we won't have to do that again."

"I suppose you're right. If that was *your* only intention, there won't be another reason for us to kiss." He watched for her expression to change, but it didn't.

Back at the house, Andrew cut his time with Samuel short. He found himself looking for Judith, not concentrating on the project at hand. But Samuel didn't seem to mind after Andrew promised to take him on a furniture delivery in the morning.

Before he could take his leave, Judith appeared at the back door, one fisted hand on her hip. "It's time to eat," she said. "My *mamm* insisted that I invite you to stay."

Andrew bent to pick up Samuel from the porch while Judith held the door open. He stopped in the threshold and peered into her eyes. "Is Levi staying also?"

"He's gone."

"Then you won't need me." He smiled wider than he should have, by the look of her knitted brow, and continued into the kitchen.

Mrs. Fischer pulled out a chair from the table. "I have your place set next to Samuel."

"*Denki*, but I need to be going." He patted Samuel's shoulder. "I'll pick you up early *meiya*."

He kept his head down when he passed Judith at the door. He opened his mouth to apologize, but closed it just as fast. He had stirred that boiling pot enough to know she was about to hiss like a kettle if he even uttered a word. Besides, what was he sorry for? That the softness of her lips and the taste of apple made him linger? That he'd acted out in the boldness he'd prayed for?

She wouldn't view either of those reasons as an apology. Besides, she had responded. She made him breathless. He had summoned every fiber within him in order to separate their embrace.

Andrew climbed into his buggy and plopped down on the seat. Praying for boldness had a powerful effect on his mind-set. What had he done? He'd cemented his shunning. Disobeying the bishop's order was punishable. He couldn't go home until he settled his nerves.

Andrew flicked the reins and directed Patsy onto the paved road. He'd only been to the cabin once since Esther died, and that was to close it up. Today was as good a day as any to start working on it. He might be taking up residence there soon.

He turned onto the bumpy road leading to the cabin and pulled back on the reins, forcing Patsy to yield to the birch trees that narrowed the lane. Once he reached the cabin, he sat in the buggy for a moment and stared at the dilapidated clapboard house. He'd bought the old hunting cabin for nearly nothing. Once the county developed a paved road to Hope Falls, not far from the cabin, the wildlife had scattered, and with them the downstate recreational hunters who sold him the place.

He stepped down from the buggy and tied Patsy under the oak tree. Three years ago he'd made a list of all the tasks needing attention. Now by the looks of the vines creeping along the wood siding and covering the windows, he'd have to amend his list. Fortunately the hunters never had the electrical or plumbing installed. What they termed "roughing it" Andrew called a way of life.

The rotten boards on the porch steps dipped under his weight. He glanced around the overgrown yard and suddenly locked eyes with a man traipsing around the side of his house.

"*Gut* day." Andrew stepped off the porch and walked toward the man.

"*Jah*, fine day." The man came closer. "I wondered who owned this *haus*. Since it's on the border of the district, I wasn't sure if you'd be an *Englischer*."

"I'm Andrew Lapp."

"*Jah*, I know who you are." He gazed around the surroundings. "*Jah*, this is a *gut* plot of land."

Andrew nodded. He'd forgotten about the clearing he planned to plow for a garden. He sighed. After the winter season he would have a better idea of how involved his father would allow him to be in the community.

"Moving in with a *fraa*?"

"*Kumm* to *redd-up*." Andrew studied the man but couldn't place him at any of the church meetings on this side of the district. Even so, word would get back to his father that he was fixing up the place.

"Fine place to start a family." He paused, his blue eyes shining like the uncluttered sky. "How long have you owned it?"

"Three years." Andrew meandered over to the back side of the buggy and unlatched the pine box in which he carried miscellaneous tools to repair a broken harness or wheel axle if needed. He pulled out a pair of leather gloves and headed to the house.

"Mind my asking why you haven't moved in sooner?"

"I suppose it wasn't meant to be." Andrew slid on his gloves. If the man insisted on prying into his life story, Andrew decided, pulling weeds would allow him to hide some of his sorrow.

"Things are not always how we want them." The man came up beside him and pulled out the vines encroaching on the windows. "Sometimes we let worries choke out life." He pointed to the edge of the property. "Look at the apple tree over there. If you cut the weeds back, it'll grow and be fruitful."

Andrew walked over to the apple tree.

The man followed. "It will find life again. You like apples?"

The flicker in the man's eyes caught Andrew off guard. It seemed as if the man knew how much Andrew liked the taste of apples on Judith's lips.

The man gazed at the house. "With a little work, this could be everything you've dreamed about."

Andrew cocked his head sideways. Suddenly the man didn't sound too Amish. "I thought maybe I had neglected the *haus* too long . . . My dreams died three years ago." His mind whirled. Why was he telling this to a stranger? He squatted to grab another handful of weeds.

"A man's life will wither if he lives too long in the past." He patted Andrew's shoulder. "But I see you are moving forward. After all, something brought you here after three years." He took another long look at the cabin and nodded. "*Jah*, a fine *haus* to raise a family." He looked at Andrew. "Your dreams have not died. If you look closely, you'll see they are the same. It's you that has a new view." The man turned away.

Andrew stood, dropped the bundle of weeds from his hands, and followed. "Wait," he called, but too much distance separated them, and the man continued without acknowledging Andrew's call.

Andrew shook his head and returned to cleaning up the area. The man's words, however, continued to replay in his thoughts.

My dreams are the same, only I have a new view. How can that be?

Judith tossed back the covers and slipped out of bed. She knelt on the floor and folded her hands. "Lord, forgive me. I tempted Andrew. I wanted him to kiss me." Judith jerked her head up. She'd kissed a man she hadn't even courted. Her mind drifted back to the firmness of his lips against hers, the tightness of his muscled chest. *Focus . . .*

She squeezed her eyes closed and clasped her hands tighter. "Have mercy. Forgive my actions." She stayed on her knees long after she said amen and long after she tried, but failed, to erase Andrew's kiss from her mind.

Crawling back into bed, she wrestled several hours with the

memory of how his lips moved over hers. She struggled to dismiss the tingle he caused, until exhaustion made its claim. Her eyes grew heavy . . .

It was snowing. At first fluffy snowflakes fluttered from above as she twirled, arms spread, head tilted to the sky, her mouth open to catch the falling flakes. Quickly the flakes turned to pellets of ice and melted as they formed a thick armor that kept her from moving.

Then a man with his face obscured, carrying a hammer and chisel, walked to the angel standing guard over her. The man received permission from the angel to chip away at her icy armor. Diligently working, the man worked to break off the thick ice shell that kept her bound.

Before her, a three-pronged road appeared. Encouraged by the man nudging her forward, she took a step, then looked back— Samuel lay pounding the heels of his hands against the lake of ice under which he was trapped. The angel's thundering voice boomed. "Choose a path."

Judith bolted upright in the bed. Her eyes burned from the sweat that rolled off her forehead. She scanned the darkened room. "Tobias," she whispered.

Silence.

Chapter Nineteen

M amm said to bring you inside."

Andrew craned his neck from his seated position on the porch to look up at Judith, who stood on the other side of the screen door. He smiled.

She did her best to ignore eye contact, darting her eyes away from his every time they connected. "I thought you could use some cooling off, but *Mamm* said she saw your buggy arrive more than an hour ago and insisted that I bring you in."

"I was early, so I took a walk." Andrew stood. He had hoped a night of sleep would have softened Judith's attitude. "You still angry?"

She motioned with her head to his wagon filled with furniture. "Do you have a tarp? The sky is gray. It might snow."

Following her gaze to the sky, Andrew sighed. In his rush to see her, he hadn't thought about the possibility of the weather changing. By the looks of the darkened sky, perhaps she was right. It wasn't like him to forget such important matters. He would stop at home and gather something to cover the furniture.

Judith had disappeared inside the house, leaving him cloud-watching alone. When she returned, she held out two quilts. "You can cover the wood with these."

Most women didn't part with their handiwork for use in bad weather, unless the article was worn and ratty. But eyeing the quilts she handed him, Andrew knew these were not ready for the rag bag. "Are you sure your *mamm* won't mind?"

Judith shrugged. "They're mine. I made them."

Andrew had never been one to study the handwork on quilts. They were functional, mostly recycled articles of clothing, a practical commodity within their community. But holding something that Judith had perhaps spent the better part of the summer hand-stitching changed his view. "These are too nice to cover furniture." He held them out for her to take back.

Judith took the bundle without a word, then stepped off the porch and climbed up into the back of his wagon. Andrew followed and waited as she unfolded a navy, gray, and black checkered quilt.

She ran her hand over the top of the chest of drawers. "You do *gut* work."

"So do you." He motioned to the quilts. "I'm going to feel bad if they get wet," he said.

Judith shrugged. "I have better ones. Besides, I can spread them in front of the woodstove if they need drying." She tapped the covered furniture. "You'll have much bigger problems if your furniture gets wet."

Andrew fastened rope over the quilts to hold them in place and gave her a broad smile, hoping for a response. "*Denki*."

The corner of her mouth twitched, then at last she offered him a brief smile—enough to warm his core.

She glanced at the house. "Samuel should be ready."

Andrew jumped off the side of the wagon and hurried to the back to assist Judith down. He held her arms long after her feet touched the ground. Unable to turn his gaze away from her shining sapphire eyes, his breath caught. He never thought she'd allow him so close again.

She looked upward. "You need to get going before the *wedder* changes."

The sky hadn't darkened more. She must have felt the connection too. Maybe she was fighting butterflies. He wasn't sure how he'd describe what was happening in his stomach. He wasn't sure if it felt like he'd eaten a whole shoofly pie or a container full of wood glue. He followed Judith into the house.

Samuel looked up from where he sat at the table. "I finished my breakfast." He turned his attention to his mother. "Can I go with Andrew *nau*?"

Mrs. Fischer wiped her hands on her apron. "If you promise to listen and obey his instructions."

"*Ich fashprecha.*"

Andrew picked Samuel up. "I'm holding you to that."

Samuel nodded as Andrew carried him outside to the wagon.

Judith followed with a smaller lap-sized blanket. "Do you have a strap to secure him on the seat?"

"*Jah*." Andrew lowered Samuel onto the bench. He lifted the end of a leather strap and weaved it around a metal ring to make it tight around Samuel's waist.

Judith spread the blanket over Samuel's lap. "Be mindful of Andrew."

She'll make a fine mother one day, he thought as he climbed to the seat. He glanced at Samuel's eager smile and nodded before he released the wagon brake.

As he made a wide turn over the lawn, he saw Judith staring off in the direction of the river. He looked at the sky, hoping the weather would stay clear until after he made his delivery. He hoped to ask Judith to go for a walk later.

Samuel glanced at the load in the wagon. "How many places are we going?"

"Today, only one." He noticed Samuel's frown and tapped the top of his hat. "But next week I'll have more items to deliver."

Samuel's eyes widened. "Can I go with you again?"

Andrew nodded. "If your *mamm* says *jah*."

Samuel's infectious gap-toothed smile made Andrew laugh. He couldn't blame the boy for not wanting to be closed up inside the house all day. If he wasn't careful, the women would have him helping to sew quilt blocks.

"So you think you want to be a craftsman. Have you been sanding your lap table?"

"*Jah*, but once it's finished, Judith said I have to do my schoolwork on it."

Andrew laughed again. Judith turning the boy's fun project into a chore cemented Andrew's thought that she'd make a perfect mother. *"Shul* is *gut.* You need to know math to measure the wood correctly."

"I don't want to read and write English."

"That is important as well." Andrew understood Samuel's dislike of reading. He'd done the required eight grades and found them tiring. He would have rather worked in the field or cleaned barns. His mother encouraged him, using his desire to whittle small animals out of scrap wood. She said the *Englischers* bought Amish wood products, but he'd have to study hard while he was in school if he planned to run a business.

His father took the biblical approach, instilling the fear of God into him. The man's duty was to learn to read High German so he understood God's word. Without reading skills, his father had said, he would struggle with his responsibilities as head of his house once he married.

The clopping of the horse's hooves on pavement snapped Andrew out of his reverie. Once they reached Willow Trail, Andrew had the horse veer onto the gravel road, then he withdrew a folded piece of paper from his pocket and handed it to Samuel. "How many houses down the road do the directions say to go?"

Samuel's face contorted. "I can't read this. I'm only five." He handed the paper back.

Andrew chuckled. *"Jah,* I suppose I didn't read at your age either." He looked at the notes he'd jotted down. "The eighth house should be stone and on the right-hand side of the road."

Counting the houses, spaced several acres apart from each other, kept Samuel busy. They were a mile down the road before the stone house came into view. Samuel pointed with excitement. "Eight! There it is, on the hill."

Andrew nodded and slowed the horse before reaching the driveway. The front wheel dipped into a rut, tipping the wagon downward on Samuel's side. Andrew put his arm around Samuel's waist as the boy started to slide. The belt would keep him on the bench, but Andrew didn't want him afraid of the rough ride. The wagon rolled backward before the horse gained traction. Then, with a forward lurch, Jack moved the load over the furrows created by the washed-out gravel.

Once they were on level ground, Andrew glanced behind them to check the furniture. The rope was tight, and the items hadn't shifted. He breathed easier and turned toward Samuel, relieved to see the boy's wide smile. "Frightened?"

Samuel shook his head. "That was fun."

Andrew chuckled. "Next time you can drive."

Samuel's eyes sparkled. "Really?"

"Not when we're loaded with furniture." Andrew looked again at the cargo, thankful for having Judith's quilts to protect the wood from being nicked. If he had to sand out imperfections and reapply another coat of varnish, he'd be delayed from renovating the cabin. He planned to repair the porch steps and even thought about enlarging the porch once he collected his earnings.

Mrs. Stanly met them near the back door. When he saw her salt-and-pepper hair wound in rollers and her fuzzy pink housecoat showing under her winter jacket, Andrew bowed his head to ward off the temptation to gawk. But when his eyes caught sight of her pink painted toes, he raised his head, thinking it was easier to look at her hair spun around the bristled rollers. He just needed to stay focused on unloading the furniture and completing his transaction. An *Englischer's* worldly attempt to enhance her appearance wasn't his concern.

Andrew was uncovering the first piece when Mr. Stanly came outside. Dressed in a business suit and a brick-colored tie, he put on a thin pair of leather gloves and came around to the back side of the wagon.

Mrs. Stanly gasped, and both men stopped what they were doing to see what had startled her. "That quilt is beautiful," she said. "May I see it?"

Andrew handed it to her over the side of the wagon.

Mrs. Stanly stroked the fabric. "This is lovely. Did your wife make it?"

"My sister Judith made it," Samuel said proudly.

Andrew gave Samuel the same stern look he had received when he was growing up. Pride was sin, and compliments from man were not to be treasured.

"*Nay*, she's not my wife," Andrew said to Mrs. Stanly.

"Very fine craftsmanship," Mr. Stanly said, then added, "I don't know anyone else who is as talented as you."

"A blessing from the Lord." Andrew viewed Samuel from the corner of his eye. He'd use the opportunity to demonstrate to Samuel how the glory belongs to the Lord. But his response hadn't been rehearsed words to tickle God's ear. He believed his talent was a gift from God and thanked Him daily.

"I have a cookie for you, if you'd like to come inside," Mrs. Stanly told Samuel.

The boy started to push off the seat, then stopped. He couldn't just jump off the wagon and go inside. Disappointment spilled from his eyes as though for the first time he realized his limitations.

Balancing the dresser off the back end of the wagon, Andrew explained, "We're in a bit of a hurry today."

With Mr. Stanly's help, it didn't take long to unload the furniture. When it came time to leave, Mrs. Stanly walked with him to the wagon. She handed Samuel a cookie and Andrew the folded quilts.

"Do you know if they are for sale?"

Andrew climbed onto the wagon bench. "I'll ask."

"She has more," Samuel added.

The woman touched Samuel's arm. "*Ach*, please tell your sister that I'd love to see them."

Andrew's heart warmed when he saw Samuel nod enthusiastically. He was a devoted youngster and the kind of son he'd love to have one day. Andrew touched the brim of his hat and nodded to Mrs. Stanly, then waited until she was inside before flicking his reins on the horse. Maneuvering Jack so that the empty wagon wouldn't travel too fast down the driveway required both concentration and skill. Samuel's hands gripped the bench, but the boy remained quiet until they were off the hill.

After they were on flat ground, Samuel snickered.

"What's so funny?" Andrew glanced at him sideways and smiled.

The five-year-old covered his mouth. "Judith made a quilt for her marriage bed."

Andrew looked at the quilt draped over Samuel's shoulders and the others folded on the bench beside them. "Which one?" He found the thought of his furniture covered with her wedding quilt unsettling.

"*Nett* these."

Andrew couldn't explain the hint of disappointment he felt. He would have been honored if one had been the wedding quilt. Yet he couldn't help but wonder if Judith would marry Levi once she'd forgiven him.

"Why aren't you married?"

Samuel's question jolted Andrew.

He cleared his throat, thinking how he should phrase his words. "I'm waiting on God to prepare the woman's heart."

Samuel's face crinkled. "What does that mean? She doesn't like you?"

"Something like that."

"My *mamm* says everyone should pray they find a mate."

Andrew blew out a breath. "It's complicated when you get to be my age."

Samuel mimicked Andrew's long exhale. "I wish you'd marry one of my sisters."

Andrew snorted. "Does it matter which one?" It mattered to him. He could never marry someone as vain as Martha. But hearing Samuel categorize them together fed Andrew's curiosity.

"Either one. There are too many girls in my *haus*."

Andrew chuckled. "That's understandable." Not that he knew what it was like, having grown up with only brothers.

He pulled into the Fischer driveway, set the brake, and jumped off the wagon. After releasing the strap, he lifted Samuel into his arms.

Judith opened the back door. "Did you have fun?"

Samuel nodded. He looked at his sister, then at Andrew. "I know which one," he said.

Andrew jostled Samuel in his arms so that he could whisper into his ear. "Let's keep that our secret."

But he wondered how long a five-year-old could keep silent.

Mrs. Fischer came out of the kitchen. "Andrew, the physical therapist will be here soon. Would you mind carrying Samuel to his bedroom?"

Samuel crinkled his face.

Andrew gave the boy a gentle shake as he carried him down the hallway. "You work hard for the medical person, and I'll take you on my next delivery."

"And I can drive?"

Andrew removed Samuel's hat and ruffled his hair. "If you're gentle with Jack. He's an old horse."

He left Samuel in his room and went to the door to hang the boy's hat on the hook. Then he stepped into the kitchen where Judith, Martha, and their mother were seated at the table peeling apples. Andrew watched the thin skin of the apple Judith held fall to the table. He licked his lips, recalling the taste of their kiss.

Mrs. Fischer looked up from coring the apple she held. "*Denki* for spending time with Samuel. He gets lonely being the only boy in the house."

Andrew nodded and looked at Judith as she continued to shave off the peeling. "Mrs. Fischer, may I take Judith for a walk?"

Mrs. Fischer's paring knife stopped, and she looked over at wide-eyed Judith and smiled. "*Jah*, I think she could use some fresh air."

Judith's expression wasn't as inviting. The look she'd given her mother narrowed when she looked at him.

"That's not fair. These stupid apples are for her singing," Martha grumbled.

"Hush!" Mrs. Fischer locked eyes with Martha before selecting another apple from the pile. She turned to Andrew and smiled. "Give Judith a minute to wash her hands."

Judith put down the paring knife and stood. "We won't be long," she told her mother as she wiped her hands. She placed the towel on the counter and walked to the door.

Andrew followed.

Once outside, she turned to him. "Why did you put me on the spot in front of my *mamm?*"

"I have to talk with you about yesterday."

She glanced over her shoulder at the house and walked toward the barn. "What about?"

About the kiss, he wanted to say. Did she feel the same connection?

Mr. Fischer came out from the barn and nodded at them on his way toward the house.

Andrew directed Judith toward the pasture. Neither spoke until they were at the orchard. Judith jumped to pick an apple out of her reach. Andrew pulled the branch closer. She picked one, handed it to Andrew, then picked another for herself.

"What about yesterday?" Judith took a bite of the apple.

Distracted by the juice from the bright red apple collecting in the corners of her mouth, he stammered. "I, um . . ." She took another bite, and he completely forgot what he'd planned to say. He motioned toward the path to the river. "Let's keep walking."

Her next bite was noisy, and he couldn't restrain his laughter.

Judith stopped.

He dropped his gaze to the ground. "Your lips . . . tasted . . ." He looked up at her and cringed. "Like apple yesterday."

Judith's eyes widened and her breath sounded like it caught in her throat. She resumed walking.

Andrew had brought her on a walk to explain his action, and now he couldn't find the right words. "I didn't mean to kiss you like that."

Judith stopped.

"I, um . . ." His stomach flipped as he peered into her piercing eyes. He waited for her to speak. "I'm sorry. I didn't mean to. It just happened."

"In other words, if I hadn't encouraged you—"

He reached for her hand holding the apple. "I do like the taste of apples."

She flung the apple into the woods like it was poisonous and stared at him without blinking.

Andrew chuckled, but stopped when she dropped her head and stared at the ground. "Hey, I was joking."

"I thought I'd only share that kind of kiss with my husband."

Andrew swallowed, stunned by her honesty.

She lifted her head. "I'm sorry. I shouldn't have brought that up."

Andrew couldn't process the meaning behind her statement. "Why are you apologizing?"

"I know you're *nett*—" She bit her bottom lip and cut off her statement.

He stepped closer. "*Nett* what?"

"Interested in courting anyone."

His gut twisted. "Who told you that?"

She looked down at the ground. "Levi."

"And he knows all about chasing women, doesn't he?"

She stared off in the direction of the woods. And just when it seemed she planned to drag out her silence indefinitely, she spoke. "I didn't mean it to sound like a jab just because you're unmarried."

"I suppose Levi told you why he calls me Bishop Junior."

"*Nay*. I thought because you're always so serious and . . ."

"And uninteresting." He brought her into his arms and leaned toward her ear. "Should I be more like Levi?" He moved his mouth within a fraction of an inch from hers. "He would kiss you again."

She wiggled loose and steeled her eyes on him. "I meant since Esther died, you haven't been interested in another woman."

Her heavy breathing made him wonder if her heart rate raced as his did. She took a step backward.

"And one more thing. I'm only interested in kissing the man I marry."

A rush of air left his lungs. What had gotten into him? He hung his head. "I'm sorry." He removed his hat and raked his fingers through his hair. "I didn't mean to upset you." He replaced his hat. "I'm a bit touchy about Levi calling me Bishop Junior. Especially since he knows that my father is . . . more than disappointed over the matter of me not being married. It seems I don't measure up to the standard of a godly Amish man. I won't ever be cast into the lot for ministry." He scuffed the ground with his boot. "I wanted to marry Esther. I even bought a cabin." He glanced up. Judith's sympathetic eyes studied his without prying into his silence. "I never thought I could fall in love with someone again."

"They say time heals old wounds."

He opened his mouth, then clamped it closed. He wanted to ask if it meant her wound from Levi had healed, but he lost his nerve. Instead, he motioned toward the river. "I watched you when I left with Samuel. I know you want to see if Tobias is there." He waved his hand. "Go on. I'll wait here for you."

Her warm smile caused his chest to swell. He'd already told her too much. He needed a few moments alone as well.

Chapter Twenty

From a hidden section on the path, Judith looked back at Andrew. He tossed stones into the river as though releasing something pent up inside of him. "Don't become like Levi," she whispered before turning to the trail.

She strolled along with her hands clasped behind her back. She had almost turned to mush in his arms, again. Her heart thudded when he said she smelled like apples. Unlacing her fingers, she placed her hand over her heart. Andrew wasn't in sight, and her heart continued to knock against her ribs. She willed herself to take captive her thoughts. Andrew Lapp had made it plain that he'd never fall in love again. His warning, no doubt, not to make more of their friendship—more of their kiss.

She reached the river's bend, anticipating the appearance of Tobias. Instead, she noticed a wooden box on the boulder and ran to see what it was. Judith picked up the box and touched the smooth sanded wood. It had to be Andrew's handiwork. With suspended breath, she opened the lid. There was her rock.

Judith removed it from the box. In the palm of her hand, it glowed with shades of emerald and jade greens, sapphire and cobalt blues, and her favorite color, ruby. She felt the love of God wash over her, and joy sprouted like tulips after a spring rain.

A gentle breeze kicked up some fallen leaves, and she looked for Tobias in the direction of the wind. If he was there, he didn't make himself visible. Judith waited a few more minutes, then placed the rock back into the wooden box and lowered the lid. Returning to the path, she had a sudden urge to run. She wanted to show Andrew the rock's vibrant colors.

She sprang out from the wooded path, and as she approached him, his eyes widened.

He craned his neck to look behind her. "Something wrong?"

"*Nay*, I was excited." She pushed the box against his chest. "Look inside."

He smiled, lifting the lid.

"Isn't the kaleidoscope pattern almost hypnotizing?"

He cocked his head sideways at her.

"I could look upon it all day, it's so beautiful."

He pulled the rock out from the box and rolled it over his palm. "It's only a river rock, *jah*?"

"*Jah*, and when the sun hits it a certain way . . ." She looked up in the sky. With the developing gray clouds, the sun wouldn't produce enough light to show him.

"You're beginning to worry me." He turned it over again, then clenched it in his fist.

"Don't——" She cringed.

"What?" His brows furrowed. "You're placing a frightening amount of emphasis on a stone." He plopped it back into the box and closed the lid. "The Bible warns about false idols. You said the angel gave you this?"

He was concerned about her putting too much emphasis on a rock, but he'd built a box to put it in? No one else had his woodworking precision, and he'd certainly left the box down by the river knowing she would find it.

His posture shifted, and the lines between his eyes took root. "Judith," he said, "it says in the Bible to test all spirits." His eyes glazed. "Satan was an angel too. He's the Great Deceiver."

She cleared her throat. "You think I'm being deceived?"

He closed his eyes, tipping his face toward the sky, and his Adam's apple bobbed when he swallowed.

"Why aren't you saying anything?" Her voice grew louder. "I know what I saw."

"So you say, but were you spellbound? You sound as though you're worshipping a rock."

She caught a glimpse of the fast-moving clouds. "It's going to rain. We better get back." Without waiting for him, she headed for the house.

He mumbled something under his breath, trekking behind her. Once they reached the back of the barn, he stopped her from continuing to the house.

"Promise me you'll pray about this."

She lowered her head, but he lifted her chin.

"Promise me you'll read the passage in Second Corinthians about Satan masquerading as an angel of light . . . There are fallen angels who pretend to be angels of righteousness." He brought her closer to him.

She closed her eyes, hearing the worried tone in his voice.

"Promise me," he whispered.

She swallowed. His breath was warm against her face. What was she doing, allowing him this close? Of course she planned to pray.

"I will." She expected him to move away once she'd agreed. He didn't.

He stared at her mouth the same as he had the day he kissed her. Then he sucked in a breath and leaned back. "Did Tobias say why God sent him?"

Judith shrugged. She could tell him about the dream, but even she didn't understand the three roads and why she was told to choose. Besides, with him moving closer again, it was hard to concentrate on any one thing in particular.

As Andrew leaned toward Judith to kiss her, thunder boomed and lightning flickered across the dark sky. He stepped away. "I have a confession."

Judith glanced nervously at the sky.

He cleared his throat. "When I kissed you, I knew Levi had already gone. I shouldn't have . . . I'm sorry." He cocked his head sideways. "I didn't intend—"

Another bolt of lightning ignited the sky. Pelted by

marble-sized hail, he grabbed her hand, and they ran toward the house. Before they reached the porch shelter, sleet had saturated their clothing.

"You can come inside and sit by the woodstove."

Andrew looked up at the sky. "I should go before it gets worse." Besides, the longer he stayed, the more he would want to kiss her again.

She seemed to accept his apology, but deep down he'd hoped for more, an admission of her own as to why she had kissed him back. He stepped away from her.

"I forgot to tell you. Mrs. Stanly, the woman who bought my furniture, is interested in buying one of your quilts."

"I've never sold one. I don't know how much to charge. Surely a quilt made with a machine would be far superior to my hand-sewn blocks."

Andrew shrugged. "She examined them closely. I know she liked them." With his hair dripping beads of water down his neck, he wanted to shake himself dry like a wet dog. He removed his hat and shook the water from its brim instead.

Judith pulled a rag from her cape pocket and dabbed her face. Her wet hair looked darker, but he could still see the red-dish streaks the summer sun had made. Her head covering lay flat against her hair, and now her teeth chattered behind purple lips.

"I see you're cold. You need to go inside." He reached for the doorknob and paused. "If you want, I'll drive you to Mrs. Stanly's house at the beginning of the week so you can show her your quilts." He didn't add that Samuel had told him about the one she was saving for her wedding bed.

Judith smiled. "*Jah*, that would be nice."

Andrew looked at the gray clouds. As cold as it was, the sleet would turn into snow. He hoped it would hold off until after Judith's singing. "I should go." He turned his gaze to Judith. "Pray about what we talked about." He waited until she nodded before he stepped off the porch. "I will pray too."

Her expression was stiff. Maybe she didn't like the idea that he would be praying. But how could he not? With so many of the community against her, the enemy was already involved in isolating her from others.

Andrew climbed onto the bench and looked back at the house. Judith had already gone inside. He shuddered. If they were not diligent to keep watch, Satan could deceive God's elect.

Judith went straight to her bedroom. She gazed at the intricate details Andrew had put into the box. By worldly standards, the box would be considered plain, but to her, the dovetailed joints and the unstained birch wood were perfect in every way. But why hadn't he said anything about making it for her? She ran her hand over the sanded bare wood as her thoughts drifted to Andrew's confession.

He admitted he was sorry for kissing her. His regret made sense after he explained he could never fall in love again. Judith had known Levi was no longer standing there—she'd wanted to kiss Andrew, but not under those circumstances. Now thoughts of his firm lips pressing against hers would taunt her memory.

"Forgive me, God, for putting him in that situation." She

placed the box on the dresser. "I shouldn't have been so forward with a man not my husband." Judith sighed.

Her legs were icy to the touch and her knees knocked to a different cadence than her chattering teeth as she changed into a dry dress. She brought the wet garments out to the sitting room and spread them over a wooden rack in front of the woodstove, then proceeded into the kitchen.

Mamm poured steaming water from the kettle into a cup. "Would you like some tea?"

"*Jah*, please."

Her mother placed the drink on the table, and Judith forced the floating tea bag to the bottom of the cup with a spoon.

"How did Samuel do with his exercises?" Judith sipped the hot liquid, feeling the warmth make its way to her stomach.

"He was so tired after his morning with Andrew and then his therapy, that he fell asleep as soon as the man left." Her mother dunked a tea bag into her cup of hot water.

Judith blew gentle ripples over the steaming tea. "A man? I thought a woman came the last time."

"He said he was filling in today." *Mamm* shrugged. "I hope the exercises help. I'm sure they will cost plenty."

This was the first time Judith had heard anything mentioned about the medical expenses. She studied *Mamm's* expression. Mulling over the hospital costs in her mind, no doubt. Samuel's accident had taken its toll on her too.

Martha entered the kitchen then, with a basket of eggs. Teeth chattering, she placed the basket on the counter, then tugged at her wet dress. "I suppose I should eat more so the wind doesn't blow me away." She swept the fallen strands of hair away from her face and eyed Judith. "I should think you'd want to fast a few meals."

Judith glanced at her mother, expecting to hear *Mamm* rebuke Martha for such a worldly, not to mention unkind, comment. But her mother continued to stare into her cup, oblivious. Judith stood. That her sister was far prettier than she was easy to see by anyone's standards—but she didn't have to sit here and listen to her jabs. She placed her cup in the sink. "I'm going to look in on Samuel."

The door creaked. Not wanting to awaken him, Judith eased it open just wide enough to squeeze inside.

Samuel's lids fluttered. He brought his hand from under the blankets and rubbed his eyes. "Is it morning?"

Judith tiptoed to the bedside. "You can sleep longer." She sat in the chair next to his bed and combed her fingers through his hair.

He stirred again. "I'm not tired. The man told me to close my eyes and dream that I was running."

Judith ran her hand along his cheek. "And how fast were you running?"

He yawned. "First I couldn't stand, but a bright light made me try harder, and before long I could." He stretched his arms over his head. "I heard singing, but I couldn't understand the words."

Judith gulped. "Tell me what the man said."

"He told me to believe I was running." He frowned. "My legs wouldn't move, so how could I believe?"

Judith stood, went to the foot of the bed, and lifted the covers. She touched his feet, and heat rose off the surface of his legs and penetrated her skin. "Did your legs feel warm when he touched you?" She eyed him closely. "Do you feel how hot they are *nau*?"

He shook his head slightly, and his mouth turned down into a frown.

Judith pulled the covers back over his feet. "What did the man look like?"

"Like a *doktah* in a white coat."

"Is that all you remember? Could you look into his eyes? What color were they?"

He shrugged. "*Bloh*, I guess."

She scooted the chair closer and leaned toward him. "How tall was he?"

Samuel's face crinkled. "Big, like David." His lips trembled. "Why?"

"No reason." She leaned back into the chair. "I was just curious." She waited until he settled. "Did he say if he planned to *kumm* back?"

"*Nay.*"

Judith tapped his hand. "*Drauwa* God, Samuel."

"That's what he said too."

Judith tilted her head to the side. "Really, the man said that?"

"He also told me about Samuel in the Bible. How God called to him when he was young. But I told him I knew that."

She stood and kissed his forehead. "You close your eyes and see yourself run some more. I will bring you supper when it's ready." She turned to leave.

"Judith."

She turned back. "*Jah?*"

"I want to be like Andrew when I grow up. Do you like the furniture he builds?"

She smiled. "Very much."

He opened his mouth as if he wanted to say more, but then he snapped it shut.

"Is there something else?" She returned to his bedside.

"Do you think that I'll walk again?"

"*Jah, Ich* do." She stroked his cheek with the back of her hand. "Remember when I told you in the hospital that I saw an angel?"

His eyes widened. "*Jah.*"

"I think if you close your eyes, you'll see one too."

Samuel snapped his lids shut.

She tiptoed to the door and looked back. "I think you already have," she whispered.

Chapter Twenty-One

The freezing rain left a thin icy coating over the puddles in the furrows of the muddy field. Judith sidestepped what wet areas she could avoid on her way to the orchard. After Samuel woke and the two of them shared a cup of hot cider, she decided to pick more apples to make a batch of cider for Sunday's singing.

She wished she had worn her gloves. The wind carried a light spray of sleet, and picking the wet apples left her hands stiff. She emptied the apron full she'd collected into the basket and paused to warm her cupped hands with her breath.

Andrew's words had stayed with her throughout the day. While she did her chores, while she sat next to the woodstove reading her Bible, and even now the promise she'd made to pray that her heart wasn't deceived remained on her mind.

"Lord, forgive me. I was stubborn when Andrew asked about Tobias. I know after reading Your word why he was concerned. Satan is a great deceiver. Show me if I've been wrong, but I believe Tobias was sent by You."

Judith picked another handful of apples off the tree and placed them into the basket.

"God, Andrew is a man after Your heart. His desire is to serve You in ministry, but unless he's married, he will not be chosen. Please show him how to love again, and honor him with a good wife."

Judith wasn't expecting the words of her prayer to sting, yet asking God to give Andrew courage to pursue marriage pricked her heart as though it were a pincushion. Perhaps her forwardness had confused Andrew. She thought, by the way he had lingered, that he wanted to kiss her, and yet he apologized. She turned at the sound of twigs snapping underfoot.

"*Mamm* sent me out here to help you." Martha crossed her arms and glanced around the orchard. "I don't know why I have to pick apples for *your* singing."

"You don't have to help." Judith emptied her load into the basket. "I'm almost finished anyway. And I'm not picking only for the singing. With the *wedder* changing, the trees need to be picked clean for apple butter."

"Levi plans to attend."

Don't take her bait. Judith continued picking without replying.

"Won't that bother you?" Martha persisted.

Judith yanked hard on a stubborn branch. "It's open to all the youth."

"I'm sure he wants to see me."

Judith tossed an apple into the basket and turned to Martha. "What have I done to you? Why do you always want to hurt me?" She sighed. "Go on back to the house. I don't need your help."

Martha shrugged. "I just wanted you to know that if Levi attends, it isn't to spend time with you. He loves me."

Judith sealed her lips to keep from saying something she'd regret. Once her sister was out of sight, Judith sank to the ground and wrapped her arms around her knees. She had paid heed to not speak her thoughts, but that didn't keep her from sinning as animosity festered within her soul.

The dried branches snapped again, and Judith looked up.

Tobias knelt beside her. "Your soul shall find rest after you lay your burdens down." He placed his hand on her shoulder. "You were not created to carry this yoke, but to praise the Lord for the work His blood completed. Search your heart, and you will find those matters that condemn the soul."

"You're telling me to forgive them. But I don't know how," Judith whispered.

"Strength comes from the Lord. Was not Jesus betrayed?"

Judith nodded.

"He who knows your pain has overcome the world, so that in Him you may find peace during times of tribulation."

Judith bowed her head and wept. Her tribulation wasn't anything in comparison to how Jesus suffered.

Tobias patted her shoulder, then stood. "I will leave you to talk with your Savior."

Judith looked up, and Tobias was gone.

"Please forgive me, Lord. I've allowed my heart to become tainted by bitterness. I want to forgive Levi and Martha. I want to be free of the sin I carry . . . Show me how to lay my burdens at Your feet, Jesus. I will follow You all the days of my life."

Inside the Fischers' new barn, the church service concluded. With the weather turning cold, instead of eating outside, they would set up the tables inside the barn. Judith was grateful that Samuel was home to attend. She left him seated near the tables to go inside the house to help with the food preparations.

She stopped inside the entry when she heard her name mentioned.

"Judith is confused, and we need to pray for her," one woman said.

"It's best to keep the children away from her, though. Until she stops with her storytelling," another added.

"My niece is a fine girl," *Aenti* Lilly said. "She feels enough guilt for yelling at Samuel while he was on the roof."

Judith cleared her throat and walked into the kitchen. It was nice that *Aenti* stood up for her, but the majority of the lot wished to condemn her. She glanced around the kitchen, thankful not to see her mother. "Where's *Mamm*?"

Aenti Lilly's eyes widened. "I have a stack of plates you can take out to the barn." She picked up the dishes and thrust them toward Judith. "Go on *nau*. The men should have the tables set up." *Aenti* Lilly waved her hand toward the door. "Your *mamm* is getting more preserves from the cellar."

Judith took the dishes. The air outside wasn't as cold as the atmosphere in the kitchen anyway.

Andrew walked up to the table as she set the plates down. "Will you meet me at the river? I'd like to talk with you."

Judith glanced around to see if anyone was within earshot. "When the meal is over," she replied. After hearing the comments from the women, she wasn't hungry. But if they were not at the meal, people would become suspicious. Andrew didn't need to become a victim of scandal. It was best to meet later, while the men were involved in their fellowship and the women were inside cleaning up.

Andrew had his plate cleaned in no time. He turned down sweets, saying he was full. As a few others left the table, he shared a smile with Judith and then disappeared. Judith found her escape from the crowd a few minutes later.

Once she entered the apple grove, Andrew stepped out from behind a tree and startled her. "I thought you said the river," she said, clutching her chest.

"I was waiting for you."

They meandered for several minutes, Andrew kicking a stone along the path. He stopped. "Did you pray about what we talked about?"

Judith studied him a moment. "I did."

"And?" His brows rose.

"I believe in my heart that God sent Tobias. I still don't know why." She chewed her bottom lip as his stare held her captive.

"And the rock?"

"I found it while I was sitting by the river. I tossed it into the water, and the next time I saw Tobias—" She looked Andrew in the eye. "You're the only friend I have, but if I say any more—"

"Stop trying to protect me." He reached for her hand. "Tell me, please."

She took his gentle hand squeeze as a prompt to continue. "Tobias gave it back to me. Only . . . it glowed."

He didn't look alarmed by her statement. Although his eyes did widen for a brief time, he nodded, encouraging her to continue.

"He told me that's how God sees His children when their hearts are pure." She held her breath, waiting for his reaction.

"I understand why it's important to you."

"You believe me?" An unexpected ease washed over her, and she blew out her held breath.

He smiled. "I don't have any doubts about you, Judith."

Thank You, Father, for giving me Andrew.

This time she kicked at the dirt. "I wanted to tell you, but I feared you wouldn't believe me."

He squeezed her hand, then released it. "I'm glad you trusted me."

Judith lowered her head.

"What's wrong?"

"People are gossiping. I'm to blame for their sin."

"*Nay, nett* so." He crossed his arms and blew out a breath. "They can choose not to pass judgment."

She welcomed Andrew's friendship, his acceptance of her, but she was to blame—he knew that. "It's about not believing me," she whispered.

He brushed his hand on her cheek. "Let God deal with them."

"But—"

He pressed his fingers over her lips and shook his head. "Leave it to God."

She closed her eyes and nodded. *Cast all your cares* . . . A quiver settled in her core at the thought of Andrew's kindness.

Andrew removed his hand. "We should get back."

Judith nodded, and they turned to walk back to the barn. "*Denki.*"

"For what?"

"Being my friend."

He chuckled. "That isn't a chore, you know."

Judith glanced at his sheepish grin and smiled. Andrew Lapp was her friend. And friends didn't hold back the truth from each other.

As they reached the side of the barn, her conscience would no longer suppress her guilt. "I have a confession." As she gazed into his eyes, their sparkle invited her to continue. "I knew Levi had left . . . when you kissed me."

When he swallowed his reply, she could see he was stunned. "I'm sorry. I should have told you. I should have—"

"Andrew." It wasn't so much the bishop's tone, but seeing his white-knuckle grip on the Bible that hinted of a pending sermon.

"We can talk more tonight," Andrew whispered without looking at Judith. He walked away from her and met his father. When the bishop demanded to know his son's whereabouts, Judith hoped Andrew wouldn't be forbidden to attend the evening singing.

Andrew followed his parents to the buggy in silence. He glanced at the Fischers' house before climbing in, but Judith had already gone inside. A smile spread across his face. Judith's response to kissing him had nothing to do with Levi.

"I didn't see you eat much, Andrew," *Mamm* said once they were en route home.

"I ate plenty."

"Did you like the *yummasetti*?"

"Jah," he replied. Although in truth he'd virtually inhaled his portion—the sweetened meat in the casserole wasn't in his mouth long enough for him to savor the taste.

His father's silence tore at his heart. He had seen Andrew and Judith walking back to the barn together. It didn't matter that they were both of courting age—his father the bishop viewed Judith's outspokenness about the angel as defiance to the *Ordnung.* Andrew had seen his father poring over the laws several times during the past week. Fearing the bishop was preparing a formal rebuke of Judith, Andrew had prayed for his father to seek God's wisdom in the matter.

His father parked the buggy next to the house. "You have chores to complete before attending the singing this evening."

Andrew nodded. He wasn't sure why his father brought up doing chores. It wasn't their custom to work on Sunday except to tend to the needs of the animals, and he had never once neglected to milk the cows or feed the livestock.

Andrew changed from his Sunday black vest and pants into his work clothes and went out to the barn. He milked the cows, fed the calves, and tossed a bale of hay over the fence for the horses. He was priming the handle of the water pump when his father came out of the house, his Bible tucked under his arm.

His father walked over to Andrew. "You've been spending a lot of time at the Fischers' *haus*."

"*Jah*, Samuel and I are still working on projects." He splashed water on his face and around the back of his neck.

"Have you other motives?"

Andrew kept his focus on the water collecting in his cupped hands. After washing, he stood upright and towel-dried his face. "Samuel shows promise of becoming a carpenter. I want to encourage him." He kept his tone even. If he appeared too eager, his father would suspect his interest was in more than just teaching Samuel the cabinetmaking trade.

His father studied him. It seemed apparent there were accusations seeded in the bishop's thoughts, yet he hadn't shaken his finger yet, demanding repentance.

Andrew prepared his defense. He and Judith were both of age to court, to marry should they choose. *Lord, I don't want to be forced to choose between pleasing my father and continuing my friendship with Judith.*

"I've made arrangements for you to escort the King girl home from the singing."

Andrew lowered the towel from his face. When he looked up, his father had laid his hand over the pages of the opened Bible. Andrew waited, assuming his father planned to read the scriptures pertaining to children obeying their parents.

His father closed the book. "The Bible is clear about not being unequally yoked. You will accompany Clare King tonight. Her parents expect you to bring her home."

Andrew wanted to challenge his father's comment, fearing it meant Judith's application for baptism would be rejected, but he held his tongue. He had nothing against Clare King. She was a fine baptized girl. But knowing how she'd voiced her interest in him months ago, he didn't want her to get the wrong idea tonight.

Andrew recalled the church gatherings in Clare's district. He had commented that the food was good, and Clare's mother made a point to tell him which dish Clare had cooked. He never repeated that mistake. Clare and her mother had followed him like flies on honey, coaxing him to eat more of the rice pudding.

His father cleared his throat. "The King girl is of marrying age."

Andrew sucked in a ragged breath. He'd agree to accompany her home after the singing, but he would never marry her—even to gain his father's approval. Didn't he remember her family's failed effort to marry her to a third cousin from Pennsylvania? Even the promise of farmland didn't keep the man in Michigan.

Andrew hung the towel around his neck. "I'll make sure she gets home." He held the ends of the towel, thinking it was a noose slipped around his neck. His father gave a satisfactory nod, then walked away. Andrew followed in silence. Once he entered the house, he went straight to his room.

Andrew tried to focus on what he would tell Judith as he clasped the hook-and-eye on his vest. He dreaded attending the singing now. He sat on the edge of his mattress to pull up his black socks and shove his feet into the snug-fitting shoes.

Before his father broke the news that he would be escorting Clare, he'd worried that the courting buggy hadn't been fixed up the way he wanted. Now it almost seemed fitting for it to be grungy tonight. He certainly wasn't out to impress Clare.

Chapter Twenty-Two

Andrew climbed into the courting buggy and gazed at the clear night sky. The ride home from singing would be cold, and the open buggy didn't offer any shield from the wind. He was glad he'd remembered to bring a blanket. The heat of guilt spread over him. If he were driving Judith, he'd offer her his coat—his embrace to shield the wind. He couldn't make any encouraging advances toward Clare. She needed to know, in a tasteful way, that he wouldn't be calling again.

He made a clicking sound, signaling Patsy into a trot. He wanted to be the first to arrive at Judith's house, hoping he'd have a moment alone with her. Clare's family had arranged for her younger brother to bring her to the gathering.

Seeing Levi's buggy parked near the barn, Andrew growled

under his breath as he tethered Patsy to the post. He drew a deep breath. He wasn't sure how the night would play out, but he had no intention of pairing up with Clare . . . and he hoped Levi's plans were not to mingle with Judith.

Andrew tugged his vest into place, then tapped on the door. He craned his neck as he tried to view the sitting room from the door window. Neither Judith nor Levi was in sight.

When Judith opened the door, the aroma of apple pie baited his senses. Distracted by the memory of their kiss, he couldn't think of what to say. All he could think about was how much he liked the taste of her sweetened lips that day.

Judith waved her hand toward the wall hook and smiled. "You can take your hat off and stay if you wish."

He slid the hat from his head and placed it on the hook. Once composed, he turned back to her and licked his lips. "I smell baked apples." He raised his brows. "I remember how tasty they were in the orchard." He studied the fullness of her lips.

"Andrew Lapp," she scolded under her breath.

He leaned closer. "My *mamm* adds *Thomas* when she wants to make her point clear."

Levi poked his head around the corner of the kitchen. "Bishop Junior, I see you've decided to join us."

Andrew followed Judith to the kitchen and stopped near Levi. "I like to sing."

Levi rolled his eyes. "But does anyone like to hear you?"

"Levi, stop that." Judith's brows furrowed.

Andrew groaned. Public protection by a woman would only feed Levi's insults. A knock on the door drew Judith's attention, and she excused herself.

Levi motioned toward the door. "Hiding behind the skirt, Bishop—"

"Has Andrew arrived?" Clare's question drowned out Levi's words.

Levi raised his brows. "You have a date?"

Andrew didn't want to call her a date, but he didn't want to admit that his father had made the arrangements either. He was stuck, and the expression on his face must have made that plain.

Levi crossed his arms and chuckled. "You dog."

Andrew rolled his eyes. He didn't know what being a dog was in Levi's eyes, but he didn't like the thought. Andrew stepped around the corner as Clare continued to question Judith.

"What time do you think the singing will end?" She didn't wait for Judith's reply. She turned to Andrew when he came into view. "*Mamm* asked that you have me home by ten o'clock."

"Sure." Andrew studied Judith, wishing he could decipher her expression. Her posture hadn't shifted; her smile remained warm. If he had arrived sooner, he could have explained. But the longer he watched her, the more convinced he became that she wasn't disappointed. The situation wasn't awkward to anyone but him.

Judith glanced at Clare, then at Andrew. With a slight tilt of her head toward Clare, Judith widened her eyes at him.

"*Ach*, I'm sorry. Judith Fischer, this is Clare King. She lives in the south district." Andrew traveled every other Sunday with his father for the services held in Clare's district. It had slipped his mind that Judith wouldn't know her, since not all the families attended services held outside of their own community.

"My brother Timothy is tending to the horse." Clare looked at Judith. "I hope you don't mind if he joins us."

"It will be *wundebaar* to have you both," Judith replied.

Clare cringed. "Three, actually. He brought a friend." She turned to Andrew. "Sadie Hartzler. You know her, she's my neighbor."

Distracted by watching Judith for signs of discomfort, Andrew failed to acknowledge Clare, and she continued.

"We don't count the *Englisch* farms in between us. The Hartzlers are my Amish neighbors."

Andrew nodded, more pretending than following her explanation. He studied Judith's natural smile.

Clare held up the covered dish she'd brought. "I made rice pudding. I know how much you liked it the last time I made it."

Andrew offered a half smile. He remembered eating the pudding and thinking he might choke.

More arrivals drew Judith's attention away from them as she greeted the newcomers.

Andrew motioned to Clare. "I'll show you where you can leave the dish." He stepped into the kitchen, and Clare followed.

Levi and a few others loitering in the kitchen came closer when Clare placed her dish with the others on the counter.

Levi craned his neck around Andrew's shoulder. "What's that?" He smiled at Clare as she removed the lid. "Rice pudding?"

"Jah." Clare clasped her hands behind her back and swayed as she looked at Andrew. "I was told before it tasted *gut.*"

"I look forward to trying some." Levi glanced at Andrew, then turned back to Clare. "I'm Andrew's cousin Levi."

"I've seen you before, but I don't think you noticed me. Last year"—she leaned closer and lowered her voice—"at the bonfire party near the Weavers' stone pile."

Levi cocked his head and grinned.

Clare's face reddened. "I'm baptized *nau*. I no longer participate in *rumschpringe*."

Andrew cleared his throat. "I'm going to say hello to Samuel."
He left Clare talking with Levi and silently prayed that they
would find a connection tonight. Maybe if he left them alone
long enough, Levi would offer to drive her home when the singing ended.

Maybe he would keep Samuel company and listen to the idle
chatter in between songs from his room. But when he opened the
door he saw Martha in the room.

"I just wanted to say hello to Samuel."

"Andrew." Samuel tapped the mattress beside him.

Martha closed the book she'd been reading and stood. "I'll
be back in a few minutes."

"I haven't heard any singing yet," Samuel said.

Andrew sat next to the boy. "I'm sure it will start soon."

Samuel positioned his hands on the mattress so he could
raise himself into an upright position. "Are you going to come
over so we can build *meiya?*"

Andrew ruffled Samuel's hair. "You need to have a *gut*
night's sleep first."

"I will," Samuel promised.

The door opened, and Martha came back in with a frown on
her face. She plopped down on the wooden chair next to the bed
and let out a long sigh.

Andrew smoothed out Samuel's hair with his hand. "I'll see
you *meiya*. Sleep well." He glanced again at Martha, then slipped
out of the room.

Levi met him at the end of the hallway. "Help me out, will you?"

"Depends."

Levi looked both ways and leaned forward. "Fix it up so I can be alone with Judith."

Andrew shook his head. *"Nay."* He took a step forward, but stopped when Levi's hand pressed against his chest.

"I've *kumm* to my senses," he whispered.

"Have you *nau*?" He motioned toward Samuel's room. "Have you told that to Martha?"

Levi shrugged. *"Nett* so direct." He looked again toward the bedrooms. "Martha wants me to take her away. Leave the faith." His eyes widened. "I thought about it. Until last *nacht*. A car pushed me off the road, and the buggy nearly flipped." Levi tapped his chest. *"Ich kumm* to *mei* senses *nau.* I'm not leaving the faith. Besides, Judith will make a fine *fraa.* And if she's got a wedding to plan, she'll drop the angel talk . . . The community will accept her again." Levi made a sharp nod. "Help me out, *jah*?"

"You stay away from Judith. She's over you." At least he'd been praying she was.

Perhaps Levi did have a sobering incident—but he hadn't mentioned once that he loved Judith. Andrew moved past him and continued to the kitchen. This wasn't a good night to be obligated to give someone else a ride home.

Judith thought she could be happy for Andrew. He'd found the courage to ask Clare to the singing—that was a start. But the poor guy looked so uncomfortable. He squirmed in his seat as if he had a burr in his pants. He sat between Levi and the man who had introduced himself as Clare's brother, Timothy. Timothy seemed pleasant enough, as did his date, Sadie.

As they sang the song Clare suggested, a cheerful tune with a fast beat, Judith scanned the row of men seated across the table from the girls. Andrew's shoulders were the broadest of all. Dragging fallen trees out of the woods and lifting the furniture he made had built his rugged stature. Judith's thoughts drifted to the memory of Andrew holding her in his arms, the ticking of his heart against her ear . . .

"Judith?" Levi tapped her hand. "It's your turn to pick a song."

She sat upright and turned to Deborah on her left. "Why don't you choose one? All I can think of are slow hymns."

Deborah picked a song, and they all joined in. Judith gave her friend a grateful smile. She knew she was the only one who had never attended an evening of singing before.

They sang several more songs before people stood and stretched. Judith took that as a sign to prepare the refreshments. The men wandered out to the porch, and the women clustered around the kitchen counter sharing recipes and talking about who was driving whom home.

Judith wanted to avoid that topic. The bright side, if she dared to think there was a bright side, was that she didn't need a ride home. As she placed the pot of apple cider on the stove to warm and tossed in a few sticks of cinnamon, she overheard Clare say to Leah, one of her good friends, that she'd been baptized last month and hoped to marry soon.

"Do you think Andrew will ask you?" Leah asked.

Judith kept her back to them, stirring the cider, but made sure her metal spoon didn't scrape the pot so she could hear Clare's reply.

"I overheard my parents talking to his father," Clare said. "They've all given their approval."

Judith's heart grew as heavy as a laundry basket full of wet towels.

Deborah tapped her shoulder and nodded toward the sitting room. Judith followed her friend out of the kitchen.

"You all right?" Deborah said. "You seemed upset by Clare's comment."

Judith swept the wrinkles from her apron. She couldn't confess that she and Andrew had kissed. Not even to her closest friend. "I would think we would have met her before tonight, is all."

Deborah lowered her voice. "Is *nett* all. You've fallen for him."

"He's a friend." Judith brushed her arm as if her sleeve had balls of lint attached. She'd made the mistake of thinking her camaraderie with Andrew was something more than mere friendship. That he wasn't pretending when he kissed her.

"*Nau* what I overheard after service makes sense."

"What did you hear?"

Deborah looked over her shoulder. "I heard the bishop was upset when you and Andrew disappeared after the meal."

"We met on the path to the river and talked."

"I heard he forbade Andrew to spend time with you."

Forbidden. Judith swallowed. "That means he plans to shun him?"

Deborah shrugged. "I sure wouldn't think he would shun his own son."

"*Jah*, the church is first." Judith saw how much David had changed, and he was only a deacon. *Ach, why did you have to befriend me, Andrew?*

Her eyes welled and she wished she could hate him for stealing her heart. Andrew Lapp had intruded in her life. He'd sought her friendship. Judith sucked in a deep breath. He could have pretended that her lips didn't touch his cheek and not responded with such a heart-melting kiss. Now his relationship with the church was in jeopardy.

"It shouldn't be an issue, *nau* that Andrew is getting married." Judith motioned to the kitchen. "I should finish preparing the cider."

Being the hostess helped Judith to keep out of uncomfortable conversation. This night could not end quickly enough for her liking.

The front door opened then, and the men came back inside. Levi helped himself to a healthy portion of Clare's rice pudding, while Andrew took a spoonful.

"I thought I should leave enough so that everyone could sample it," he told Clare after she protested.

Judith ladled apple cider into coffee cups and passed them out before she fixed a plate of food for herself. She spooned some of Clare's pudding onto her plate and scolded herself for thinking it was runny.

When everyone took a place at the table, Levi insisted that "Bishop Junior" lead them in prayer. Andrew's jaw tightened, but he did as Levi asked. Judith didn't pay attention to his words.

Her thoughts drifted to how Levi wouldn't be able to tease him once he'd married Clare and became eligible for a ministry role.

Once Andrew finished the prayer, he took his seat at the table and picked up his fork. Judith watched to see what he would eat first. When he chose her apple pie, her exhaled breath caused him to pause and gaze at her before getting the fork to his mouth.

Andrew chewed leisurely. If he was savoring the flavor or aware that Judith was waiting for a sign of his approval, he didn't show it. She asked herself why it mattered. But she knew. All the women wanted their dish to be the best. A silent vying for a husband.

"*Gut* pie, Judith." Levi lifted his fork in salute.

"*Denki.*"

Another man added that he liked the crust.

Andrew continued to eat.

Judith found herself mesmerized by the rhythmic movement of Andrew's square jaw. She forced herself to redirect her focus and turned sideways in her chair toward Clare.

"Your rice pudding is very tasty." Levi poured out compliments the same way he layered hotcakes with syrup—sweet, sticky, and oozing with charm.

Clare's giggle became a muffled background to Judith's thoughts. Levi's flirting was predictable, and it didn't even hurt. The bitterness, the envy, the anger of betrayal—they were gone. "Thank You, God," Judith whispered under her breath.

Andrew scraped his fork across the plate to gather the last crumb. Judith caught him staring at the dollop of rice pudding shoved to the side. He readied his cup of cider in one hand and his fork in the other and gulped as she'd seen Samuel do a hundred times before he choked down turnip greens. Andrew shoved the bite into his mouth and chased down the pudding with a cup-draining drink of cider. His eyes closed.

Judith's chair screeched against the wood floor as she moved away from the table. She filled a fresh cup of cider and brought it to Andrew. "Thirsty?" She exchanged cups with him and took the empty one to the sink. "There's plenty of food. Andrew, would you like more rice pudding?"

Levi jumped up from the table with his empty plate. "I'll eat another helping."

Judith spooned a generous portion onto Levi's plate. She shrugged at Andrew. "Sorry, you didn't speak up fast enough." She turned to Clare. "You'll have to make him another batch."

Clare looked across the table at Andrew and sighed. "Next Sunday, I will." Clare's trusting smile slapped Judith with guilt. Teasing Andrew was one thing, but she never intended to poke fun at Clare's pudding.

She studied the other young woman's high cheekbones, her straight white teeth, and even the daintiness of her earlobes. Judith touched her own ears. They flared out from her head and her lobes were fat. Bringing her hand down to her lap, she noticed the dirt embedded in the cracks of her knuckles. She glanced at Clare's smooth hands, wondering if she ever worked in the garden. Her hands were not calloused from pulling weeds as Judith's were.

Several people stood at once and began to make their exit. "*Denki* for hosting the singing," they took turns saying.

Judith walked them to the front door and helped them with their coats.

Leah leaned toward Judith. "*Denki* for *nett* talking about . . ."

Judith arched her brows. "About what?"

"You know . . . the stranger. My *mamm* told me if you started talking about him, I had to leave."

Judith swallowed. The lump in her throat continued to grow. "Please." She cleared her throat and forced a smile. "Tell your *mamm* the topic didn't come up."

Leah nodded. "I hope you'll be able to come to my *haus* for the next Sunday singing."

Judith opened the door. "I hope so too." She followed the guests out to the porch and waved as they climbed into their open-topped buggies. The lump growing in Judith's throat swelled with a suffocating grip. Leah's *mamm* might not want Judith to attend her daughter's singing. The thought made her wish she had the safety of Andrew's arms to comfort her.

Deborah came up beside Judith while Ben went to pull the buggy around. "This was a lot of fun. Maybe we can get together for sewing later this week."

"*Jah*, that would be *gut*," Judith replied, but her attention was on the porch where Andrew and Clare were talking with Timothy and Sadie.

"Watch over *mei* sister," Timothy said.

Andrew nodded soberly.

Clare leaned toward Andrew. "I'm older, and he treats me as though I'm the *boppli* sister."

Deborah tapped Judith's arm. "Here's Ben. I mustn't keep him waiting," she said and walked away.

Judith said good night to Timothy and Sadie, and as they headed for the buggy, she continued to the house. Clare chattered to both Andrew and now Levi, who had joined them on the porch. As Judith climbed the porch steps, Clare broke from her conversation and directed her attention to Judith.

"I had a *wundebaar* time," Clare said.

Judith climbed the steps. "I'm glad Andrew brought you."

"*Ach nay*, I forgot my dish." She went back into the house, leaving Andrew and Levi on the porch with Judith.

Levi stepped forward. "Can I talk with you?" He placed his hand on her lower back and directed her off the porch.

Andrew followed. "Judith—"

"I'll be fine." She meant what she said. Now that she no longer held animosity toward Levi, she would no longer be influenced by his charm. So she hoped, anyway.

"I have to talk with you first." Andrew reached for her arm and gave it a slight tug. "It's important," he said with an urgency she'd never heard.

Levi snorted. "Andrew, do you mind?" He motioned to the porch. "Your date is up there."

Andrew crossed his arms, planted his feet, and glowered at Levi. At the depth of Andrew's icy stare, bone marrow could freeze. "You talked with her all evening. Why don't you go keep her company while Judith and I have a few words?"

Judith glanced at Levi. "I'll only be a minute." She turned to Andrew. "What's so important?"

He guided her several feet until they were under the maple tree, and even the moonlight couldn't be seen on his face. "Are you in love with him?"

"Andrew, such a personal question."

"Don't fall for his lies."

"You don't need to worry about me." Despite her attempt to keep her voice calm, it quivered. She flinched when he touched her arm. She'd already caused him family strife, she couldn't allow him to be seen touching her arm.

"I'm sorry that I didn't have a chance to tell you about Clare. I tried to get here early."

Judith turned when she heard Levi clear his throat. He and Clare walked up to Judith and Andrew.

"Your date is cold, Andrew," Levi announced.

A chill ran down Judith's back.

Levi placed his hand on her back. "You were finished talking, right?"

"*Jah,*" Judith answered. She turned to Clare. "It was nice meeting you."

Andrew scratched the back of his neck. He turned to Clare. "Are you ready?"

Clare nodded. A gust of cold air caused her to shiver, and she stepped closer to Andrew. "I think the ride home might get a little chilly."

Andrew held out his hands, offering to carry her dish. Judith thought it strange he didn't offer to shield Clare from the wind or rub her arms as he had done with her by the river.

Judith watched them walk toward Andrew's open-top courting buggy. A pang of sadness at seeing Andrew help Clare into the buggy took Judith by surprise. Her prayer had been for Andrew to find courage to fall in love again. So why couldn't she rejoice for him?

Levi cleared his throat.

She turned toward him. "What did you want to talk about?"

The wind sent a chill down her back. Levi reached his arm around her shoulder at the same time Andrew's buggy drove past, and Judith noticed Clare sliding closer to Andrew. An unsettling thought passed her mind—only Andrew could provide the warmth Judith longed for, the type that penetrated the soul and kindled the heart. She sidestepped Levi's arm. He was no substitute for Andrew, even if Andrew and she were only friends.

"We can sit on the porch," Judith suggested, already walking away.

Levi followed. His playful nature had turned serious. "I treated you badly," he said once they sat on the step.

Her hands were dry, her heartbeat steady; even her breathing hadn't fluctuated. No longer would his long lashes or blue eyes cause her to stammer. She was free.

Levi reached for Judith's hand. "I'm sorry. Will you forgive me?"

Judith placed her other hand over his, gave it a gentle squeeze, and then pulled both of her hands free. "I forgive you." The words came easily. In her heart, she had already forgiven him.

"I'm so ashamed." He closed his eyes for a brief moment, and when he opened them again, he cracked a smile. "I've repented of my sins, Judith. I'm turning my life around."

"I'm happy for you, Levi." Her words caught in her throat as she realized she was truly happy for him.

"I plan to be baptized. I really have changed."

Judith smiled. "I believe you." She was glad to see that he looked genuinely pleased about his decision to commit his life to God and join the church.

"There's something else I need to ask." He gazed up to the sky for a moment, then brought his focus to her and searched her eyes. "Will you ever find it in your heart to forget how badly I hurt you?"

"I already told you. I forgive you."

"I want to marry you," he blurted.

Judith's breath caught in her throat. She'd waited for two years to court Levi. She'd dreamt of his proposal and longed to see their names published in church. She glanced in the direction of the garden, thinking of how she had planned to plant extra celery to serve at the wedding.

He shifted, then finally stood. "Judith . . ." His voice turned husky. "I'm asking you to marry me."

Chapter Twenty-Three

Andrew turned the horse into the Kings' driveway. He stepped out of the buggy and helped Clare down.

She dipped her head into a slight bow. "*Denki* for the ride home."

"No problem." He walked her to the front door. "I hope we made it before ten."

Clare gazed toward the barn. "My parents are not back yet." She pointed to the empty lean-to joined to the barn.

He rubbed the back of his neck. "I should be heading home. Are you going to be all right here alone?" He glanced over the yard but didn't see any sign of Timothy's buggy.

Her smile turned into a frown. "I thought you'd like to sit

on the porch swing with me." She motioned to the two-seater bench suspended by chains.

"I, uh . . ." He looked at the dark house. It would be rude for him not to wait until her parents returned home. "Sure." He motioned for her to lead the way to the swing.

"I had a nice time at the singing tonight." She sat and tapped the bench beside her.

Seeing the narrow section, he hesitated until she tapped her hand against the bench again. Andrew sat down but bounced back up to his feet when he realized there wasn't enough space for his arm other than around Clare. He moved to the porch railing. "I'll be over here."

He leaned against the post. He could breathe easier with some distance between them.

"I wouldn't mind your arm around me."

He crossed and uncrossed his arms. "I'm *gut*," he explained, tapping the wooden rail before crossing his arms again.

"Isn't the moon large tonight?"

Andrew turned to look at the moon, and when he turned back, Clare was beside him.

"I like it when the moon is full, don't you?" She nudged her shoulder against his side.

"It sure sheds light." Enough light, he tried telling himself, that she shouldn't be frightened to sit alone.

"Andrew." Her arm came up under his. "You can kiss me if you want."

He blew out a breath. Her parents wanted her home by ten, and they weren't even home to receive her. He glanced at her as she closed her eyes and puckered her lips.

He turned and tilted his head toward the sky. "Maybe we should count the stars." That would keep them busy.

Clare sighed. "Wouldn't you like to kiss me before you ask?" She leaned forward.

He leaned back. "Ask what?"

Her eyes widened, and she planted her hands on her hips. "Andrew Lapp."

He cringed. With her back against the moonlight, her face was shadowed. But the frustration in her tone wasn't masked.

"My parents gave their permission."

So much for counting stars. "Clare, I'm not sure what we're talking about."

"Don't you want to kiss me before we're married?"

He lifted his hands to his face and massaged his temples. He hadn't even held her hand all night. How could she think . . .

"Clare, could I have a drink of water, please?"

She looked annoyed, but she disappeared into the house and came back with a glass.

He gulped the water down. "*Denki*," he said, handing her the glass.

"Do you want more?"

"Sure." He'd be waterlogged at this rate if her parents didn't arrive soon.

When she returned, Andrew sipped the water, prolonging the silence. "We don't know each other well enough to kiss." He couldn't say the word *marriage*. She needed to know he wouldn't be kissing her tonight or ever.

Hearing buggy wheels grinding on the gravel driveway saved him from any further discussion. Clare's mother stepped out of the buggy and climbed the porch steps. Andrew wanted to tell Mrs. King he delivered her daughter on time.

Instead, he looked at Clare. "*Denki* for attending the singing with me."

"I enjoyed myself very much, Andrew."

"*Guder nacht,*" he said, already stepping off the porch. He wasted no time climbing onto his buggy seat and driving off without looking back. It wasn't until he was home and putting the buggy away that he noticed her rice pudding dish on the floorboard. His stomach sank at the thought of having to return it to her.

As he entered his house, he met the Fischers leaving. Their long faces startled him. Why were they here tonight? As a baptized member of the church, he would have known about a special meeting had one been planned.

"How was the evening singing?" his father asked.

"Fine," he replied and walked straight to his bedroom. He had too much on his mind for conversation.

Judith had made it clear that she didn't need his protection from Levi. She might be strong enough to resist Levi's charm, but what worried Andrew was, did she *want* to? She had a soft heart. Maybe she was ready to give him another chance. Andrew's gut tightened. He'd seen the determined look in Levi's eyes before. Levi intended to move back into her good graces.

Andrew needed to close himself off and pray. Judith might not have wanted his physical support, but spiritually, he was going to intercede on her behalf.

He prayed into the early morning hours, until sleep released him. In his dreams, he and Judith knelt together, seeking God.

Chapter Twenty-Four

J udith swallowed. Levi had steadied his eyes on hers, awaiting her answer. Every hope she'd had revolved around planning a wedding. Celebrating an event, rather than concentrating on the holy union between two people—joined by God. The doleful truth choked her airway. She hadn't been told by God to marry Levi. Freed of the misconception, a shiver traveled through her.

"I can't."

He leaned closer. "But . . . but we've always planned to get married. When you turned nineteen. I thought—"

"I thought that's what I wanted too." Her voice broke and she bowed her head. *Lord, please give me the words to say.* "I was in love with the idea of marriage." Judith looked into his eyes. "I can't marry you, Levi. I don't love you."

Her dreams of marriage and children were no longer reachable now that her eyes were opened. She could never marry someone she didn't love.

"*Ach*, here you are, Levi." Martha stepped out from the house and onto the porch. "I didn't interrupt anything, did I?"

Judith groaned at the sound of her sister's sarcastic voice. *Father, I pray Your grace that enabled me to forgive Levi will also extend to Martha.* She stood. She'd given Levi her answer, and she wasn't about to hang out on the porch explaining anything to Martha.

Levi followed her up the steps. "Judith, I wanted us to talk more."

Judith turned, but from the corner of her eye, Martha glared at her. "I have *nay* more to say, Levi," Judith said, reaching for the doorknob.

Martha walked up the steps. "Levi, you promised on the *nacht* we spent together we would go away."

Levi tossed his head. After a quick sheepish glance at Judith, he turned to Martha. "We can't leave. What would we do? Where would we go?"

Judith pushed open the door. "I'll let you two work out your plans." She escaped into the house and leaned against the inside of the door to catch her breath. How could Martha speak so boldly about her sin? At least Levi had the decency to appear ashamed. Martha seemed to take pride in her blatant transgressions.

"Lord, I pray for my sister's soul. I don't think she sees herself sinking into a miry pit, yet the scriptures are clear. In the last days some will fall away . . . Please, show her Your hand that she might turn from her wicked ways and follow You."

The doorknob jiggled, and Judith stepped aside.

Martha entered. "What were you doing, trying to listen through the door?" She smiled. "We'll probably get married. After everyone hears about us spending the *nacht* together, I'm sure Levi will speak to the bishop."

Judith's breath caught in her throat. "You threatened to tell everyone?"

"Well, Levi says *nau* that he doesn't want to leave the community. He had some kind of experience on the road that frightened him into keeping the faith, or something like that. *Nau* he won't leave."

Maybe Martha hadn't realized it yet, but to speak with the bishop regarding marriage meant Martha and Levi would have to be baptized and live according to the *Ordnung*. Judith only hoped that her sister's words of commitment would be toward God and not to tickle Levi's or Bishop Lapp's ear.

Martha sauntered toward the kitchen. "Who would have guessed I would marry before you." She glanced over her shoulder. "This is probably what happened to Ellen's sister Katie. I wonder if she fell in love with men who wanted other women too. What was the name of that girl Andrew took home from the singing?"

"Leave Andrew out of this." Judith clasped the back of her neck. *Keep your words . . . Don't take her bait and sin.* She wouldn't have guessed Martha was capable of such cruelty. Following her sister into the kitchen, Judith realized that losing Levi wasn't what hurt. But the profound awareness of her love for Andrew weighted her heart.

Lord, help me, please.

Judith sucked in a deep breath and released it slowly. "I forgive you, Martha." She paused, giving Martha a chance to respond. When she didn't, Judith continued. "I've held resentment toward you, and I asked God to cleanse my heart."

Martha turned to leave the kitchen.

Judith raised her voice. "I'm *nett* letting *mei* bitterness separate me from God's plan."

Her sister still made no response.

Judith heated a pot of water to soak the dishes. Even if Martha continued to ignore her willingness to mend their relationship, she had followed God's word and forgiven Martha. When she heard her parents' voices, she met them at the door. Rebecca was asleep in *Mamm's* arms. Her mother carried her sister to the bedroom, while her *daed* placed his hat on the wall hook.

"There's apple pie left over. Would you like a slice?" Judith asked.

He looked up at Judith and paused before removing his boots.

"*Nay.*" He stood and tapped his stomach. "I've eaten plenty."

"I could warm some cider?"

He shook his head. "I'm going to bed."

It wasn't unusual for her father to retire early, but tonight he seemed distracted. Before they left for the Lapps' he'd commented on how good her pie smelled and how he hoped she'd save him a piece. Now he seemed anxious to retreat. Her mother, too, hadn't come out to the kitchen after putting Rebecca to bed.

Judith rinsed the last dish and placed it on the towel to dry. It was good that her parents were tired. If her mother had come out to the kitchen, she would have asked how the evening went, and Judith didn't want to slip and say something about Martha's problems.

She paused at Martha's room. Under the door, a hint of light meant her sister wasn't asleep. Judith raised her hand to tap on the door, then stopped herself. God would have to deal with Martha's situation. Until then, Judith would pray for her. Pray for them both, Martha and Levi.

When she moved away from her sister's bedroom, Judith heard weeping. She moved to her parents' door. It was wrong to eavesdrop, she knew—but what was wrong? Was there worse news about Samuel that she hadn't heard?

"I'll put in a larger garden this year," her mother said.

"That won't raise much money," her father replied. "At our age, we might never return the money to the district for the hospital bills."

Judith hadn't given much thought as to what delayed her parents, but now their reason for going to the bishop's house was clear. They needed a community offering to pay for the medical bills.

"If we hadn't built the barn, we would've had the money."

"Be thankful we had the money to replace the barn. If we can't take care of our livestock, our entire income will be devastated."

"I don't want to believe we've fallen into disfavor with God like Bishop Lapp suggested."

"Hush *nau*."

Her mother mumbled something Judith couldn't make out, and then the room fell silent. Judith slipped into her bedroom and changed into her nightdress, deep in thoughts of how she could earn money. Pulling the covers up around her neck, she had her answer. She would sell her quilts. It wouldn't bring in much, but she had to do something. Judith jumped out of bed and knelt to pray.

"Father, You have cattle on a thousand hills and supply the sparrow its food. You will provide for us too. We need money to pay for the medical expenses. I pray I will find favor with selling my quilts. *Aemen.*"

She went to her closet and pulled the stack of quilts down from the shelf. She folded the quilt she'd made for her wedding and placed it on the pile, then grabbed it back up and draped it over her shoulders. How could she part with this quilt?

She drew in a deep breath. Her parents needed the money. Besides, she had no use for a wedding quilt. She wasn't getting married anytime soon.

Chapter Twenty-Five

Judith shot up out of bed, clutching her chest and panting. Another dream of Samuel pinned under ice filled her night. This time only his legs were frozen, and his arms were free to chip away at the frozen block. *Why does the same dream repeat? The same path choices* . . . Logical thinking, if that were possible during a dream, would lead one to choose the paved road, but her heart clearly was swayed toward the narrow, vine-covered path. *What does it mean?*

Judith dressed before dawn and slipped out the back door. After learning of Andrew's likely engagement last evening, she'd spent her waking hours trying to rebuke envy and her sleeping hours fretting about how to free Samuel.

A low-lying fog covered the ground, and the morning dew

saturated the hem of her dress. When her teeth started chattering, she wondered if slipping away this early was wise. Judith came to the boulder and sat. She gazed at the sunrise, marveled at the sweet chirping birds, and suddenly she felt alone. Even the birds had companions. She had no one.

"You have never been alone, Judith."

She spun around. Tobias stood a few feet away, and his smile warmed her soul. Judith pushed off the boulder to meet him. "Why did God send you?"

"Someone has petitioned God for you."

"Who prayed for me?" She heard the panic in her voice, yet she hoped Tobias accepted it as a plea of desperation rather than a demand for knowledge. Who could have prayed for her that God would send an angel with His message?

"The answer is before your eyes, if you will see with your heart." He knelt beside her. "I come to encourage your faith. Child, I come to show you the paths from which to choose. I cannot choose for you."

"Where are the roads? When must I choose?"

"Continue in faith."

"The measure of my faith has faded." She bowed her head, ashamed.

"When you give all, more will be given. And when you have done all to stand, continue to stand. There is no trouble in this world that Christ has not overcome."

Judith lifted her head to see into Tobias's frosty-blue eyes. "And Samuel? He's frozen in my dreams."

"What you've been shown is not Samuel's path to choose." Tobias turned to go.

"But Samuel's accident is my fault. I must know if he will walk."

He turned and faced her. "Child, you do not see Samuel the way God sees him. God's plan is perfect." Tobias stood and spread his arms, indicating the vast area. "Your path is before you. Let the light from God be a lamp unto your feet."

Judith studied the ground, turning a circle, searching where Tobias indicated.

No path.

No light.

Nothing. "Where——?"

Tobias was gone.

Judith stayed awhile longer, hoping, praying, begging Tobias to return. Sure that he wouldn't, she walked home.

She came from behind the barn as her father stepped out from the house.

He met her in the driveway. "Where have you been?"

"I went for a walk by the river."

His eyes hardened, but before he could speak, a car pulled into the drive. Her father nodded to Mr. Thon, their *Englisch* neighbor, then turned back to Judith. "I have errands in town. I'll talk with you later." He walked to the car.

Her father must have a long list of tasks. Usually he didn't ask Mr. Thon to drive them in his automobile unless it was an emergency or the weather conditions were too harsh for the horses.

Her father eased into the front seat, and through the windshield she caught a glimpse of his down-turned mouth . . . a warning of his displeasure over her morning disappearance.

❖

Andrew rushed to complete his morning chores. He'd spent a good portion of the night wrestling with his feelings and trying to release them totally to God. Judith's heart was full of compassion and forgiveness. Levi's charm could easily move her again. If he had come to his senses as he claimed, his cousin would propose. And why wouldn't she say yes if she was still in love with Levi?

Andrew harnessed Patsy to the buggy. He wanted to leave before his father returned from the market and questioned his plans. Over the past few days, his father's tolerance had thinned for Andrew working with Samuel.

Judith was hanging clothes on the line when he pulled into the yard. He tethered Patsy to the post and walked over to her.

"*Guder mariye.*" She continued to pin the towels on the line.

"Need help?"

"*Nay*, I can handle it." She glanced at the house before reaching for another towel. "Samuel is busy with the physical therapist."

"*Jah*, I figured so when I saw the car."

"She just arrived. You probably should *kumm* back later."

"I thought you wanted me to take you to Mrs. Stanly's *haus*. She's the one interested in your quilts."

Judith glanced at the house. "If you give me a minute, I'll go inside and get them."

"Sure." He crossed under the clothesline, where she had hung a wet towel between them. "I liked your apple pie last night."

She smiled briefly, then picked up another towel and gave it a snap before lifting it to the line.

"Am I not supposed to remember the day in the orchard?"
He stepped closer, not caring who saw them together. "I couldn't
think of anything else when you drank that apple cider. Your lips
were wet, and I couldn't think of anything but—"

"Andrew, stop." She lowered her voice. "What's gotten into
you? I'm shocked you would say something like that." She made
another quick glance at the house. "That kiss shouldn't have
happened."

He gazed into her piercing blue eyes. "*Jah*, I know. You want
only to kiss your husband like that."

"*Jah*, and you should only want to kiss your *fraa*—"

"*Ich* do." He wanted to kiss only her. But hearing the sharp-
ness in her rebuke, his words caught in his throat. After a moment
he asked, "What did Levi want last night?"

She moved to the far end of the line where several articles
of clothing already hung and started feeling them for dampness.

"Judith, I want to know." Andrew moved in front of the
clothing.

"He said he's changed, and he asked my forgiveness."

"And you wholeheartedly gave it to him."

Judith tossed a pair of stiff pants into the empty basket. "I'll
go fetch the quilts, if you're still willing to take them." She didn't
wait for him to reply.

Andrew sighed. He shouldn't have said anything about the
apple cider on her lips. He peered up at the cloudy sky. *Forgive
me. I still struggle with envy. You know the condition of Levi's heart.
You know if he will hold true to Judith. I don't want to stand in the
way of her happiness, so set me aside if it is Your will.*

The screen door snapped as Judith came back outside, her

arms loaded down with blankets. Andrew met her in the drive to take the bundle from her hands.

"*Denki.*" She followed him to the buggy.

When he set the quilts on the seat, the middle blanket caught his eye. He pawed through the pile and lifted the quilt. "Isn't this the one you were sewing the day the barn was built?"

She nodded.

"Are you sure you want to sell this one?" He was probing, he knew. If she had made this quilt for her wedding, why did she plan to part with it?

She didn't respond, but her eyes locked on the material.

"You seem hesitant," he said softly.

Judith touched the blanket's binding. She dropped it just as fast. "My parents need the money for Samuel's hospital bills."

Andrew swallowed. "Are you sure?"

She nodded. "It's all I can offer."

He motioned to the buggy. "Climb in, and let's take them." He waited, but she didn't budge. "You do intend to ride along, right?"

She shook her head. "It would be best if I stay."

"Mrs. Stanly wanted you to *kumm* also. She wants to meet you."

"We shouldn't be seen together." She lowered her chin to her chest.

Andrew's gut twisted. "So you believed him. Levi tells you he changed, and you believe him."

Judith lifted her head. "This isn't about Levi. I know your father has forbidden you to see me."

He followed her gaze as a car pulled into the drive. Her

father stepped out from the car, thanked the driver, and headed into the house carrying a long envelope.

"*Daed's* back from town. You should go."

The screen door snapped. Judith's *mamm* and the physical therapist stepped onto the porch.

Andrew looked puzzled. "I thought she just arrived."

Judith glanced at him. "*Jah*, she did. What do you suppose happened?"

Before he could reply, Martha came outside and walked toward them.

Judith sighed. "Wonder what she wants."

Andrew shook his head. By the looks of Martha's smile as she glided toward them, it couldn't be good.

"Last night I told her I forgave her . . ."

"And?" He clamped down on his bottom lip.

Judith's brows arched, and she locked eyes with him. "She didn't even acknowledge it." She sighed and looked away. "I don't know that anything will bring about a change in her."

Martha came up and stood between Judith and him. "*Daed* wants you inside *nau*."

Judith turned to Andrew. "*Denki* for handling the quilts." She walked away with her head turned downward.

Martha's eyes followed Judith walking to the house. "She's done it again. This time she's stirred up Samuel, talking about that angel." She looked at Andrew. "She's doing it for attention. That's all it is."

The burn of acid rose in Andrew's throat. "Leave her alone. You're not one who should pass judgment. You're the one who seeks attention."

"If you're referring to Levi, he thought Judith was dull."

"Haven't you heard? He's changed. He asked for Judith's forgiveness." Resentment threaded his words.

"He won't stay that way." She crossed her arms. "Besides, why should it matter to you?"

"You broke your sister's heart. That matters to me." He wagged his finger at her. "Don't you . . . persuade him . . ." He blew out a breath. If he didn't stop, his words would only serve to provoke her. Levi wouldn't have the willpower to avoid her temptation. "I'm going to pray that God gets ahold of you."

Andrew climbed into the buggy. The only chance of derailing Martha was to inform David of his sister's actions. No brother wanted to hear that type of news, but David was the deacon. In the end, it would be his duty to set his sister straight.

Chapter Twenty-Six

"Is there something wrong?" Judith gazed at her parents seated at the kitchen table, but couldn't decipher their dismal expressions.

Her father motioned to the empty chair. "Judith, sit. We must talk." He waited until she sat before continuing. "Samuel refused to do anything for the therapist today. He kept insisting he wanted the angel to come back."

Judith folded her hands in her lap and looked down at the table.

Her father rolled a long envelope in his hands, then tossed it on the table. "We asked you not to give Samuel false hope. You disobeyed us."

Her brother needed encouragement. She hadn't acted in defiance, but she had disobeyed. No wonder God hadn't healed Samuel. She'd blocked the blessing by her sinful disobedience. A lump lodged in her throat. She swallowed, but the swelling remained. "I'm sorry."

"We don't know what to do with you." Her father glanced at *Mamm*, then looked again at Judith. "You were instructed not to see that *Englischer* again. Yet you were at the river this morning. Why do you disobey us?"

Judith shrugged. "I believe . . ."

Why is it so hard for them to believe, God? They taught me what I know. They instilled Your laws into my heart.

"What gave you the idea that Samuel saw—" *Mamm's* voice turned hoarse and she cleared her throat in order to continue. "An angel?"

"Something he told Samuel." Next, they would ask what the angel had said. But Judith was drawing a blank. Why couldn't she remember? If the man was truly an angel, why couldn't she remember what he told Samuel that made her think he was Tobias? It was all too confusing.

Her father pressed the bridge of his nose between his index finger and thumb. "What did he say?"

"Other than for Samuel to imagine he was running, I don't remember," she whispered.

The envelope next to *Daed's* coffee cup bounced when he pounded his hand on the table. "That's the problem. You've told so many stories, you don't even remember them." He shook his head. "What has happened to you?"

Judith cringed. "But Samuel described his looks as identical to the man I saw . . . As God is my witness, I believe he saw Tobias—"

Her father held up his hand. "Who is Tobias?"

"The angel."

Mamm gasped. "He has a name?"

"God named the stars. Why wouldn't He have named His angels?"

Mamm started to cry, which caused her father to tap his hand against the table again.

"Judith, that's enough." He gazed at her across the table. "We've decided to send you to live with *Mamm's* second cousin in Ohio." He motioned to the envelope. "The ticket is bought."

Judith's eyes widened. "What? I don't even know them."

"They are family. There you'll have an unblemished reputation." He picked up the envelope from the table and glanced at it. "You will stay and find a husband in Ohio."

"I don't want to live in Ohio." Judith's gaze flipped to her mother. "*Mamm*, please." Her stomach rolled, and her throat burned.

Her father tapped the envelope against the table as though moving its contents to one end. "This decision was made by the bishop." His words grew softer. "He requested you leave the community."

"I'm being shunned?" What happened to those not baptized having leniency? *Rumschpringe?* Why couldn't they turn their heads as they did when other youth tested worldly temptations? Why was this different—worse than the sins others had received forgiveness for?

"You paid no heed to rebuke. You've not changed any of your ways. If you go to Ohio, you can continue in the faith."

"I'm allowed to continue in the Amish faith in Ohio, but not here? When did sin become different depending on what state you live in?" She clutched her throat and squeezed her eyes closed.

"You have caused others to sin."

Judith's eyes shot open. Her father looked across the table at her mother and sighed. "You must go."

"Who sinned because of me? Samuel? I didn't mean to—"

"Andrew Lapp. He will be punished if you stay."

"*Nay*, Andrew did nothing wrong." She turned to her mother. "*Mamm*, he only befriended me."

Daed shifted on the chair. "We've sent word. The relatives know you're *kumming*. I suggest you pack your things," he announced, his tone final.

Everyone knew her fate but her. Relatives she'd never met knew she was coming. Her parents must have planned her departure days ago.

Judith stood and fled out the door, then began to run as fast as she could toward the river. "Why, God?"

She reached the patch of ferns, then pivoted and paced back to the river's edge. "Why am I the only one who sees Tobias? Why am I the only one who believes?" She turned again. "He told me I would have to stand, but do I have to stand alone?" She threw her hands up into the air and looked at the sky. "I've used all the faith I've been given. How will I continue to stand?"

Except for the rushing sound of river water, there was only silence.

"My thoughts are simple. How am I expected to make the right choice?" Judith fell to her knees and then to her face. "Please don't leave me. Show me the path and the way I should go. Guide me with a lamp unto my path. Open my eyes that I might see."

Everything she remembered Tobias telling her, she repeated over and over until exhaustion overtook her words and silence hung in the air.

She drew in a deep breath and closed her eyes. She knew. "It's the path to Ohio, isn't it, God?"

Judith wasn't surprised to see David's buggy parked in front of the house when she returned. She wasn't anticipating what she heard, however, as she stepped into the house.

"So you did spend the night with Martha?"

She walked into the kitchen as Levi lifted his head to reply. "*Jah*, we talked . . ." His eyes locked a moment on Judith, then drifted back to David. "And we drank whiskey."

Mamm sobbed into her handkerchief and *Daed* lowered his head into his hands while David paced the floor. He stopped in front of Levi and crossed his arms. "You've marred her reputation."

Martha grabbed David's arm. "I love Levi."

Her father shook his head. "You've disgraced your family. The church. Have you no shame?"

Martha's bottom lip trembled.

She had them all fooled, thought Judith, playing remorseful. Even Levi looked taken in by her act. He shifted in his seat.

Judith leaned against the cabinet and folded her arms across her chest. Her heart ached for her parents. *Daed* held a somber glare and stroked his beard while *Mamm's* shoulders shook as she wept. Hadn't Martha considered the pain she would cause them? *Ach*, her pretending to be distraught created quite a predicament for Levi.

"We shouldn't have spent the night together." Martha turned toward Levi. "I wanted you to know how much I love you."

"Did you—" *Daed* began.

"Nay!" The color drained from Levi's face. "We never had relations." He turned to look at David. "I'm telling the truth. We kissed, is all."

"Did you think about her reputation?" David crossed his arms.

Levi slowly shook his head. "I'm sorry." He cleared his throat. "I'll marry her," he said softly. He briefly gazed at Martha. "If you're willing to join the church." Then he looked at David again. "If the bishop will still baptize us *nau*."

"Your commitment to the church must be genuine," David said. "Since you're *nett* already members, you probably won't be required to do a kneeling confession in repentance of your transgressions." He looked hard at Martha. "But are you willing, if asked?"

Martha exchanged glances with Levi and nodded.

Daed glanced over his shoulder and noticed Judith. "Your sister has admitted her sin. I wish you would consider making a kneeling confession also."

Judith gulped. She had been praying about the matter. "Truly, *Ich* have *nett* intentionally sinned against God." Still, she had caused Andrew to disobey the bishop. She was guilty.

Daed's eyes narrowed. "Go on your way."

Judith turned. Her eyes burned as the tears pooled. *He's casting me away, God. I'm a disappointment—a shame.*

She ran to her bedroom, flopped on the bed, and buried her face into her pillow to muffle her sobbing.

When she had no more tears left, she wiped her eyes and pushed off the bed. She opened the dresser and pulled out her clothing, remembering the time she spent with her mother sewing each article. She gazed around the room. The bare walls, the braided floor rug . . . she would miss every inch.

You wanted me to choose, God, but leaving my district would never be my choice.

Her eye caught on the wooden box she'd placed on the dresser. She ran her hand over the smooth birch, remembering the day she found it at the river. Opening the box, she lifted the rock.

Her heart sank. It looked like an ordinary rock.

She needed the glimmer of hope of the vibrant colors, but the rock no longer shone. Judith lowered it into the box, closed the lid, and went outside.

David stood at his buggy, harnessing his horse, when she stepped out on the porch. He waved her over to him, and her heart raced. Would he rebuke her too?

David pulled the leather strap from under the horse's belly and looped it through the metal ring. "I understand you will be going to Ohio."

"*Jah.*"

He faced her. "I wish you would have listened. I don't want to see you go." He motioned to the house. "*Mamm* and *Daed* are heartbroken."

Judith lowered her head and nodded.

He touched her arm. "I'm sorry, too, about Levi. Ellen told me how you had dreamed of marrying him."

Judith shrugged. It seemed a long time since she'd had any dreams of marriage. "Who told you about Martha and Levi?"

"Andrew stopped by the *haus*. He sounded worried about you." David sighed. "He's protective of you. He came to your defense the night you disappeared too."

Judith raised her head. "He did?"

"*Jah*. He stood up for you in front of the bishop."

Her chest grew heavy. "He shouldn't have done that."

"Judith, perhaps if you talked with the bishop and made a kneeling confession, you wouldn't be sent to Ohio."

"Confess I never saw an angel? Confess I no longer believe Samuel will walk? Confess what?"

"Tell the bishop what he wants to hear. Tell him you were confused, that you won't make up any more stories."

"If it were only a story, I would have already said so. But I didn't make it up."

David sighed. "I wish your conviction was a worthy one. *Ich veiklich* do." He climbed into his buggy. "I will talk with the bishop once the talk has settled and see if you can return." David motioned to the house. "*Daed* and *Mamm* are sad. They don't want to send you away."

The house door opened, and Levi and Martha stepped outside together.

Judith turned away. "I feel awful, but I will accept their decision. Tell Ellen I will write her."

Judith meandered along the trail, and when she reached the

river, she sat on the large boulder. Once again she opened the box with suspended breath. Again, the rock didn't glow as it had before.

"I accept Your will." She closed her eyes, desperately wanting to talk with Tobias. She needed to know if it was something she'd done that caused the rock not to shine. Judith waited with her eyes closed.

Silence.

Even the birds stopped chirping, and the breeze stilled.

Tobias was gone, and now God was gone too.

Judith stood, set the box on the boulder, and walked away.

Chapter Twenty-Seven

Andrew held a tight grasp on the money from selling Judith's quilts as he knocked on the Fischers' door.

Judith answered, but the moment their eyes connected, she lowered her head. Her face was puffy and her eyes were red.

"I sold your quilts," he said, stepping into the house.

"Denki." Her reply wasn't more than a whisper.

Andrew glanced around the room. Mrs. Fischer looked up from her sewing hoop. Her eyes were also red. Mr. Fischer sat in the rocker. He glanced up but quickly continued reading the Bible on his lap.

Andrew cocked his head to get a view of Judith's eyes. "Are you all right?"

She nodded.

"Can you go for a walk with me?"

"Nay," she mumbled.

He leaned closer. "I have to talk with you."

She made a sideways glance at her parents and shook her head.

"Is it about Levi?" A tinge of guilt spread through him for involving David.

She shook her head in denial.

Andrew held out the money. "Mrs. Stanly will have the rest of the money *meiya.*"

"Denki." She glanced up but quickly averted her eyes. "If I'm gone, will you see that my parents get the money?"

"What?" He looked over at Judith's parents, and seeing their lack of interest in their conversation, he stepped closer to her. "Come with me to the river, please."

"I can't."

He touched her arm. She tensed, and he dropped his hand. "Don't shut me out." He looked over at her parents again, and when Mrs. Fischer looked up from her needlework, he bade them good night.

"Guder nacht." He turned but paused long enough to look back at Judith. "The river," he mouthed, but she made no indication that she would meet him there.

Andrew crawled out of bed and stretched. He hadn't slept much during the night. After waiting several hours for Judith to meet him at the river, he finally left, brokenhearted and discouraged beyond measure. The remainder of the night he spent on his knees petitioning God.

He fastened his suspenders and cringed as a knot tightened his lower back.

"Lord, I've asked You so many times, and I thank You for Your patience with me, but why can't I let Judith go? My heart aches for her. I dreamt that we were praying together at the cabin. Lord, I don't understand any of this. Is she upset with me over involving David? Does she still believe that Levi has changed? Is she willing to marry him? If so, I cannot continue to stay in this community if I covet another man's wife. Please show me how I can escape the temptation. *Aemen.*"

The scent of frying bacon brought him out to the kitchen. His mother dished up a large portion of eggs, potatoes, and bacon and placed the plate on the table as Andrew pulled out the chair.

He smiled at his mother. *"Denki."*

"You *muscht* be hungry. You didn't eat supper last night," she said, returning to the stove to prepare another dish.

"I wasn't hungry." Andrew glanced across the table at his father. With his Bible next to his breakfast plate, his father was engrossed in his studies. Andrew poked his fork into the eggs and stirred the runny yolks into the potatoes.

His father looked up from his reading. "I understand you've been working on the cabin?"

Andrew nodded. He wondered how his father knew, but decided to leave the matter alone.

"What are your plans, to sell it?"

"*Nay*, to move into it."

Zechariah pushed his reading glasses higher on his nose. "*Gut*." He nodded in approval. "I've made arrangements with Abe King for you to marry his daughter."

Andrew choked on a forkful of potatoes. He coughed longer than he needed to as he tried to register his father's words.

"I'm not marrying her."

His forceful tone startled his mother, who scurried to calm the clattering plates that she'd dropped on the counter.

His father's brows furrowed. "What reason is there to move into the *haus* if you have no plans to marry?" His voice deepened. "Every man of God has the responsibility to *abvoahra* in ministry. How will you serve if you do not marry?"

"I plan to marry Judith Fischer." His words were out before he thought of how it sounded, loving the woman his cousin intended to marry.

"*Nay!* I won't allow it."

"I've fallen in love with her." Andrew bowed his head, ashamed of his inability to guard his heart—inability to turn from his feelings.

Bishop Lapp groaned. "Your heart will mend once she's sent to Ohio and you've married the King girl."

"What do you mean . . . Judith's being sent to Ohio?"

"She has relatives there."

Andrew's jaw tightened. "When was that decided?"

"The meeting was amongst the deacons and myself. I will not discuss—"

"Why is she being forced to leave?"

His father's eyes narrowed. "I am the bishop. She will not

cause division in the church. In my *haus*! I forbade you to see her, and you disobeyed my order."

Andrew pounded his chest. "Then I'm the one you should send away."

"Stop it. I will not allow my son to talk in this defiant manner."

Andrew slid his chair back from the table and stood. "I won't let her go."

His father's eyes hardened. He pointed to the chair. "Sit down. You don't know what's best."

Andrew walked to the door and paused. Looking back at his father, he pointed to his Bible. "If you read in there what pleases God, you'll find out it's faith. This district has ridiculed Judith for her faith, and they've mocked God in doing so." Andrew opened the door. "I want your blessing to marry her, *Daed*." He didn't give his father time to deny his request, but continued. "And I'm willing to marry her without it, even if it means moving to Ohio."

"Andrew Thomas Lapp," his mother said.

Andrew stopped and turned. "*Mamm*, I love Judith."

She met him at the door and leaned toward him. "Work out your rebellious ways with your father. God wants us to live in unity with one another, not carry strife."

"Please don't worry about me. I am prayerful of such important matters. Judith is a *gut* woman. She loves God."

He waited, wanting her acknowledging smile, but knowing in submission to her husband she wouldn't outwardly go against his father's word. Andrew turned and twisted the doorknob, silently praying that his mother's large brown eyes wouldn't haunt him forever.

His hands trembled as he harnessed the horse. He should

have known not to risk meeting Judith after Sunday services. This was all his fault.

The driveway's gravel crunched, and Andrew turned to see Levi pull into the drive. Now was as good a time as any to approach him about Judith. Andrew left his buggy to walk over to meet Levi.

"Is your *daed* home? I need to talk to him about baptism and marriage."

Andrew drew a deep breath. "So her answer was *jah*?"

Levi chuckled. "She was practically all over me to ask." He twisted his lips. "Not that I had much choice. Her family says I ruined her reputation."

Andrew gulped.

Levi chuckled. "Maybe all this is too much for you to hear, Bishop Junior."

Andrew's chest expanded. "Do you love her?"

Levi shrugged. "I suppose eventually— *Ach*, settle down." He planted his hands on Andrew's chest. "You're the one who got David involved. Besides, I told Martha if she joined the church I would marry her."

Andrew blew out his breath. "Martha? I thought you were planning to propose to Judith."

"I did." Levi clapped Andrew's shoulder. "She said *nay*. She's in love with you."

"She said that?"

"She said she's never loved me . . . said something about not even knowing what love was until recently." Levi dug his hands into his pockets and shrugged. "I put two and two together."

"I do want to marry her."

Levi's brows rose. *"Ach,* then you better hurry. She's leaving for Ohio."

"Jah." Andrew's stomach flipped. *"Jah!* I've got to go." He turned and sprinted to his buggy, then remembered something he needed from the workshop.

"Where are you going?" Levi called.

"I forgot something important." Too important to leave behind.

Chapter Twenty-Eight

Martha poked her head inside the bedroom door. "Judith, can we talk?"

Last minute send-off, was it? Couldn't Martha let her leave for Ohio in peace?

Martha entered the room. "I'm sorry, Judith. I've treated you badly."

Judith continued emptying out her dresser drawer.

Martha sat on the bed and folded her hands in her lap. With her down-turned mouth, she almost looked convincing.

Almost.

"I don't want you to leave without knowing how sorry I am. I truly am."

Judith tossed a dress into the suitcase with the others, then crossed her arms. "You won. You have everything you wanted. Besides, I'm not upset with you. You have to live with yourself."

"Levi had a long talk with me. He helped me to see how poorly I've acted. I've been acting like a child."

Judith bit back the urge to agree. If she said anything, she would point out how at seventeen, Martha was a child. Instead, she resumed packing. She didn't know what time she needed to be at the bus station, and she still wanted to say good-bye to Samuel.

"He wants me to confess before God . . . and you. I was jealous of you."

Judith stopped midway to the closet and turned. "Jealous of me? Why?"

Martha's eyes filled with tears. "You're older. And never in trouble . . . and allowed to date." She sucked in a deep breath. "And Levi had teased me, saying I'd be his little sister-in-law soon."

"When was this?"

"At the barn raising." Martha lifted her gaze to meet Judith's. "It's all my fault. I was angry he called me a child, and I . . ." She hung her head low. "I wanted to prove I wasn't a child. *Ach*, I'm sorry. If I hadn't convinced him to teach me how to kiss like *Englisch* girls . . ."

"It's okay, Martha. What's done is done. I forgive you."

Her shoulders shook and she cried harder.

Judith sat beside her on the bed and put her arm around her sister's shoulder. "Don't cry."

"I don't want you to leave because of me."

"It's God's plan."

Martha's tears coursed down her neck. She lifted her head. "Samuel falling was never your fault. If I hadn't been teasing Levi . . . *Ach*, Judith, please forgive me. I've blamed you and I've been angry at you and it wasn't your fault." Martha folded into Judith's arms.

Judith patted her sister's back. "In God's time, He will reveal His plan."

Judith had told herself those same words throughout the night. She'd spent numerous hours begging God for answers. Then when she learned about Ohio, she begged God for a different plan. But her request was useless. Her dreams of the three roads stopped. Tobias hadn't returned.

A heavy knock on the door sounded, and Judith wiped her watery eyes. *"Jah?"*

The door opened, and her father looked into the room. "We must *geh* soon."

Judith nodded.

Daed closed the door, and Judith patted Martha's back. *"Ich* must finish." As she pulled away, a peaceful warmth passed over Judith. Was God showing her that things would work out in Ohio too? She had to trust Him. Having witnessed the miracle of Martha's heart softening, anything was possible.

"Martha, will you take *mei* suitcase out to the buggy while I say *mei* good-byes to Samuel?"

Judith wiped her face. She didn't want Samuel to see her crying. But outside his bedroom door, she had to dry her eyes once more before entering.

"What's wrong, Judith?"

She forced herself to smile and walked closer to his bed. "I'm going away to visit relatives for a while."

"How long?"

She shrugged, knowing she wouldn't be able to hold her voice steady.

"I'll miss you."

Kneeling, she reached over to him and combed her fingers through his hair. "I'll miss you too."

"I had another dream," he said. "I heard a voice telling me I could get up *nau*."

"*Jah*, so did you?"

"I followed a golden glow. I was walking."

She kissed his forehead. "That'd be *gut*."

Behind her, *Daed* cleared his throat.

Judith's heart sank. She hadn't heard him open the door. Now he would accuse her of convincing Samuel he could walk again.

"The buggy is ready."

Judith nodded. She turned back to her brother. "It is time I go. You be a *gut* boy." Her voice cracked.

"*Kumm* home soon."

"*Jah*," she replied without looking back. Closing his bedroom door, she could hear him whimpering. Her heart grew heavy. *Provide him comfort, Lord.*

Outside, *Mamm*, Rebecca, and her father had already loaded into the buggy. She hugged Martha on the porch, then climbed inside. As they pulled out from the drive, her vision blurred, hindering one last look at the farm. At her life left behind.

"Judith is gone, Andrew," Martha informed him at the door.

Andrew pushed past her into the kitchen. Empty. "Where is she?"

Martha trailed behind him. "I told you, she's gone."

He studied her red and blotchy face. She wasn't gloating, and her eyes didn't have the same haughtiness. Still, he didn't trust her.

"Andrew?" Samuel called out from the bedroom.

He opened Samuel's bedroom door.

The boy's eyes brightened as he hoisted himself upright. "Are we going to build today?"

Andrew squatted at his bedside. "*Nett* today, Samuel. I'm looking for Judith. Have you seen her?" Even though he didn't want to delay a second more than necessary, he spoke with a calm tone so as not to disturb the little boy.

"She's going to visit relatives. Why would that make her cry?" Samuel started to sniffle. "It's about me, isn't it?"

Andrew ruffled Samuel's hair. "Don't get upset. You didn't do anything."

"I don't think she wanted to go."

"Remember what I told you about Judith?" Andrew brushed his hand over Samuel's messy hair, flattening out the static. "I'm going to ask her to marry me, and I'm going to bring her back."

"I want to go with you, please."

"I can't take you. I'm sorry." Andrew stood. "But when I come back, we'll do some more building."

Samuel rubbed his fists over his puffy eyes.

"Okay?"

Samuel nodded, but his lips puckered and he started to cry again.

Andrew patted the boy's shoulder. "Samuel, pray that God gives me enough time to stop her."

As he left the room, Martha met him in the hallway.

"They left for the bus station more than an hour ago. You'll have to hurry if you want to catch her." She pressed her hand against his back, nudging him forward. "Andrew, Judith needs you. I hope it's not too late."

What was up with Martha? He paused at the door. "I find it hard to believe. You suddenly care about your sister?"

"I asked her to forgive me, and I meant *mei* words." She looked toward Samuel's room. "He's been crying since they left. I don't know how to console him." She turned back toward Andrew. "Can you go in the Shady Pine Drive direction? I don't think you'll make it unless you do."

He'd already considered the option. Taking the route would shave forty minutes off the trip. "I'll have to," he said, rushing out the door.

Andrew's chest grew heavy as he approached the road Esther had lived on. The road he traveled every day that summer to see her, even after the kitchen cabinets were built. During the three years since he'd come down the road, the red pine trees along the roadside had matured. Now their needles bent with the northeastern wind. Storm clouds hovered overhead, and inside, his core chilled to the bone.

His thoughts drifted to the times he and Esther had sat beneath the cluster of birch trees. She wasn't physically able to enjoy the outdoors often. The doctor wanted her to stay calm and inside so as not to stress her heart.

Andrew's throat tightened, remembering the day he'd convinced her to go for a buggy ride. The dust from the dirt roads put too much demand on her lungs, and once she started coughing, she couldn't catch her breath.

His eyes burned. Why did her heart finally give out in his buggy? He could still feel her body slumped over against his shoulder as he urged Patsy to run faster than she'd run before. It didn't help. The woman he'd believed would be his wife had died seated next to him.

He hated the dry gravel road. Hated the dust kicked up by the horse. Hated that he had convinced her to take the drive.

Andrew peered up into the sky. "God, I don't understand Your ways. I don't think like You think. I loved her . . . I bought that cabin."

His vision blurred, and he swiped his shirtsleeve over his eyes. As he neared her father's farmhouse, the cluster of birch trees came into view. While he was trying to clear his sight, the buggy wheel dipped into a deep rut.

A loud snap. The splintered wheel skidded across the gravel.

The horse struggled for traction, but Patsy, a driver, didn't have the strength that Jack, his Belgium, had for hauling unbalanced loads. She couldn't pull the buggy with a broken wheelbase.

Andrew steadied the horse and stepped out to look at the damage. Under most circumstances, he traveled with spare parts.

But not complete wheels. It would take hours to hobble back to the house and change buggies. Hours he didn't have.

He rubbed the back of his neck. *Think* . . .

Andrew squatted next to the wagon. With the hit the wheel took, he wouldn't be able to limp home on it. He unhitched Patsy and led her to the side of the road where he tied her to a tree.

He scanned the area. Esther's family wouldn't own a phone, but maybe . . . The next farm had a tractor in the field. Perhaps the *Englisch* who lived there would let him use their phone to call Mr. Thon for a ride.

A buggy came up behind him and stopped. Andrew turned to greet the man. "*Gut* day."

It was anything but a good day, but he didn't want to sound rude.

"*Jah*." The man pointed to Andrew's debilitated buggy and Patsy tied to the tree. "Your buggy?"

"*Jah*, the wheel broke."

The bearded man nodded. "*Kumm*, I'll take you to your *haus*."

"*Denki*." Andrew climbed in and took a good look at the stranger. He was no one Andrew had ever seen before. "You from around here?"

"*Nay*, just passing through on a visit."

Andrew cocked his head sideways.

The man's blue eyes sparkled.

"You look like someone . . ." *The man at the cabin*. He had seen the stranger before.

The man kept his focus directed at the road. "Where were you headed?"

"The bus station."

"Going away?"

Andrew shrugged. *"Nett* so sure myself." When the man's brows furrowed, Andrew continued his explanation. "The woman I want to marry is leaving . . . I wanted to stop her or . . ." He looked out the window opening. Judith was probably already on a bus.

"Or go with her?"

"Jah." Andrew patted his pockets, hoping his travel money hadn't fallen out. He'd emptied the money jar he kept hidden under the floorboard before leaving his *daed's* house. He glanced back at his buggy and his heart sank. He had forgotten the box.

"Is something wrong?"

"I forgot something in my buggy, is all."

The man stopped the buggy.

"Nay, please, there isn't enough time to go back." Andrew's heart skipped. Time was running out.

The man stepped out.

Did the horse need to rest? Andrew glanced back at the *Englisch* farm they had passed. He could walk back, ask to use their phone, and . . . Andrew gulped. What was the stranger doing, whispering in the horse's ear?

The man returned to the window opening. "Take the buggy, Andrew. You will not miss Judith." He walked away.

Andrew . . . He knows my name. Had he given his name to him at the cabin? *Jah,* at that time the man said he knew who Andrew was . . . but Judith?

Andrew swung sideways on the seat, but the man was gone. It took him a few moments to get the feeling back in his feet. The length of his spine tingled as the words repeated in his mind.

The horse tossed her head and pawed at the ground.

Andrew slid into the driver's place, and without his having to say anything, the mare broke into a racing pace down the road.

Pulling into the bus station, Andrew saw the Fischers' buggy parked under a lamppost. His heart swelled. After tying the horse next to theirs, he ran into the building.

Inside, he skidded to a stop on the tiled floor. Both Mrs. Fischer and Rebecca in her arms were crying. He scanned the waiting area. Judith's father was talking with a worker at the loading area. Judith was . . . gone.

Andrew blew out his suspended breath. *I'm too late, God.* His eyes welled and blurred his vision. He looked up at the slate-colored ceiling, hoping the tears would stay in his eyes and not roll down his face. *Now what do I do, God?* Andrew rubbed the moisture from his eyes. He took a few steps toward the family, not sure what he would say or if begging for her whereabouts would gain their sympathy.

From the corner of his eye, he saw the door to the ladies' room open. Judith stepped out, wiping her tearstained face.

She glanced up and saw him, and her face paled. Her eyes darted to where her mother sat, then to where her father stood.

"What are you doing here, Andrew?"

"Were you going to leave without saying good-bye?"

"It's not as though I had a choice." She bit her bottom lip and closed her eyes.

"I don't want you to go." He reached for her hand but noticed her *daed* approaching and released it.

"The bus has been delayed six hours." Mr. Fischer looked at his wife, then to Judith. "We might as well wait at home."

Andrew stepped forward. "Mr. Fischer, I'd like your permission to take Judith home."

Her father stared at him.

"Allow it please, Jonas," Mrs. Fischer said.

He nodded his consent. "Don't be too long. She needs to catch that bus."

Chapter Twenty-Nine

J udith kept her back as straight and stiff as the buggy bench
she sat on. Andrew made a few sideways glances at her, but
she pretended not to notice. He kept his comments to himself until they were outside the city limits.

"Why didn't you tell me?"

Judith shrugged. She knew why. Andrew would try to stop
her parents from sending her away. But he couldn't protect her
from them or from the bishop.

"I thought we were friends."

Judith drew in a long breath and gazed at the houses. "I don't
think I've been on this road before."

"Don't change the subject." He touched her hand as she held
tight to the bench. "I'm glad you didn't leave."

She looked down at his hand covering hers, then lifted her eyes to meet his. "I still am . . . in six hours," she murmured, turning away from the intensity of his stare.

"Change your mind and stay."

She couldn't change God's decision. She'd already tried. "How *kumm* you took this route?"

His expression saddened and she closed her eyes, remembering how he avoided the main route when they visited Samuel in the hospital. Levi had asked the same question, and something painful stirred in Andrew's eyes that day.

"I took the other road on my way into town." He kept his focus on the road. "Besides, this way I can show you a quilt."

Judith lifted her brows. "A quilt?" She was leaving in six hours, and he wanted her to see a quilt.

"This one is special—you'll want to see it," he said, then whispered under his breath, "I hope."

Judith looked at the *Englisch* houses. Thanksgiving hadn't passed, and their houses and lawns were already decorated for Christmas. She sighed. It would be difficult not celebrating Jesus' birth with her family.

Andrew glanced at her. "What are you thinking about?"

Judith dug her hands into her cape pockets and dabbed at her eyes with a tattered tissue. Even if she admitted to feeling sad over leaving, Andrew couldn't do anything about it. "Where did you say this quilt is?"

"I didn't say." He turned his head and concentrated on the road.

Judith shifted in her seat. If the bishop caught the two of them together, surely Andrew would be punished. She was surprised that her father had allowed them to leave the bus station together. She twisted to look out the window opening.

He chuckled. "Why are you so nervous?"

She focused on the passing houses. "Worried, is all."

"About what?"

"You don't have to hide the truth from me. I know why you chose this route. So your father won't see us together."

Andrew shook his head. He cleared his throat. "Esther lived down the other road. I haven't gone that way in three years. Not since—"

"I'm sorry. You don't have to explain."

He forced a smile. "We were on a buggy ride when she died."

Judith touched his forearm. "I'm sorry. Driving that way today *muscht* have been painful. I don't blame you for not wanting to go back that direction."

He patted her hand. "I had to reach you. I couldn't let you go."

She snapped her hand off his forearm. "I only have a few hours before I have to be back at the bus station." She looked out the opening. The ride into town was difficult, but this was too much to bear. While at the station, she had time to reflect on all the people and activities she'd miss. Baking pies with her mother, the community suppers, walking Rebecca to *shul*, reading to Samuel . . . and mostly, she would miss Andrew. His strong arms, his grin. She dabbed the tissue against the corners of her eyes.

"Are you okay?"

She nodded, but deep down she knew she would never be okay. How had Andrew come to mean so much in her life? It occurred to her then that during the long ride into town, and the time she'd spent waiting for the bus, Levi hadn't once crossed her mind.

"What are you thinking about?"

"Levi."

Andrew's expression hardened. "Sorry I asked."

"I was thinking about how I didn't think of him . . . I mean, when I was waiting at the bus station."

Andrew's brows rose and his head cocked to the side as though he was unscrambling her statement to make sense of it.

"When I thought of missing everyone when I was in Ohio, Levi never came to mind."

Andrew rubbed the nape of his neck. "I don't think he would be the first to come to my mind either." He looked at her a long moment, then said, "I heard he proposed."

"*Jah*, he did." Judith fumbled with the tissue in her hand. "I heard all my life that God's purpose for me was to marry and have children."

"And now?"

She shrugged. "I don't see myself falling in love with someone in Ohio." She didn't see herself loving anyone other than Andrew.

Judith had replayed Clare's words a hundred times since the evening everyone gathered for singing. How she said the bishop had given his approval of marriage. Andrew and Clare wouldn't have sought the bishop's approval unless there was a commitment between them.

She bit her bottom lip to keep it from trembling. No, if her purpose was to marry and have children as Amish women were taught growing up, she didn't know if she had any purpose at all.

The recurring dream of the footpath with its glittering leaves didn't help. The narrow road, she'd come to believe, meant she would walk it alone—in Ohio. And she was all right with that decision, knowing it was God's will.

Judith looked at the farms. They had entered the Amish district—Clare's district. She looked at the space on the bench between her and Andrew and slid over to the side, increasing the distance between them.

Andrew slid closer to Judith. "Close your eyes. I want it to be a surprise."

Judith raised her eyebrows at him, but complied. Having her eyes closed made it easier to avoid acknowledging that he'd moved closer to her on the bench. A few minutes passed before she felt the pavement end under the buggy wheels and the seat bounce over the bumpy road. What sounded like tree branches swept the roof of the buggy, and Judith fumbled for the edge of the bench. Her hand met Andrew's, and he gave hers a gentle squeeze.

"Your eyes still closed?"

"*Jah.*"

"Whoa." Once the buggy stopped, he nudged her. "Okay, you can look."

Judith opened her eyes. A small wood-sided cabin came into view. She turned to Andrew as he jumped out. Her eyes followed him as he tied the horse and came to her side of the buggy.

"*Kumm mitt mich.*" He reached for her hand.

Judith slanted her brows. "Is this—"

"Where the quilt is? *Jah.*"

She eased off the seat, still not understanding. A stiff breeze caused the leaves to clatter overhead. She gazed up, seeing the glistening golden hues shake against the blue sky.

Following Andrew up the porch steps, Judith paused as he opened the door.

"It's okay." He motioned for her to come inside with a wave of his hand.

After her eyes had adjusted to the darkness inside, the empty sitting room came into view. "I don't understand. Who lives in a house with no furniture?"

"That will take a little time." He guided her toward a narrow hallway.

Without a lamp, she couldn't see anything down the dark hallway. She walked close behind Andrew as he led the way. "Whose *haus* is this? Why isn't there anyone here?"

"You ask a lot of questions." He stopped at the end of the hall and opened the door, then stepped away to clear her view.

Judith stared at the wooden bed. The quilt she'd sold to Mrs. Stanly was spread neatly over it. "I don't understand."

"I bought the quilt." He studied her eyes. "I bought this *haus*."

Her hands began to tremble. He'd bought a house in the adjoining district. It made sense, buying a house in Clare's district. But what was her box doing on the bed? She had left the box and the rock at the river.

Andrew rushed to the bed and picked up the box. His eyes widened as though he, too, was surprised. "I, um . . ."

Judith bolted down the hall and didn't breathe again until she was standing on the porch.

Andrew stepped outside. He reached for her hand. "It's

small. But it borders the south district and—" He brushed his hand over her cheek. "You don't like the *haus*?"

"Will you take me home *nau*?"

Andrew came closer. "What's wrong?"

She squeezed her eyes closed and dropped her gaze to the sun-faded boards of the porch.

"Why did you leave the box at the river?"

Unable to look at him, she turned away, but his strong hands redirected her. "Andrew, please." His uncompromising stare continued until she sighed. "The rock no longer glowed. *Ich muscht* have done something . . ." She dried her eyes. "I got you into trouble with the bishop. I was selfish. I . . . I was filled with envy. You shouldn't have made the box for me. I couldn't possibly take it with me." Her voice quivered. "I had to leave *you* behind," she whispered.

His hand brushed her cheek. "Why? Judith, you're special to me. Can you really leave me behind so easily?"

Her silence agitated him. "I know the *haus* is small," he said. "I'll put on an addition. I'll increase the number of bedrooms. I'll—"

"Andrew, the house is nice. I just wasn't prepared to see my quilt on a bed that you made, that's all." She paused. "I'm happy for you. I really—"

He moved closer. His eyes focusing on her mouth, he leaned toward her.

"We shouldn't—"

He brought her against him and, disregarding her dutiful objection, kissed her. A steady, mesmerizing kiss that suspended all reason to pull away. She lifted her hand to his jaw, touching the prickle of whiskers. She pushed away and cringed as she gasped for air. Why hadn't she seen his jaw shadowed with hair growth before this? Before she kissed a man about to be married.

"What's wrong?" He tried to reach for her, but she stepped away.

"Don't touch me." Without giving heed to self-restraint, she had melted with ease into his arms. She couldn't allow him that close again.

"What did I do?"

"I told you not to kiss me like that!"

He eased closer, and she backed up until she was up against the porch banister.

She pointed to his face. "You're getting married."

"I hope so." He scratched the whiskers. "I was in a hurry to get to the bus station, but I like the idea of not shaving." He reached for her hand. "You kissed me too, and neither of us was pretending."

"It was wrong." She bowed her head. "Andrew, I know about Clare. She told me you and her—" It hurt to say the words.

"What about us? There's nothing."

Judith lifted her head and met his eyes in a stare. "The bishop—your father—gave his approval of your marriage."

Andrew slowly shook his head. "I'm sorry you heard that." He came closer and drew her into his arms. "I didn't hear about that arrangement until today." He kissed her forehead.

"Andrew, please stop. It's wrong."

He kissed her cheek. "I don't think so." The tips of his fingers followed her jawline. "You still only want to kiss your husband the way you kissed me?"

"*Jah.*"

His warm breath created a stir. The hairs along her arm stood in the wake of his feather kisses. She found it impossible to breathe normally. "Andrew."

"Then marry me so I can kiss you again." His whiskers brushed against her face. "Marry me, Judith."

She pulled away before their lips met. "I can't." Her throat tightened. Glancing up, she noticed his blank stare and closed her eyes. "I can't, Andrew."

"I love you, Judith. I thought you had feelings for me too."

Lord, I love him, but he'd have to leave the church if he married me.

Andrew blew out a breath. "I wore out the knees in my pants praying for you. Asking God for you."

Judith opened her eyes. "You were asking God for me?"

He nodded. "I prayed for us. For children. I prayed that your eyes would be open." He cupped her face. "I love you." He tipped her chin up with his thumb. "I'll sell this *haus* if you want to move to Ohio. But I'm coming with you."

"You don't know what you're saying." She moved her head sideways to avoid looking into his eyes. If she wasn't careful, she'd be vowing her love to him, and it would never work.

Andrew brought her head back to face him. Resting his forehead against hers, he whispered, "I'm asking you to marry me, Judith Fischer."

"Your father won't allow it."

"This doesn't have anything to do with him." He raised his head. "Tell me you don't love me."

She swallowed. "Andrew."

"I know that you do. I see it in your eyes."

"*Jah*, I love you. But it doesn't change anything. We still cannot get married. Your father—"

Andrew's mouth captured her words again, and she surrendered in his embrace. He broke from the kiss. "Are you going to marry me?"

"You know my heart wants to answer *jah*. But I still can't."

When she tried to break loose from him, he held her tight.

"I won't leave God for you, but I'll leave the community and my family. I would like my father's blessing, but he won't stop me from marrying you." He wiped his hand against her wet face. "Don't you understand? I haven't stopped loving God, and I won't, ever. But my life here in this community would not be complete without you."

"Don't say that. You wanted ministry."

"Not without you." He dropped his arms from her and shrugged. "I had a dream of us praying together, only instead of your outer *kapp*, you wore a sleeping prayer *kapp*, and I had a beard. Don't you see? God showed me *us* praying together, *married*."

"He showed me a dream also. I saw a road, and then it split three ways, and I was told to choose."

Andrew swallowed. "Which way did you choose?"

"I was directed toward the one in the middle. A mere footpath." She lifted her hand to cover her face. "Andrew, it *muscht* lead to Ohio."

Andrew laughed. *"Kumm mitt mich,"* he said, taking hold of her hand. "The center path, you say?"

"*Jah*, but don't laugh. I'm afraid."

He squeezed her hand. "I won't let you go *nau*."

They walked past the buggy. "Where are you taking me?"

"Your eyes were closed when we pulled in." He continued to chuckle as he led her out of the wooded trail and out to the main paved road.

Judith gasped. The road was split just like the one in her dream. She pivoted around, taking in the glimmering golden leaves. Unable to speak, she closed her eyes. *Is this true, God? This path leads to Andrew. But what about the bishop?*

Andrew motioned toward the house. "The center path is with me."

Judith's eyes watered. *"Ach*, Andrew." She wrapped her arms around his neck. *"Jah*, I'll marry you." Just as Tobias had told her, her eyes were opened—she understood the dream— the right path.

As they kissed, the snow began to fall. Wet snowflakes canvassed the sky and covered their heads.

"This is my dream, Andrew. Ice pellets were falling from the sky and—" She'd forgotten about Samuel.

"And what?"

"In that same dream, I saw Samuel, only he was frozen under a sheet of ice."

"Shh . . . It's okay." He guided her head against his chest and rested his chin on her prayer cloth.

"I think I was wrong about Samuel walking."

He lifted his chin and pulled away enough to look into her eyes. "Why do you say that?"

"My dreams were to show me you. You prayed for my eyes to be open, and I think they are *nau.*" A lump formed in her throat. "Andrew, maybe I've been wrong this entire time."

"You're not making sense. None of this means Samuel won't walk."

"I think it does mean that. Samuel never got his legs free from the ice in my dreams. God knows how many hairs are on one's head, He knows how many steps Samuel will take. *Ach*, why am I just *nau* understanding this? Tobias said his steps are ordered, but he never said how many steps he would take." She chewed her bottom lip. "I'll tell your father I was wrong, and maybe he will give us his blessing."

"Why do you say that?" His tone turned stern.

She turned her head, but he rested his hand on her cheek and guided her back to face him.

"Are you saying you didn't see an angel?" He locked his gaze on her.

"No. I saw him. But the dream—" She paused when his jaw tightened. "I'll tell your father I was wrong about Samuel walking."

"No, you will not." His brows furrowed. "He'll want you to say you were wrong about seeing an angel." He shook his head. "You're not telling him that. We've got to stand on faith." He tipped her chin. "We'll pray for God's mercy as long as it takes until we see Samuel walk." He kissed her forehead, then peered into her eyes and smiled. "You might be patching holes in your dress, but we'll keep praying." He dropped to his knees and reached for her hand. "Let's pray *nau*."

Judith knelt with him. Andrew clasped her hands, and the cold ground no longer chilled her bones. Instead, her core warmed. As she closed her eyes, a golden glow filled her view. While Andrew prayed for her surety of her convictions and for

Samuel's complete healing, a faint hum of chanting sounds filled her ears.

"*Denki*, God. *Aemen*."

Judith lifted her head. "I believe God gave me a new measure of faith."

A wide smile spread across Andrew's face. "Hold on to that belief," he said, reaching for her hand to help her off her knees.

"*Jah*, I'm convinced. No one can change *mei* surety *nau*."

He tugged her hand. "*Kumm*, let's tell Samuel first about us getting married. I need to tell him that his prayers were answered." Andrew chuckled. "He prayed that you wouldn't leave the bus station until I reached you."

"He knew that you wanted to stop me?"

"He knows I want to marry you too." He tugged her arm. "He asked me to. He said something about having too many girls in the house."

"*Ach*, so honorable of you to help him in his dilemma." Judith looked up at the falling snow. "We had better hurry. At the rate of this snow *kumming* down, the roads will get slippery soon."

Chapter Thirty

To Judith's dismay, several buggies lined her parents' driveway. "Why do you think everyone is here?" She pointed to the bishop's buggy. "Your father's here."

Andrew reached for her hand and gave it a reassuring squeeze. "That's *gut*. We'll tell them together." He parked the buggy next to the others and turned on the seat to face her. "Whatever happens, I love you. If they oppose us getting married and joining the church, we leave together."

Judith nodded. "Whatever happens," she repeated.

During the buggy ride, she had prayed for a miracle. She wanted to be accepted and wanted Andrew to be eligible for ministry. She asked God to show them the way. Andrew's silence didn't surprise her. A man after God's heart, Andrew would have also continued praying. Judith smiled with the thought of knowing that even in silence, they were before God in one accord.

She accepted Andrew's hand to help her from the buggy, knowing the menfolk were watching nearby. Andrew smiled without so much as a hint of fear.

"Lord, if it be Your will, show them the truth," she whispered, then directed her gaze to the sky. "It's snowing hard. Why do you suppose they've gathered outside the barn?"

Andrew shrugged. "Let's find out."

David came out of the barn and rejoined the other men. "He isn't in there."

The urgency in his voice caused Judith's heart to pound wildly.

"How can a paralyzed boy go far?" *Daed* inquired. His slumped posture made him look years older. With his head bowed, his shoulders shook.

Judith increased her pace. "What's happened?"

David rubbed his beard. "Samuel's missing."

"How can it be so?" She scanned the snow-covered yard. "Where's Martha?"

David cleared his throat. "Don't know."

Andrew stepped closer. "How long have they been gone?"

"We came back from town and found the house empty." *Daed* drew a deep breath. David's arm came around his father's shoulder. "I'll keep looking. You should—"

"I cannot wait with the women while my children are missing." *Daed's* voice rose, but his mouth trembled with every word.

Zechariah cleared his throat. "Perhaps we should all pray."

Certainly God had spoken to the bishop's heart. Outside of

service, she hadn't heard him pray much. Usually he offered to seek the scriptures.

The bishop eyed each of them gathered, gave a stiff nod, then clasped his hands in front of him and bowed his head. The others followed.

She exchanged looks with Andrew, who lifted his right shoulder in a slight shrug. She bowed her head, but heaviness penetrated her limbs. She felt pulled away, and the bishop's voice grew distant.

A golden haze lifted from the earth and shards of icicles sprayed a distant form. Moving closer, she could see Samuel. He pulled on his legs, then stopped. He took gasping breaths, his face contorted. Finally, as he began to recline, a voice called out, telling him to stand. Without effort, Samuel rose to his feet . . .

Chanting sounds grew louder as the dream faded. Judith opened her eyes and scanned the area. Tobias stood at the edge of the apple orchard, beckoning her to come. Although the bishop's prayer hadn't ended, she took a step away.

Andrew grabbed her hand, his eyes wide and searching. She motioned with her head toward the apple orchard.

The bishop had just breathed *aemen* to conclude his prayer when Judith blurted, "Did anyone search by the river?" She pivoted without waiting for their reply and bolted from the group.

Andrew and David both kept stride while the others followed at a slower pace.

Once they reached the river, Judith slid to a halt. Martha was lying on the ground, and Samuel was seated alongside her, patting her back.

Samuel looked up. "Judith!" He pushed off Martha's shoulder to stand and made a few tottering steps toward her.

Judith reached out her arms. "Be careful." Then reality sank in. Samuel was walking. Taking steps without assistance. Tears flowed freely, clouding her vision, but nothing could take from the miracle happening before her. *Denki, God. Denki.*

Andrew boasted a wide smile.

"Look what God has done," she said, turning to Andrew and David.

Andrew nodded. *"Ach,* what a glorious sight, *jah?"*

David's mouth hung agape. Then, slowly moving toward Samuel, he released a pent-up sob. "Samuel, you're walking!" He gathered Samuel into his arms and twirled him in a circle.

Daed and Bishop Lapp arrived together.

"Denki, God. *Mei* boy is safe," *Daed* choked.

The bishop stepped forward. "Is he all right?"

David nodded at the older men. *"Ach,* more than *fine."* He gazed at Samuel and asked, "Feel strong enough to show them?"

"Jah, put me down."

David gently lowered Samuel to his feet. "Watch him *nau.* You'll see."

The boy's smile widened as he made his way toward his father.

"Ach!" *Daed* covered his mouth with his hand and bent to one knee.

Bishop Lapp's mouth hung open. He looked at Judith, but broke eye contact and lowered his head.

Andrew moved closer and tentatively patted Judith's back. "It's a *wundebaar* miracle, isn't it?" He reached into his pocket, removed a handkerchief, and offered it to her.

Judith looked around the clearing. The long afternoon sun

rays cast a golden hue over the freshly fallen snow, reminding her of the glow she'd seen in her dream. The light softened everyone's features. *Daed's* wet face held a sparkle as he cuddled with her little brother.

Then her eyes stopped on Martha, still lying on the ground. With all the excitement over Samuel's miracle, Martha hadn't moved. "Samuel, what happened to Martha?"

"She went to sleep. I couldn't wake her."

David rushed to Martha and jostled her shoulders. "Martha, can you hear me?"

Their sister moaned and fluttered her lashes a few times before she opened her eyes.

David helped her into a seated position.

Daed brushed Judith's shoulder. "Hold Samuel," he said, passing her brother from his arms into hers. He knelt beside David and Martha. "What happened?"

Martha squinted, blinked a few times, then slowly shook her head. "It was odd. While I was praying for God to forgive me . . . I heard singing." She looked up, scanned everyone, then locked on Judith. "I didn't understand any of the words. They weren't *Englisch* or *Deitsch*." She turned to *Daed*. "Then I heard the door slam, and it brought me out of my stupor. Samuel wasn't in his room. By the time I ran outside, I saw him *walking*—right beside a huge *Englischer*. I called out, but neither of them responded, so I followed them here." Her eyes grew bigger. *"Daed*, when the *Englischer* turned to look at me, his eyes were mesmerizing."

"Do you remember walking with a man, Samuel?" *Daed* asked.

Samuel lifted his head off Judith's shoulder. *"Jah*, Tobias."

"Who is Tobias?" the bishop asked.

The little boy beamed. "He's the angel who told me I could walk."

Daed gulped. "Tobias, you say?"

"*Jah.*" Samuel turned to Judith. "He came to me in *mei* dream. Only he had a golden glow surrounding him. I heard his voice telling me to stand, so I did. Then I followed him."

Joy bubbled up from deep within Judith, and a sound between a sob and a laugh escaped her lips.

Andrew, eyes glistening now, breathed deep and smiled.

"He's the largest *Englischer* I've ever seen." Martha stood with David's help. "I couldn't believe my eyes. Samuel walked."

Her father shook his head slowly. "I don't understand. The doctors said the nerve damage to his spine was too great. They were sure he would never walk."

The bishop made a sweeping scan of the area. "Where is this Tobias?"

"He vanished." Martha looked from *Daed* to David. "I saw a brightness reflecting off the snow."

Samuel nodded. "*Jah*, I saw it too. And Martha fell down." He pointed to the clearing. "He went that way. I wanted to go, but Tobias said to watch over Martha." He looked at his sister. "I couldn't wake you."

Martha nodded. "*Jah*, the singing started again, and still I didn't know the words."

Bishop Lapp cleared his throat. "We've seen a miracle today. I suggest we go back to the *haus* where you can give us the details." He turned, then after a slight hesitation, he walked up to Andrew and Judith. His gaze lifted to the sky. "Samuel's steps were ordered by God."

"Judith was right." Samuel hugged Judith's neck. "He was an angel."

Bishop Lapp leaned toward Andrew's ear and whispered something Judith wasn't able to hear.

Andrew nodded.

Before his father rejoined the others heading back to the house, he held Judith's gaze, nodded, then turned to his son and clapped his shoulder.

Daed stopped in front of them. "Samuel, *kumm mitt mich. Mamm* will want to see you walk."

Judith passed Samuel to her father's waiting arms.

The boy motioned for Andrew. "Are you *kumming?*"

"Shortly." He leaned closer. "I have to talk with Judith first." He glanced at Judith's *daed*, and his face turned a shade of pink. "That is, if it be all right with you?"

Daed made a stiff nod. *"Jah."* He turned and followed the others toward the house.

Martha gave Judith a teary-eyed hug. "I'm glad you're not going to Ohio."

Judith nodded. Her heart was so full of happiness, she couldn't speak. She brushed the tears from her eyes as Andrew settled his strong arm around her shoulder.

Once they were alone, Andrew turned Judith toward him. "Samuel walked." He kissed her forehead. "Our prayers were answered." He kissed the tip of her nose and rested his forehead against hers. "My father gave me his blessing."

"He did?" Her heart fluttered as his kisses feathered along her cheekbone.

"It looks like God got a *gut* hold of them all, *jah?*"

She clung to him tighter. "*Jah*."

Andrew brought her out to arm's length. "You sound sad."

Judith sniffled. "Tobias is gone. I wanted to thank him."

Andrew shook his head. "It's God we must thank. He sent Tobias." Andrew cupped her face and lightly stroked his thumb along her cheekbone. "I have so much to give thanks for."

Judith nodded. "I do too. He opened my eyes and showed me you." She sighed. "I suppose there are more reasons than Samuel walking as to why God sent Tobias."

Andrew looked at her, a slight smile on his lips. "*Jah*, I suppose we may never know all the reasons." He drew her closer to him. "I want us to marry once you're baptized."

Joy spread through her as she gazed into his eyes. "If I had *mei* way, I would be baptized today."

Discussion Questions

1. How do Judith and Martha react differently to their brother's accident? Was there a time when you lashed out at a close friend or relative? Did you recognize your action immediately?

2. Have you experienced a time when you've taken a stand on something, only to feel as though you were standing alone? Maybe a friend took a stand and you were able to offer support or help?

3. Even though Judith believed she was following God's direction, how did she behave when she thought God was silent? What does the scripture John 14:18 mean to you?

4. Although Judith wasn't always aware of Andrew's support, he still held her up. What are ways we can hold each other up during a time of need? Can you think of others outside your circle of friends and family whom you could help?

5. In John 16:33 what does Jesus tell us we can have? How is this possible?

6. What do the following scriptures say about God's faithfulness? Psalms 89:24; 89:33; 101:6; 119:90; Hebrews 10:23.

7. Can you think of a time when God sent some form of encouragement to you that helped you to keep the faith? Perhaps something someone said or the words of a certain song helped remind you of God's promises.

8. When Samuel arrived home from the hospital unable to walk, Judith felt hopeless. Have you ever felt disappointed when God's plan is different from your own? The Bible tells us that His timing is perfect. Can you see how His timing in Judith's life was perfect?

9. Has there been a time when while you were waiting for God's direction in a situation, you took the matter back into your own hands? What happened when you did? When we continually worry after we have prayed about something, are we taking the matter back into our own hands?

10. Andrew told his father that Judith's faith pleased God. What does the Bible say about those who diligently seek Him?

11. How did Andrew help Judith the most? Have you ever prayed for someone and felt strengthened yourself?

12. What does the Bible say about angels in Psalm 91:11?

Acknowledgments

I thank God for His grace. Without His unmerited favor, and the people He has placed in my life, I wouldn't have seen my dreams materialize. I thank God for my husband, Dan, and our three children, Lexie, Danny, and Sarah.

Dan, thank you for the times you've pushed me beyond my abilities. You're an awesome soul mate to swing for the bleachers with. Thanks for being a great husband, wonderful father, and for doing your own laundry. Your love and support are incredible.

Lexie, your help around the house and encouragement have been a godsend. Thanks for cooking. You've officially mastered all dishes that include rice and beans. Thank you for taking the book photo and hiding my double chin.

Danny, as I watch you grow, I know God has been good to me. From a newborn needing a liver transplant to a thriving young boy, I see you and I stand in awe of what God has done. He has great things in store for you, and I'm honored to be your mom.

Sarah, you're a bright girl. I'm so proud that God has called my "little gapper" to be a prayer warrior. I'm confident that God will do great things through you. Thanks for holding me up in your prayers.

Mom (Ella Roberts), you stayed up late typing my stories since I was in grade school. Thanks for your unconditional love and always believing in me. I guess you're thankful I know how to type now.

Dad (Paul Droste), growing up tagging along on your radio interviews, I've learned communication skills from the best. Kathy Droste, I'm grateful to have a stepmother who is willing to spend long hours "red-inking" my first draft. I owe you a new pen—and a lot more!

I have a large list of friends and family who have supported and encouraged me. My writing pal and lunch buddy, Jennifer Uhlarik. We've sat in the same booth, ordered the same food, and plotted and killed off characters for months. Your friendship, critical eyes, and godly support are so valuable. Quanda Watson, my prayer partner. Joy Elwell, Mary Ann Stockwell, and Joan Paisley, thanks for your ability to speed-read and give timely feedback. Susanne Dietze, we've been through many chapters together and have shared tears of frustration and joy. I'm so grateful to have you as my friend. Scribes 211: Sarah Hamaker, Virginia Hamlin, Bob Kaku, Dave Longeuay, Gail Sattler, Linda Truesdell, and Jennifer Uhlarik—we certainly are an eclectic group of writers. Thanks for your honest feedback and helpful corrections.

I'll always be thankful for Mary and Simon Thon, who introduced me to the Amish while I lived with them during college, and to my Amish friends of Mecosta County, Michigan, who invited me into their homes.

I especially appreciate my publishing family at Thomas Nelson. Natalie Hanemann, you are an awesome editor. Thanks for your support and encouragement. I would also like to thank Lissa Halls Johnson and LB Norton for all your hard work.

The beloved
Heaven on Earth series

"Ruth Reid is skillful in portraying the Amish way of life as well as weaving together miracles with the everyday."

—Beth Wiseman, bestselling author of the Daughters of the Promise series

Enjoy Ruth Reid's Amish Wonders Series!

Available in print, audio, and e-book.

Enjoy an excerpt from Ruth Reid's *A Dream of Miracles*

Chapter One

"M ei sohn needs to see *Doktah* Roswell. It's an emergency." Mattie Diener stood before the receptionist's window with three-year-old Nathan on one hip, and Amanda, her eighteen-month-old daughter, teetered on her other.

The young woman looked up from her computer screen and slid the sign-in log closer to Mattie. "What's Nathan's problem today, Mrs. Diener?"

"He's *nett* himself." Mattie gently lowered Amanda to the floor at her side in order to free her hand to sign the forms. She jotted the pertinent information on the log, then handed the clipboard back to the receptionist.

Mattie cradled Nathan tighter to her chest as heat radiated from his little body. She'd given him feverfew earlier, but this time the herb did little to bring his fever down. Mattie placed her hand on his moist forehead. "He's burning up."

The woman's eyes widened as if seeing Nathan for the first time.

"And I see he has a rash." She removed the headset that connected her to the telephone, rolled her chair back from the desk, and stood.

"*Jah*, it's a . . . heat rash."

The receptionist held up one finger. "Stay right there. I'll get the nurse." She disappeared behind the partitioned wall of file cabinets.

Little Amanda clung to Mattie's legs, her round face buried in the folds of Mattie's dress. She should have asked her best friend Grace to watch Amanda. Her daughter was shy around strangers. Although not a bad thing, it did make her daughter clingy, even more so when she was overly tired. Amanda's crankiness had started last week when the temperature had risen above eighty, a record high for the second week of June in Michigan's Upper Peninsula.

Whispers spread amongst the roomful of people. Mattie glanced over her shoulder and scanned the waiting room with an apologetic smile. Doctor Roswell's office was always abuzz with patients. Well respected in Badger Creek, the country doctor took his time listening to his patients' concerns no matter how many people waited to see him.

She'd brought Nathan into the office numerous times since his birth three years ago. Doctor Roswell always managed to squeeze her son into his busy day. She studied her sleeping son. Nathan's lips were cracked, and he was panting with shallow breaths, his face blotchy with a beet-red, prickly heat rash. *Oh, please hurry.*

A few moments later, the door leading to the back hallway opened, and the nurse ushered Mattie and the children down the hall and into one of the empty rooms. "What brings you in today, Mrs. Diener?"

"Nathan's had a high fever most of yesterday and today." Mattie lowered Nathan onto the paper-lined table. He flailed his arms, but Mattie was able to settle him by gently stroking the side of his face.

"I gave him feverfew, but it hasn't helped. The rash just started." Amanda tugged on Mattie's dress. She bent down and gathered her daughter into her arms.

The nurse eyed him closely. "It doesn't look like chicken pox to me," she mumbled.

Made sense why they had rushed her into a back room. Avoid the possible risk of spreading the virus. Only this wasn't chicken pox. She'd cared for her younger sisters when they were covered in spots, so she knew Nathan's was a simple fever rash. "I agree," Mattie said. "I think it's a heat rash."

"We'll let the doctor do the diagnosing." The nurse placed the tip of the ear thermometer in Nathan's ear and held it in position until it beeped. She discarded the plastic protective cap, then returned the instrument to the wall charger.

"He has a fever, doesn't he?" Mattie's dress was still damp from his sweat.

"Yes, it's 102.6." She jotted the number on the paper attached to a clipboard. "You said he's had a fever for two days. Any vomiting or diarrhea?"

"*Nay.*"

The nurse placed her hand on Nathan's wrist and monitored her watch. Afterward, she made a few notations on the form. "He isn't normally this quiet, is he?"

Mattie shook her head.

The nurse crossed the room and paused at the door. "The doctor will be in to see him shortly."

Mattie lifted her hand to Nathan's head and brushed the mop of wet curls away from his face. Bands of sweat dotted his forehead. "Lord, he's so frail. Please watch over him. *Mei* children are all I have," she whispered as the door opened.

A thirtysomething woman wearing a cranberry-colored dress under a long, white doctor's coat entered. As she crossed the room, her matching cranberry heels clacked against the laminate floor.

"I'm Doctor Wellington," she said, extending her hand.

Mattie shook the woman's smooth hand and tried to hide her surprise at how firm the doctor's grasp was for a woman. "I'm Mattie Diener. Where's Doctor Roswell? I hope nothing has happened to him."

The woman smiled. "He's on sabbatical."

Mattie crinkled her brows, unsure if that was good or bad.

"A much-needed vacation," the doctor explained, moving to the sink to wash her hands. Her friendly demeanor shifted to a professional nature once she approached Nathan. "How long has he had the red blotches on his face?" She began unbuttoning his shirt.

"They just appeared. I think the fever brought them on." Mattie scrutinized the doctor's facial expression. If the doctor was alarmed by Nathan's mottled chest, her expression didn't show it. Doctor Wellington continued the assessment, pressing her hand on Nathan's abdomen in several places. Her son's lips curled into a slight frown and his eyes opened. He stared several seconds, almost stupor-like, then closed them again.

"Is he normally this lethargic?"

"He's *nett* acting like himself, if that's what you're asking."

She scanned the nurse's notes. "You gave him feverfew?"

"*Jah.* Normally it brings his fever down in a few hours, but *nett* this time."

"How much did you give him?"

Mattie shook her head. "I didn't measure the exact amount. I made it into a broth. Yesterday he drank it throughout the day, but today he refused it."

She reviewed the chart. "No vomiting or diarrhea. How has his appetite been?"

"Other than the broth, he hasn't eaten anything since yesterday morning, and it wasn't much. Usually I can encourage him to breast-feed when he refuses everything else, but he wasn't interested."

"How often does he breastfeed?"

"When he's sick, restless. The attachment seems to calm him down."

Nathan stirred. He opened his eyes, then blinked a few times under the room's bright lights. As if focusing for the first time on the doctor, his eyes widened and he let out a shrill cry.

"It's okay. I'm right here," Mattie said in Pennsylvania *Deitsch*. She reached for his tiny hand and gave it a gentle squeeze. "This is *Doktah* Wellington."

His gaze slowly drifted to the opposite side of the table but darted back to Mattie, his face puckering with fear.

"*Bruder kronk?*" Amanda began to whimper.

"*Shh . . .*" Mattie kissed her daughter's temple. "Your big *bruder* is going to be okay."

Doctor Wellington leaned closer to him. "Can you tell me your name?"

Nathan ignored the doctor and locked his gaze on Mattie.

"His name is Nathan," she volunteered. "He doesn't know many *Englisch* words yet." She looked fondly at her son. His rosy cheeks brought out his blue eyes, the spitting image of his father, her late husband. Andy's cheeks would turn red after he'd worked outside in the cold weather and then stay that way for hours.

Doctor Wellington peered up from the chart, arching her thin, penciled brows. "He's three years old. He should be talking."

"He does . . . to me." Had this doctor never treated an Amish child? They only spoke Pennsylvania *Deitsch* until they reached school age. When the doctor's brows angled in what appeared to be disapproval, Mattie opened her mouth to explain, but Nathan's moan pulled her attention back to her son.

Nathan licked his cracked lips. Breathing out of his mouth had caused them to dry. She would dab some more beeswax on them once they returned home.

The doctor started to check his ears, and he tossed his head.

"Nathan." He stilled at Mattie's sharp rebuke. She softened her tone. "It's okay."

"His ears are clear. Can you open your mouth and say *ah?*" The doctor demonstrated by opening her mouth wide, exposing her perfectly white teeth, and sticking out her tongue. When he finally mimicked her action, Doctor Wellington's forehead wrinkled. She leaned closer, aiming a penlight into his mouth. "How long has he had blisters in his mouth?"

"I'm *nett* sure." Such important details shouldn't come as a surprise. What else had she missed?

The physician went to the phone on the wall and dialed. "Please pull Nathan Diener's complete medical records and bring the file to me." She washed her hands again, then reexamined Nathan's mouth. "You don't know how long he's had the blisters?"

Mattie swallowed hard. The doctor's tone had sharpened, her penetrating eyes silent accusers. Mattie shook her head. "*Nay.* Until you brought them to *mei* attention, I had no idea."

A soft knock on the door pulled the doctor's attention away. The nurse entered and handed her two thick binder files. "Here's the chart you requested."

"Thank you." Doctor Wellington took a moment to scan the stack of documents.

"He's been sick a lot," Mattie said, breaking the silence. The doctor merely nodded without looking up and flipped to the next page. When she finally closed the file, her exam became more precise, less informative. Mattie chewed her lip. She wanted to ask questions, but she also didn't want to interrupt the doctor.

Nathan's whimpering at the constant probing stirred Amanda, who soon joined the chorus of sobs. Mattie rocked her daughter in her arms, trying to soothe her before the doctor suggested she take Amanda out of the room.

Doctor Wellington pressed Nathan's tongue down with a flat wooden stick, then felt his neck and under his arms. When she pinched his fingertip, Nathan retracted his hand and tucked it under his armpit.

"Let her look at you." Mattie redirected her attention from her son to the doctor. "He's *nett* like this with *Doktah* Roswell." She stroked his sweat-matted auburn locks. "We'll be going home soon."

"He needs to be admitted to the hospital for observation," the doctor said, writing something on the paper attached to the clipboard.

"I can observe him from home. *Doktah* Roswell usually gives me a list of things to watch for."

She looked up from her notes. "He's dehydrated and needs fluids."

"I'll make sure he drinks plenty of fluids." And she would bring him in to see *Doktah* Roswell once he returned from vacation. At least his exams were never abrupt. Besides, she still had a pile of unpaid hospital bills from when Andy was admitted.

Mattie lowered Amanda to the floor, then gathered Nathan into her arms. "Can you tell me when *Doktah* Roswell will be back?"

"Mrs. Diener, your son has been seen in the clinic multiple times." She motioned to the thick files the nurse had brought her. "Don't you want to get to the underlying cause of his problem?"

Mattie squared her shoulders. "Of course I do." Was the doctor suggesting Mattie didn't care for her son? She hadn't been in the room more than fifteen minutes. How could she make such accusations? "He has a weak immune system; *Doktah* Roswell knows all about him."

Doctor Wellington removed a form from the clipboard. "This is his admission orders. When you get to the hospital, you can give them to the nurse. I'll be by to check on him later."

Mattie hesitated. Her mind was going a million directions. She couldn't very well leave the horse tied up for hours in the hospital parking lot. Usually she arranged rides from her *Englisch* friend in advance. Did she even have Cora's phone number with her?

The doctor glanced at the form, then looked at Mattie, her expression hardening. "I strongly advise you not to refuse medical care for your child."

The story continues in Ruth Reid's *A Dream of Miracles* . . .

About the Author

RUTH REID is a full-time pharmacist who lives in Florida with her husband and three children. When attending the Ferris State University College of Pharmacy in Big Rapids, Michigan, she lived on the outskirts of an Amish community and had several occasions to visit the Amish farms. Her interest grew into love as she saw the beauty in living a simple life.

Visit Ruth online at ruthreid.com
Facebook: Author Ruth Reid
Twitter: @authorruthreid